"It's a hugely fun read whether you're ogres or horrified by hobgoblins and may just be one of the sweetest love stories of the year."
Katie Clapham, Storytellers, Inc. blog

oved it' Don't know what to say but, blimey, that was my life! I'm only kidding, it still is!"
Sarwat Chadda, author of *The Ash Mistry Chronicles*

A deliciously tender story that wittily captures the ecstasy and agony of being a teenager."
Julia Eccleshare, Lovereading4kids

Adrian Mole for the Geek generation."
Faith, Sister Spooky blog

Whether you're a geek looking for some advice, or just like other people's misfortune, this is the book for you!"
age 13

Fantastic exploration of hanging on, letting go and fitting in. Terribly good stuff."
Guy Bass, author of *Stitch Head*

Geekhood is funny and insightful. Archie is a thoroughly engaging character who conveys all the awkwardness of a teenage boy's first encounter with girls."
Suzanne Wearing, *We Love This Book*

"Anyone who enjoys a laugh-out-loud, witty and moving insight into a geek's life will love this book."
Lorcan, age 12

"This is a funny, heart-delighting and utterly real tale that will have you punching the air. Get ready to embrace your Geekhood!"
Jakes, blogger and *Armadillo* reviewer

For Mum for just being her, Dad for his boundless enthusiasm, and for my mate Jim for teaching me the meaning of friendship. And always for my son, Hugh.

STRIPES PUBLISHING
An imprint of Little Tiger Press
1 The Coda Centre, 189 Munster Road,
London SW6 6AW

A paperback original
First published in Great Britain in 2012

ISBN: 978-1-84715-231-2

ANDY ROBB

GEEKHOOD
CLOSE ENCOUNTERS OF THE GIRL KIND

stripes

*"Who am I? Are you sure you want to know?
If someone told you I was just your average ordinary
guy without a care in the world, somebody lied."*

Peter Parker, *Spider-Man 2*

*"Rosie Cotton dancing. She had ribbons in her hair.
If ever I were to marry someone, it would have been her.
It would have been her."*

Sam Gamgee, *The Lord of the Rings:
The Return of the King*

IM

ONE

There are better ways to wake up. One would be to be nudged into consciousness after a night of Abandoned Passion with Kirsty Ford. (But, short of selling my virginity on eBay, any form of Abandoned Passion will have to remain a solo flight.) Another would be to have my mum and dad gently call my name, and tell me that they're back together and that everything's going to be all right. But they don't and it won't, so there's no point even thinking about it.

There are countless ways that are better than the one that I have to go through this particular morning. First it starts with a noxious smell that drifts up my nose, threatening to close my throat and make my stomach rebel against whatever I had for tea last night. Then there's the bark of a voice that shatters my slumber and catapults me into the morning sunlight that is suddenly streaming through my curtains. Basically, I'm shaking off the bad dream that I was having last night and walking straight into another one.

"Arch! Wake up, mate! It's nearly lunchtime."

It's my stepfather, Tony. Well, he's not technically my stepfather as he and Mum aren't married, but it's easier

9

than saying "my mum's boyfriend". He's standing at the window and might as well be beaming the sun's rays into my eyes with a magnifying glass. There's already a fag clamped between his lips, sporting a cylinder of ash that threatens to drop with every word he speaks. Needless to say, the room now stinks of cigarette smoke. As my brain tries to quickly relearn everything it's picked up in the last fourteen years – speech and basic motor functions, like sitting up – I get this weird feeling that I don't know where I am. It's only a split second before I remember that we moved into our new house yesterday. That would account for the pile of boxes at the end of my bed.

Tony stands, looking out of the window, a cup of tea for me notably absent from his hands. He's a big bloke in every sense of the word: tall, big gut, big voice, big pain in the backside. Only his glasses indicate that he might be human at all, hinting at a frailty that seems otherwise missing from the whole deal. He goes over to my painting desk and picks up one of my miniatures; it's a goblin warrior I've been working on, trying to paint in some detail on the shield. I unpacked them last night, to check for any damage that might've happened in the move. Tony looks at it closely and chuckles to himself.

"Nice one," he says.

Just in case you haven't worked it out, Tony drives me nuts. But he's my mum's partner, and I've got to live with him for at least the next four years, until I go to uni or he works out that he serves no other purpose on this earth than to wind me up, and then spectacularly explodes in a cloud of guilt. Or something like that. So, I tolerate him; I have to for Mum's sake. She'd hate it if I kicked up a fuss and, for some reason that I just can't get a handle on, he seems to make her happy. To cover this conflict of emotions, I've developed a VERY LOUD interior monologue that works completely independently from what my face and body are doing. For example, at the moment, while Tony is examining my prized goblin warrior, my face has crinkled into the approximation of a sleepy smile, while my hand scratches at my head in a pantomime of tiredness. Even my voice, although a bit croaky, has a friendly lift in it.

"Cool, isn't it? Just wanted to check they'd made the journey OK."

However, at exactly the same time that my exterior is sending all these signals of muzzy cheeriness, my Interior Monologue (IM) is saying something along the lines of:

Put that bloody thing down, you Tosser! It's not there for you to laugh at; it's there as an expression of my need to escape this world and embrace a realm where anything

11

is possible! And put that bloody fag out before you come in next time! And stop calling me "Arch"! It's "Archie"! Nobody else but Mum gets to call me "Arch" – it doesn't make us any more related or anything! AND WHAT ARE YOU DOING IN HERE ANYWAY?!

Does this make me two-faced? I don't think so. I see it more as a silent pressure release. If I didn't rant to myself, I'd say something stupid and upset someone. I'll concede that maybe my IM does get a bit carried away sometimes and perhaps loses a little perspective, but no one's perfect.

"We're unpacking the lounge," Tony declares, as though he's actually going to be involved. "D'you want to give us a hand?"

IM: *What kind of stupid question is that? Of course I don't want to come and unpack the lounge but, in the interests of a quiet life, I will.*

"Yeah, sure. Give us a minute and I'll come down."

And Tony leaves the room. Doesn't even say thanks. I sink back into the pillow and let out a loud sigh.

Welcome to my world.

I roll out of bed and stumble into the bathroom. Unfortunately, the new bathroom mirror is broadcasting the same picture as the old one: a mess of blond hair that looks like it would be more at home on the end of a mop frames the face of an adult trying to form, somewhat unsuccessfully, on the head of a child. Compared to some of the other guys in my class, I look young for my age, but I still get a thrill seeing the glitter of a scraggy nest of hairs sprouting out of my chin. There's even the threat of a few on my chest. We'll stop there.

Teeth brushed and clothes thrown on, I lumber down the stairs, running my hand along the unfamiliar wood of the banister. It's a fairly big house – much bigger than the one me 'n' Mum moved into when she split from Dad. There's no doubting that our lives have taken a financial turn-for-the-better since Mum met Tony (he runs his own business – something about a marketing data service), but it doesn't make him any less of a Tosser. I do, occasionally, try to step back and look at him with objective eyes, but the same answer keeps returning: Tosser.

IM: *Ah, yes. Extensive research has finally allowed us to confirm the existence of the Tosser gene…*

Mum greets me at the bottom of the stairs with a cup of tea. She's always been a big tea-drinker, but during The Split-Up, she seemed to drink even more and I sort of joined in. It was the only way I knew of offering

13

some form of support at the time. In films, you see guys drowning their sorrows with beer or whisky. Me and my mum did it with Typhoo.

"Sleep well in your new room?"

"Yeah, not bad."

I can tell she's scanning me for any worries I might have, but I've learned not to give too much away. I know she only has my best interests at heart, but if I say something's up, she'll tell Tony and, in a clumsy moment of attempted bonding, I'll be subjected to some sort of chat that neither he nor I want to have.

We go into the lounge, which is big enough to pass for the entire ground floor of our last house. Tony's sitting cross-legged on the floor, a Buddha with a fag, reading a book from one of the boxes he's just opened. Mum's already buzzing around in the background, like a well-meaning bumblebee.

"I think these are yours, Arch. D'you want me to take them up for you?" She's standing by the two boxes I couldn't find last night.

"Yep. They're mine. Don't worry, I'll do it."

They contain my game-playing gear. OK, here's where I have to clarify something else. Because of this *one* quirk, this *one* fascination, this *one* harmless little interest, I am, according to the Rules of Society, hereby branded a "Geek".

IM: *Let's not forget your ability to quote* Star Wars, *your obsession with fantasy novels, your inability to pass a comic book shop without buying something and your general hopelessness with girls. Oh – and you don't like football. Just sayin'.*

Like most people my age, I have a computer and a PlayStation, but a couple of years ago I came across the cover of a Sunday magazine – one of those that comes with the papers. On it was a photograph of a dragon – quite obviously a model, but painted in a way that made giving it a go seem like The Most Important Thing in the World. It wasn't that the model looked alive, it was that it looked like a Work of Art. The dragon in question was a Fire Dragon, and I can still remember how each of the red scales was christened with a yellow highlight that melted seamlessly into the base colour. My world was rocked.

IM: *Nothing geeky about that.*

So, I read the article, just to see what it was about, and it turned out that there was this world of gamers who painted miniatures to accompany their RPGs, or Role-playing Games. It was like I had discovered something that no one else knew about, some ancient and mysterious secret. At least that's what I thought until Dad said it was pretty big when he was growing up. And Mum told a story about some religious-types handing out leaflets at her school, saying that these games were one step away from Satan worship. And Dad admitted he knew a guy who knew a guy who might've played it while he was at college. It seems that even in the Dark Ages, RPGs had a bit of a Geek rep going: no one likes to admit that they ever sat round a table fighting pretend monsters with dice.

IM: *No kidding? Why could that be?*

Yes, we're talking Dungeons & Dragons, the great-grandaddy of all RPGs. And the best. Something in me just seemed to bite. Mum and Dad's rows had reached biblical proportions by then, and it was a cheaper escape route than the ticket to Greece I occasionally fantasized about. Even better, the article had a list of shops where you could buy this sort of stuff and – guess what? – there was one in my town! Boringsville suddenly had an adventure playground and it went by the name of "The Goblin's Hovel".

That was it: any money I came by – be it my allowance or odd-job money or birthday cash – I was straight down the Hovel. It was like an Aladdin's cave: models of every colour and description stood proudly in display cabinets; others fought battles on gaming boards mocked-up to look like forests or wasteland. Dragons stood side by side with trolls and ogres, while barbarian warriors valiantly tried to hold them off. There was a part of the showroom dedicated to the tricks of the trade: modelling knives, glues, brushes and paints with names that practically begged you to stick a paintbrush in and get cracking – who could resist "Goblin Green" or "Vampire Vermilion"? And the models themselves: sculpted heroes and villains striking poses that made you want to believe that magic is real.

IM: *"Geek Grey", anyone…?*

I s'pose the other thing the Hovel gave me was a place to hide; somewhere I didn't have to listen to raised voices or conversations cracking under the strain of civility. Even if it did mean listening to the sound of Big Marv, the owner's, 80s metal collection blaring over the in-store sound system.

And then there were the games: games in which you could adopt the persona of a character a million miles away from who you really were – heroic fighters, wily thieves, insane magicians. It called to me like a whisper from a dream.

IM: **Whispers* Geeeeeeek…*

It became my Saturday regime: pop down to the Hovel and spend hours deciding which miniature would receive the loving caresses of my paintbrush. Or, if I didn't have any money, just flipping through the rule books of various games to marvel at the mechanics of imaginary worlds that could be brought to life. I'm not even going to *begin* to talk about all the dice you can get for the rules systems. Needless to say, I hung out at the Hovel A LOT.

I guess I was a bit embarrassed at first and kept myself to myself, but slowly I started to recognize the odd face from school and a few surreptitious nods were exchanged. Some of the nods evolved into conversations and mates were made: Matt, Beggsy and Ravi – all of us united in leaving the Real World behind. Every few weeks, we'd meet at someone's house and embark on a journey together, hunting monsters, slaying the undead or double-crossing each other for a jewel with special powers. Unsurprisingly, there were never any girls there.

IM: *Just can't … figure … out … why…*

In fact, the next game is due to be staged at my new house, but I've got to find the right time: I need Mum and Tony to be out, so that we can really get involved without the fear of half-time sandwiches being delivered to the door by my mum and bringing us all crashing back to earth. It's all about atmosphere, you understand.

So there you have it: my name's Archie and I'm a Geek. But only in this world…

I'm halfway up the stairs with the second cardboard box when the landline rings; I won't be getting a new mobile until I've raised the cash to pay for half of it. According to Mum, spilling paint on the last two doesn't qualify as "looking after your possessions". Mum calls up after me, masking the mouthpiece with her hand.

"Archie! It's for you."

I dump the box on the landing and thunder back down, trying not to appear too eager.

"Hey, Archie." It's Beggsy. His voice still hasn't fully broken yet and he swings from sounding like Mickey Mouse to James Earl Jones in a matter of seconds. I'm pretty lucky: mine broke gradually, without me really noticing it.

"Hey."

"How's the new pad?"

"Cool. What's up?"

"Dude – have you forgotten what day it is?"

"Remind me."

"*Dude!* June the 9th! It's Battle-Fest! Down at the Hovel!"

Beggsy's right! It's the day when the Hovel comes into its own. I can't believe I'd forgotten! This is the day when they open up the doors for gamers to bring their prize models down to the shop and game like there's no tomorrow. There are painting workshops with visiting artists, awards for the best models and winner-stays-on war games! It's Geek heaven.

"What time?"

"Two. You coming?"

The "Yeah!" I give him is one that asks, "Are you completely nuts?" at the same time.

"Great!"

"Hang on," I groan. "I've promised to unpack."

"*Du-ude!*"

"Hang on!"

I smother the mouthpiece and call back after Mum. "Mum! Is it OK if I go down the Hovel? There's a games day on."

She comes into the hallway, holding a pewter-coloured kettle half out of its newspaper wrap.

"What about all the unpacking?"

"I'll unpack my stuff later – I promise. It's the last Saturday of half term…"

I know the answer before she says it; she does this frown thing that's supposed to suggest that she's thinking about it, but I've seen better acting in pantomimes. Without waiting to hear the "yes" that's rattling around her head, I'm straight back on the phone to Beggsy.

"See you there."

"Cool. Bye."

"Bye."

A hand on my shoulder makes me spin round: Tony's grinning at me like he knows something I don't.

"Trying to get out of the unpacking, eh, Arch?" He throws in a knowing chuckle, just to make sure that the urge to punch him becomes really unbearable.

IM: *You TOSSER! As if YOU'RE going to be doing ANYTHING other than sneaking off to read the paper somewhere!*

For some reason, I throw my appeal out to Mum.

"I've already said I'll do it later, haven't I, Mum?"

She just smiles and goes back to the unpacking, and Tony chuckles off as if he's won some kind of victory. I silently mouth "Tosser" after him, then shoot upstairs to have a root through my miniatures. What should I take? Should I take anything? You've got to understand that this is like gun slinging for Geeks; every hotshot who thinks he can use a paintbrush will be there, waving around his best offering and weighing it up against the others. To take nothing would be like admitting defeat, like the Mexican peasants in spaghetti westerns. But if I take the wrong thing...

IM: *It just doesn't bear thinking about...*

I eventually settle on a wizard I painted a couple of months ago. It's not a showboating piece, by any means, but I'm quite pleased with the flesh tones, and the detail

I've put in on his cape was researched from ancient Celtic writings. It also boasts the best varnish job I've ever done: four layers of gloss that give it the look of china. It's good enough to show that I've got a steady hand and I'm not frightened to use it. I lay it gently in a carry case and pack it with cotton wool.

Two o'clock is just round the corner. If I get my act together, I should make it with time to spare.

It's time to ride into battle.

I wonder if Mum'll give me a lift?

TWO

To be honest, I could have walked it; the new house is only about twenty minutes from town. But you don't turn up late for a games day. It's Geek Law. And even though I'm at least ten minutes early, the Hovel is already overflowing with Geeks. This means that on the pavement outside there are loads of little groups of guys my age and men in their forties, all wearing clothes that are meant to act as camouflage. In reality, their clothes are so drab that they might as well be wearing neon signs with "I'm a Geek – And So is He" flashing on and off above them. It's a weird one, but in an effort to fly under the radar, they make themselves impossible to miss. I s'pose this is where me and my mates break from the herd; we dress pretty normally. But, then again, I'm a Geek, so what do I know?

IM: *You said it, not me.*

I eventually locate Beggsy standing with Ravi and Matt beside a lamp post.

"Hey."

"Dude!" Beggsy's always the first to respond. He's got this hyped-up enthusiasm about pretty much anything you'd care to mention. If he wasn't such a nerd, he'd be really cool, if you see what I mean. It's not that he looks like a dork or anything, he's just a Geek to his teeth. The Geek Factor is a hard one to define, but you don't need to be Simon Cowell to spot it. It might be the way somebody talks or what they talk about.

IM: Star Wars *versus* Star Trek. *Discuss.*

Often, they'll be lacking the basic grooming techniques, such as sorting their hair out. The other big one is Geeks who have become Totally Immersed. Basically, this means that they identify heavily with a character from a film or book and go a bit too far in trying to look like them. Cue full-length leather coats or wispy goatee beards and ponytails. Those guys are *proper* Geeks.

IM: *And you're just a regular guy…*

He might be a Geek to his teeth, but Beggsy doesn't look like one. I don't think I do either, for that matter. But Ravi and Matt… You don't need a Geek Detector™ to single them out. Ravi's got the permanent downcast expression of someone who's heavy with hormones, and Matt is cursed with bright ginger hair and this sort of angular body language that shouts his awkwardness before he even opens his mouth. And when he does open his mouth, you get this kind of thin voice. It's broken, but he's no Darth Vader. The Touch of the Geek is definitely upon them. Matt deals with his affliction by dishing out sarcasm like a croupier deals cards. Ravi doesn't say much – he just watches people, like everyone's a potential threat: the Geek Factor in full flow. And he's also got the deepest voice out of all of us, which sounds weird coming from such a weedy-looking guy.

"Dude! What did you bring?" Beggsy asks, all enthusiasm and Mickey Mouse squeaks.

I pull out my carry case and unveil my wizard. Three sets of eyes home in on it, examining my handiwork with hawk-like precision. Matt takes the wizard in his palm and squints at it in the sunlight.

"What did you use for the gloss?" he mutters. "A roller?"

This produces a couple of snorts and knowing guffaws from the rest of the gang – me included. It's not that the guy's dry, he's more like a walking drought.

"Yeah, yeah," I say, grinning. "And what about you losers? What did you bring?"

In an instant, they present me with an ogre, an undead warlord and a goblin wolf-rider. Each of them is pretty good in its own way. Of the lot, Beggsy's wolf-rider, which has been deftly dry-brushed, then highlighted to show off the intricacy of the model, has the most chance of winning anything.

A bang on a gong from Big Marv pulls us out of our

weighing-up: Battle-Fest is underway!

We go in, Beggsy leading the way. He heads straight for the role-playing table and quickly digs into an adventure. Matt heads for the war-gaming table: it's a more mathematical game, which suits his personality, but he waits on the sidelines to size up the competition. Me and Ravi have been given the job of handing in our competition entries and, after registering them with Marv, we take some time to check out what we're up against. There's some really eye-catching stuff here, not least an Elf mage and a demon of some sort – they both look as if they could leap off their stands. Ravi raises a wry eyebrow too. It's going to be a close finish.

For me, it's straight over to the painting workshop. There's a guest artist from the miniature-making company giving away some of the arcane secrets of brushwork. There are a few stools for people who want to get in and try their hand, but they're taken, so I watch for a bit and then go and look at the new model releases "fresh from the forge".

One of them – a gargoyle – catches my eye. I think I'm going to have to buy it. As I study its bare metal form in the blister pack, imagining how I would paint it and how the finished article might look, I fail to notice that the general babble of Geek-speak around me has dropped to a hushed level. It's only a gentle tap on my shoulder that snaps me out of my artistic reverie, and I turn round to see the last thing I would ever expect to see in The Goblin's Hovel, at Battle-Fest, at 2.45 on a Saturday afternoon.

It's a girl.

If you haven't worked it out yet, girls don't do this. They don't come to the Hovel. They don't like goblins and dragons. They don't paint miniatures. They don't play role-playing games or re-enact fictional battles. And they don't come near Geeks like me.

Especially if they're pretty.

And this girl is pretty.

She's about my height and my age, and a bit of a Goth. Her hair is black and shiny, cut into a Cleopatra-style bob and there's just a little too much black eyeliner round her clear blue eyes. While she hasn't gone for the black lipstick thing, she's obviously powdered down her skin, giving it that slightly ethereal look. In contrast to her pale skin, she's dressed in black from head to toe: black top, fingerless gloves, black nail polish and a long, floaty black skirt. There's a couple of silver, Celtic-style rings on her fingers and some sort of ankh (like a cross with a hoop at the top) hanging round her neck. This is where it pays to be a Geek: I can identify obscure bits of jewellery – I've probably painted tiny versions of them somewhere down the line.

Of course, being tapped on the shoulder by a pretty Goth girl sends my Exterior Monologue (EM) and my IM into complete conflict. My EM tries to communicate the idea that this happens to me all the time – that I'm not in the slightest bit intimidated by her being of the OPPOSITE SEX and that I might not actually come to this nest of nerds that often. I do this by blushing madly, scratching my head and shifting my weight on to my back foot. Suddenly, it's like my body is an ill-fitting suit that belongs to someone else. All the moisture in my mouth evaporates and my tongue seems to swell up to the size and shape of a melon.

IM:*You'reagirlyou'reagirlyou'reagirl,you'reaPRETTY girlyou'reagirlI'mageekI'mageekI'mageekI'mageekyou're agirlyou'reagirlyou'reaPRETTYgirl...*

The Beautiful Goth smiles in a way that makes me want to stare at her mouth for ever.

"Hi." Her voice is like tinsel. I don't know any other way to describe it.

IM: *OhGodohGodohGodohGod...*

"Hi." I sound like I'm gargling with sand.

"Sorry to bother you, but ... what is this place?"

"It's a shop."

IM: *Ten points for stupidity!*

"Yes, but what sort of shop?"

IM: *Don't make it sound like you know too much!*

"It's a games shop. Role-playing games – that sort of thing."

IM: *That alone was WAAAY too much!*

"Oh, right." She looks vaguely disappointed and all my major organs feel like they're melting in sympathy. "So none of this is … it's not 'real', then? Not … you know…"

IM: *What? What do I know?*

"…to do with…"

IM: *WHAT? TO DO WITH WHAT?*

"…magic?" She says the last word quickly and quietly.

While it's a weird question, my memory bank briefly reminds me that my dad once showed me how to pull a coin out of someone's ear. This may be the wrong time. Besides, I've only got a tenner.

"No, it's not real. It's all games and models. Just make-believe. You know."

"Oh, OK. Thanks. Sorry to bother you."

IM: *It's no problem at all because I think I love you. Can we forget I'm a Geek and elope?*

"No worries." My EM gives one of those stupid shrugs that's supposed to suggest that I'm friendly and approachable, but in reality probably looks like I'm having a minor fit of some sort. She goes with a shy smile and a quiet "thanks" and a part of me leaves with her.

There's a tap on my other shoulder. I can't take much more of this.

I turn round to be confronted with a much more ordinary sight: Beggsy, Matt and Ravi.

"Dude! What was *that*?" says Beggsy, grinning.

"Just some girl."

Matt smirks darkly. "Another dream consigned to the scrapheap."

"Yeah," I sigh.

What I hate about him most right now is that he's absolutely right.

"Is that a gargoyle in your pocket – or are you just pleased to see me?"

"Ha, ha. It's definitely a gargoyle."

We are heading home, and Matt hasn't relented for the past fifteen minutes. It's not surprising, really. Given our Geek status, none of us have had any real exposure to girls, and the fact that I have just been involved in something that might almost be considered a conversation with one does make me an easy target.

But we all know it's just an unconfessed way of expressing envy.

My meeting with the Beautiful Goth has eclipsed pretty much everything else; Beggsy got a runner's-up award in the painting competition and Matt nearly won a war-game tournament. We've even forgotten our usual favourite topic of conversation: Kirsty Ford.

IM: *But now,"There is another."*

Matt's the first to peel away, firing off a few more Goth-based parting shots before he reaches his house. Ravi's next – a couple of streets later – leaving me and Beggsy. Before the move, I would've been the next to break away, cutting through Davenport Road to the shoebox that me and Mum called "home". I'm now grateful for the extra ten minutes I've got to walk to the new house; it allows me time to give all my Anti-Tosser Systems™ a quick service.

"Dude – we still gaming at yours next weekend?" Beggsy's voice covers three octaves in one question.

"Yeah, I just want to see if I can get the Olds out for the evening."

"Why? Your mum and Tony are cool."

Beggsy's got a real hate-on for his parents at the moment, which could be down to the fact that his Olds seem to be living in a 1970s time warp. He works in insurance and she is a teacher whose preoccupation with the house being *über* clean and tidy verges on OCD. It's one of those "shoes-off" houses, which always makes me a bit uncomfortable as my feet can have a way of announcing themselves – especially if I've been wearing trainers. Which I usually have. Beggsy's comment irks me slightly. I wouldn't ordinarily use the word "irk", but it just seems to suit; I'm not quite irritated enough to snap, but in my eyes there are a few variables that he hasn't taken into consideration. Firstly, that Tony is a Tosser. Secondly, that Tony is a Tosser and, thirdly, that Tony is a Tosser. And then there's all his knowing Tosser comments about the Game, like "Who's Gandalf tonight?" or "Off to slay more orcs, lads?" Yeah, yeah, we've all read Tolkien, but his only frame of reference is the film trilogy and it doesn't give him the right. Trouble is, I've got to find a way of conveying all this to Beggsy without sounding spoiled.

"Whatever."

IM: *Works every time.*

We amble along to Beggsy's house, discussing the ins and outs of our next game. As we arrive, I can see his mum twitching the net curtains in the living room. At my house, we have a lounge. In Beggsy's, they have a living room. Mrs Beggs opens the front door and waves at me. I wave back and Beggsy rolls his eyes, muttering a barely audible "Jesus" under his breath.

It's with a certain amount of relief that I notice Tony's car is missing from the drive. His absence gives me a moment to look at the new house with a different head on. I can see it as my home, rather than the place I stay with Mum and her boyfriend. And, I've got to say, as houses go, it's pretty good. The brickwork is a sort of pale pink and a hedge blocks the view to the front door. It's private, but lets you know it's there. And, although we've yet to christen it, it's got to be way better for me and my mates to game in than the house me and Mum lived in after The Divorce. That house was small and my bedroom was right next to the toilet. Here, I've got an awesome attic room, well away from the toilet, well away from Mum and Tony's bedroom…

IM: *Don't even go there!*

…and, most important of all, well away from Tony.

I let myself in and find Mum in the hallway, surrounded by balls of scrunched-up newspaper.

"Hello, love. Did you have a nice time?"

"Yeah, cool. Where's Tony?"

"Just nipped out for some cigarettes. He ought to be back by now; he's probably stopped off at the snooker club."

Figures. If there's any hard work to be done, Tony's

usually to be found at the snooker club. According to him, the best business deals are never done in the office, but over "a pint and a frame".

IM: *Whatever.*

So that means Mum's been left to man the battle stations, single-handed. Judging by the amount of newspaper all over the floor, the stacks of unopened boxes and the ornaments, books and other stuff that is, right now, homeless, she's going to need another gunner.

"D'you want a hand?"

"Don't worry, love. I'm quite happy just pottering. Go and relax."

That's my mum for you; she gives everything and never thinks it's enough. With a fond "Shut up", I help her unpack and enjoy just hanging out, me and her. Just like before she met Tony.

Over the next hour or so, we rummage through newspaper, collapse boxes and put things in one place, only to move them again a few minutes later. Eventually, Mum throws in the towel.

"Cup of tea?"

I think she's powered by tea. I'm sure there'd be some sort of economic disaster in India if she ever stopped drinking it.

"Go on, then." It's a cuddle in a cup.

IM: *It's also the right time to ask her about the*

34

Game on Friday night...

But just as we enter the kitchen, I hear the front door go. All my survival mechanisms kick into place, proclaiming that they're back online with a wave of tension that sweeps through my body and excavates a look that might just pass for a smile. Before he swaggers into the kitchen, Tony sticks his head into the lounge and makes a surprised, yet approving noise. Like the fairies have been.

"Well, that's the lounge nearly done," he announces, as though we've got no idea.

Beneath my dead-eyed grin, my IM is fully charged and operational.

IM: *Yep. That's the lounge done. And of course you're going to stand there, surveying your domain, as though you've actually been involved. Any second now, you'll be asking for a coffee, as though you've earned it.*

But Tony's got an ace up his sleeve; he always has. He suddenly swishes forward and produces a big bunch of flowers from behind his back. Mum, of course, melts and gives him a hug, before locating a vase.

IM: *Tosser.*

The amount of flowers he buys for Mum must keep the local florists in business. And Mum's always genuinely surprised and delighted. I guess that's where Dad fell down; he didn't do that sort of thing and

35

maybe that's why I hate it so much when Tony does – it's a reminder of my father's failings, a little insight into what might've driven my parents apart. Not that either of them has ever told me what happened.

"Any chance of a coffee, darling?"

IM: *Tosser.*

Mum's one step ahead of him and rewards the slacking hero with a steaming cup. I just can't work it out; she doesn't even scowl as he sparks up another fag. She hated Dad smoking and never stopped telling him. Clearly she's happy and loves Tony for what he is, warts and all. Although how anyone can be happy living with a Tosser is beyond me. Flowers or not.

Tony's steam-train voice cuts through the High Court which is in session in my head.

"Good news! I just clinched another deal! And Paul and Tina have invited us out for dinner on Friday night to celebrate…"

IM: *Result! Win! No Mum and no Tony = hassle-free Games Night! *Sound of party trumpets being blown**

Mum grins and ruffles his hair.

"Well done, love! That'd be nice. Archie?"

The gargoyle in my pocket presses into my thigh as I shift in my seat, almost insisting that I get it over with. So I do. "Could I get my friends round instead, Mum? You know – for a game."

Mum looks to Tony, even though I've asked her. He reacts with that sort of pantomime "you crazy kid" look that tells me that this fits in with his plans nicely. He didn't really want me along anyway. And, quite frankly, I'd rather spend an evening sticking pins in my eyes than watch him nosh his way through a Chinese.

"I reckon that's a deal, mate!"

"Thanks, Tony. Nice one."

Smiling has never been such hard work.

Back in my room, my shields go offline for a bit. It's not so much a strain to keep them up these days, more an inconvenience. It's certainly an irritant. Tony seems to have a knack for getting under your skin, but not in the way that Beautiful Goth did at the Hovel. My mind does the one thing I shouldn't allow it to and replays our encounter. Complete with cinematic music.

I stand in the Hovel, checking out the gargoyle. The music is like that bit in Return of the Jedi *where everyone's in Jabba's Palace – a bit edgy and dangerous. There's a tap on my shoulder. I whirl round, a coiled spring ready for action, all brooding and intense. Beautiful Goth is there and I see her try to hide the Instant Attraction she obviously feels. The cinematic music changes to that bit where Han Solo's about to get frozen in carbonite and Princess Leia tells him she loves him.*

"Hi," she says, sounding a bit nervous.

"Hi," I reply in a confident yet "I'm mildly surprised to see someone as beautiful as YOU here" kind of way. My tone and ice-cool body language suggest that meetings of this sort are probably the norm for a man of my experience.

"Sorry to bother you … but what is this place?"

"It's where I've been waiting for you." My reply comes complete with an amused smile. Beautiful Goth appears in awe of my worldly demeanour. Music swells.

"O-Oh," she stutters, taken aback at my directness. "Is any of this to do with magic?"

"It could be," I whisper, stepping forward and producing the Ace of Hearts from behind her ear. Unable to resist, Beautiful Goth steps into the kiss that is now inevitable. Music reaches a crescendo and then goes off into the Star Wars *theme, registering my triumph.*

IM: *Yeah, right. As if. Geek.*

I sigh one of those sighs that can only come from a heart that aches in vain.

IM: *You're a Geek, she's not; get over it.*

I need something to distract myself from Impossible Thoughts. It's time to start thinking about something else, something I can really focus on apart from how

I'm never in a million years going to get it together with someone like Beautiful Goth. The gargoyle suddenly seems really appropriate, like a self-portrait.

IM: *Cue the violins.*

I get out my laptop and hit the net. One of the things the internet is good for is research. As I Google the word "gargoyle" under Images, I get my new purchase out and tear the blister pack from its card. The gargoyle sits in my palm. It's a bit bigger than I'm used to painting – probably about 45mm in height. It sits hunched on a rock, its bat-like wings folded in on themselves, as though the creature is ready for flight. Beneath its heavy, furrowed brow, two perfectly round eyes glare out at me either side of its simian nose. The mouth is curled into a sneer, revealing sharp fangs. It's got everything you want in a gargoyle: pointed ears, horns, claws, goat legs and a dragon's tail. I'm going to enjoy painting this one.

The results come back and I browse images of stone monstrosities, deciding which details might be worth pursuing. It's all in the details; I could put on moss growths or paint in sinister cracks – maybe even birdshit. You've got to think outside the box before you commit the paintbrush.

More out of habit than curiosity, I hit the Facebook icon in my Favourites bar and open the home page in another tab. Out of the corner of my eye, I give my mates' posts the once-over. Nothing really to report: Beggsy's become friends with someone called Marcus and Ravi's uploaded a photo of himself as a child. Matt isn't on it – I think he's got some sort of conspiracy thing going, like if he uses Facebook, everyone in the world'll suddenly be able to see just what he gets up to when he's on his own. Like anyone's interested. It's probably more to do with the fact that, without his mates, Matt hasn't got much going on at all – which would be a pretty lame thing to broadcast over the internet. Not that Ravi and Beggsy have anything of world-rocking importance to say.

IM: *And you do?*

I return to the gargoyle images and continue my hunt for inspiration. A picture catches my attention and I click on it to get a better look. As I do so, I see my Facebook tab's flashing. It's Dad.

Hi son. Hope u r well. Can't make it 2mrw. The kids r ill & Jane needs my help. Maybe nxt wknd? L u Dad x

I hate it when my father uses text speak. I don't know why. I use it, my friends use it – but when my dad uses it, there seems something just totally … crap … about it. I read the message again. Great. So his new kids are ill and he can't make it out of the house.

Dad's inherited three children from his new wife. I think he dated her for about a year before I was allowed to meet her. Probably to protect my eleven-year-old self from anything resembling emotional trauma.

IM: *Like that hadn't happened already.*

But Dad made one major goof: he let me meet Jane before Mum found out about her. From me. Which didn't go down too well. It wasn't that Mum was jealous; between cups of tea she said she was glad he'd found someone. It was the fact she hadn't been told first so that she could tell me – help prevent Collateral Damage. And maybe she felt a bit threatened by Jane, I don't know. But her stress-outs didn't last too long – about a year later, Tony wheezed his way on to the scene and everyone was happy.

IM: *Almost everyone…*

Yeah, well, now I've got Tony and Jane in my life, and I've got to make like they're Family. Not to mention Jane's kids: Lucas, Steven and Izzy, aged nine, seven and four, respectively. Somehow, I'm expected to magically believe that these children are suddenly the brothers and sister I never had and that building Lego with them is what's been missing from my life. And that Jane, purely through signing a worthless bit of paper in a registry office, is somehow allowed to be "cool" and "groovy" with me in a way that makes my skin want to peel itself off. Her attempts at "bonding" make Tony's look positively sophisticated, and what she thinks passes as funny would make a corpse try and hang itself. Luckily, I've developed a VERY LOUD Interior Monologue.

IM: *Are we done yet?*

I guess Dad's happy, though. He's always rambling on about how well he gets on with "the kids" and how Jane is such a kind and caring person, so I guess I should be used to it by now. Perhaps it's my age; isn't that supposed to be responsible for everything that's wrong in my life right now? It's not the fact that both my parents are shacked up with idiots.

IM: *Of course not. It's your age.*

I type a reply that errs on the side of bland. Yes, I'm disappointed that I'm not seeing him "**2mrw**", but it's balanced out by the realization that I won't have to force a laugh out in the face of one of Jane's room-clearing jokes or build another house out of plastic bricks. My fingers skip lightly across the keyboard.

No worries. Next weekend is fine.

I hit Return.

Nice 1. Hows ur mum?

I don't know why he asks. Probably as some sort of pantomime attempt to show me that grown-ups can behave like adults.

She's good. Moved into the new house yesterday.

Thats nice. Hows ur room?

Cool. A lot bigger than the last one.

Good. Cudnt get much smllr! Lol!

The "lol" makes the hairs on the back of my neck yearn for freedom. Having a parent who lols is like finding out that that song you liked on the radio was by some 'tard off *X Factor*. It's so, so wrong. Best to head it off with a question.

How're you doing?

Fine, thnx. Got 2 go, tho. Mking chkn soup. Lol! FB u anthr time. L u xx.

x.

With a weighty sigh, I shut down the laptop and take

my gargoyle over to my painting desk. Already I've got a vivid picture in my head as to how this one's going to look. I open the window in the sloping ceiling above my desk and reach for a can of undercoat.

Time to make everything all white…

Once the undercoat is done, I switch the radio on and listen to some music while it dries. I need a distraction; I've already broken one of the Golden Rules of Geekdom and I don't want to go there again: never entertain thoughts about girls who are out of your league. That way madness lies. However, the radio has other ideas and it seems every song that plays has some hidden reference to Beautiful Goth. However tenuous:

Radio: *"You're beautiful, you're beautiful…"*

IM: **Sighs**

Radio: *"You're beautiful, it's true…"*

IM: **Attempts harmonies* "So true…"*

Radio: *"I saw your face, in a crowded place…"*

IM: *Was this guy watching? How does he know? It's like it was written about me!*

Radio: *"And I don't know what to do…"*

IM:
Radio: } *"'Cause I'll never be … with … you…"*

44

IM: *AAARRRGGGHH!*

As a final effort to try and put Beautiful Goth out of my head I kill the radio, unpack a few more models and locate my paint set. It nearly works.

There's a tentative knock at my bedroom door and I know it's Mum; my Tosser Tracker™ would have detected Tony lumbering up the stairs, hoiking himself up on the banister just in case his smoke-blistered lungs decided to pack in on him. Mum's brought me a ham sandwich and a cup of tea.

"Will this do for tea, love? I'll get to the shops tomorrow and we'll have a roast."

"Thanks, Mum."

"We're going to watch a DVD in a minute, once Tony's got the player wired up. Want to join us?"

"No, thanks. I'm going to try and sort out my room a bit more."

"OK. If you're sure."

I can tell by her look that she wants me to come and watch the film, but I just can't face it. For starters, the idea of watching Tony cursing at wires and SCART plugs for half an hour doesn't appeal. And actually trying to watch a film with him is virtually impossible; he has this habit of talking at the screen, and it drives me nuts. It's usually at moments of high tension, major plot points or killer lines. Like, if it's a sci-fi, and the lead guy is looking for an alien and we can see it behind him, Tony'll start saying things like "Uh-ohhh!" or "Heeerree it comes!". Or if the heroine goes into the wrong room (as they inevitably do in most films), you'll hear "You didn't want to do *thaaat*!" in this mindless, sing-songy kind of voice. Or when the hero comes out with some killer riposte, Tony'll chuckle and repeat it two or three times, almost as if he's storing it away so that he can use it. Like he's ever going to have the opportunity to tell a damned dirty ape to take its paws off him. Unless his business goes belly up, and he can only find a job as a zoo keeper and gets involved in a horrific set-to with a gorilla. One can only hope.

"No, thanks. I'm just going to hang out in my room."

"OK. You know where we are if you change your mind." And she's gone.

Absolved of my duties for the evening, I dig out my books from their box and start arranging them on the shelves above my painting desk. As you might've guessed, it's all escapist stuff: *The Lord of the Rings*, Terry Pratchett, the *Bartimaeus* books, fantasy art – that sort of thing. My gaming rule books have to go on horizontally as the shelves don't have the height for them. It's funny, when you unpack things, you end up paying more attention to stuff, almost as if its new environment might show up something you hadn't seen before. Without realizing it, I kill a couple of hours just flipping through books, dipping in and out. It's only the muffled thunder of Tony's feet on the stairs that make me notice that it's getting late and I'm tired. Mum calls through the door.

"Night, love!"

"Night, Mum."

I wait until I hear the click of their bedroom door before I get undressed and into bed. My favourite rule book has made it in with me and I hit my bedside lamp and start reading.

As I look at the pictures and reread rules that I virtually know off by heart, I can feel sleep tugging at my eyelids. Dread makes me fluff the pillows and sit a little straighter. I don't want to sleep. I'll fight it for as long as I can.

I don't want the Dream to come. Please can I dream about Beautiful Goth instead?

THREE

It begins, as it always does, with me asleep in my bed, in the same position I was in before I drifted off. With that weirdness that only happens in dreams, I can see myself on the bed, asleep, although I also feel like I'm in bed at the same time. It's like there's a camera filming me and a camera in my head, and they're both on playback at the same time. I can see both sets of footage simultaneously; no split screen, no tricks – just two sets of information relayed at once.

My duvet starts to peel back without me helping it. As I start to realize that I'm frightened beyond reason, I can feel a sense of menace emanating from something unseen at the end of my bed. The menace is intense and directed straight at me. If it had a colour it would be utterly and impenetrably black. The duvet suddenly shoots off and dumps itself on the floor. I can feel and see myself trying to move my leaden limbs and back up to the wall behind me, but I'm too slow, too heavy.

And then I wake up. I heave myself up and groan, running my hands through my hair. At least I didn't end up throwing myself out of bed this time. I've been having this dream, off and on, for a few months now.

Sometimes it goes quiet and leaves me alone for a while; sometimes it does a full cinema-release in my head, playing twice nightly for a week at a time. I hope this isn't the beginning of one of those. It makes me hate going to sleep and means that at weekends I end up sleeping in until late, and during a school week, I practically have to be winched out of bed. Luckily, Mum thinks it's because my body clock is set to "Teenage Time".

My bedside clock tells me it's six thirty-six on Sunday morning. I feel like I've been plugged into the mains, so there's no chance of me getting back to sleep. With a begrudging sigh, I pull open the skylight in the roof. It's all quiet outside, save for a few perky chirps from the trees in the street. I hope that the peace will somehow calm the noise in my head.

Later, with Tony sent off to do the shopping for lunch, the Emergency Sunday Morning Hunter-Gatherer Duties inevitably fall on my shoulders. I walk up to our new local shop for a pint of milk and a paper for Mum; it'll be a while before Tony returns and if she doesn't get a cup of tea soon, the universe may implode. The shop comes into view and, with an inward groan, I register a Pack of Grunts on the pavement outside.

They're a huddle of pale skin, dark eyes, hooded tops and crew cuts and I know exactly who they are: Paul Green, Lewis Mills and Jason Humphries. If you went to my school, so would you.

IM: *Shields up!*

Despite the fact that they're all in my year, I remind myself that they don't really know who I am. I tend to fly under their radar most of the time, but they'll have seen me around with Beggsy, Matt and Ravi, and somewhere behind those muscular brows they'll have me marked down as a nerd. Which shouldn't bother me, but right now I'm the only nerd in the street.

Trouble is, if I cross the road and walk in another direction, not only will I have to arrive home empty-handed, but somehow, in some way I don't understand, my seemingly innocent actions will mark me out as a target. I'll have flagged myself up as the injured gazelle, the bleeding fish – the Lone Geek. So, there's no choice but to go through them and into the shop. The trick is to avoid eye contact, but not look like I'm avoiding eye contact. At the same time, I've got to keep watching them for any telltale signs that I've figured on their all-too bleak horizons.

The cigarettes are coming out and being passed round, like apes with bananas. Suddenly I'm conscious of my natural desire to curve my shoulders and blend into the surroundings. Can't do that – any display of submission means they've won the right to make my life difficult anytime and anywhere they like. Trouble is that walking too tall could be interpreted as a challenge.

If I had a mobile, I could fake a conversation. Instead, I opt for the old hands-in-the-pockets routine and an expression that says I'm really thinking hard about something.

I get closer and, like an automatic response, one of them looks up in my direction. I catch my breath, but I know it's too late and so does he. A dull recognition dawns in the shadowed eyes of Paul Green. There's the rumour of a dark smile on his lips. I'm committed, so I've got no choice. But then suddenly one of the Pack who's got his back to me – Jason – slaps Paul on the chest and jerks his head in the direction of the shop. Paul and Lewis follow his lead.

What happens next is a bit like any scene from *Star Trek: The Next Generation* where Worf has to register surprise. It's the sort of facial pantomime that only a true brain-donor can master. The three hoodies have it down to a T.

I briefly wonder what they're looking at, but to tell the truth, mostly I'm just relieved that something else has got their attention. And then I find myself having a similar moment, as Beautiful Goth steps out of the shop and walks towards me. Smiling.

IM: *Two to beam up.*

I'd love to report that at this moment the hoodies fade into the background as Goth Girl practically floats over in slow motion, eclipsing everything around her. The reality is that her presence – glorious though it is – only serves to make the Pack of Grunts more aware of us both. One of them, Jason, barks something, leering over his shoulder. His mates seem to rock back, as though they're hinged at the pelvis, laughing and crossing their arms. But their dead, dark eyes work her up and down like the coils of three boa constrictors.

In one world, I am a Level 5 Mage, capable of summoning an undead army to do my bidding. In this one, I'm a nerd who stands about as much chance of facing off these jerks as a fart in a hurricane.

Thankfully, Goth Girl is made of sterner stuff. With a flick of her alabaster head, she snaps back with a retort that is packed with more swear words than you'd have thought possible. She throws "the finger" in for good measure and then, I could be wrong, but I'm sure that her walk morphs into a strut that accentuates the swing of her hips. She stops in front of me and fixes me with her ice-blue eyes.

IM:...*Eep.*

"You were in that funny shop yesterday, weren't you?"

I silently damn my nerdishness and nod like I've been possessed by the spirit of a woodpecker.

"The Hovel, yeah."

"Can we talk for a minute?"

IM: *God and Baby Jesus.*

"Yeah, sure."

With that, she quickly links arms with me and walks me away from the shop. I'm ashamed, but not too proud to admit, that this is the most contact I've ever had with a girl in my whole life. It's as if I've suddenly inherited Peter Parker's spider-sense; every patch of my skin (that is in contact with my sweatshirt that is in contact with her tight black top that is in contact with her skin) is suddenly suffering from heightened awareness. Not to mention the faint blooming in my nether regions.

We keep walking away from the shop, my mother's milk becoming a distant memory.

IM: *Dear Sigmund Freud…*

"So … uh … what do you want to talk about?"

IM: *Just shut up for a minute. Let her do the talking. Mouth closed; ears open.*

Beautiful Goth stops suddenly and swings me round in front of her.

"Have they gone?"

For a moment, I haven't got a clue what she's on about and then it clicks. I peer past her and look at the

Pack of Grunts. Even from here, I can see their foreheads rippling. All three of them are looking at us now, and the muscular nodding that is taking place can only spell bad news. Then, to my relief, they pull their bikes round in a motion that reminds me of cowboys on horseback, and vanish in the other direction, leaving cigarette smoke in their wake.

"They've gone." It's only two words, but I try and inject them with as much Han Solo as I can.

Beautiful Goth seems to put all her weight on one leg and lets half her body slump. I've never seen anyone slump so elegantly.

IM: *Come on! She's stressed! You might be able to get your arm round her!*

I silence the newly awakened predator that seems to have moved into my body and search my extensive database of films for the appropriate thing to say.

"Were they bothering you?"

Goth Girl unslumps and looks me dead in the eye with a smile that would make Clark Kent order a kryptonite sandwich.

"Why? You a ninja or something?"

IM: *She knows you're a nerd! Abort! Abort!*

This causes my EM to react with an all-systems shutdown. Without a film quote or a terminal one-liner to fall back on, all I can do is blink excessively, stutter a

54

bit and blush. Goth Girl's expression changes to one of concern.

IM: *Pity'll do...*

"I'm sorry, I didn't mean it! I've just got a bit of a funny sense of humour. Look – let's start again. Hello. I'm Sarah and thanks for helping me out with that bunch of losers."

Out comes a hand. I think I'm supposed to shake it. My EM comes back online and manages a lopsided smile.

"Archie."

My hand goes up and meets hers, spider-sense tingling in anticipation. But I don't anticipate her next move: when our hands meet, she pauses for a second and then suddenly grips it tighter. At the same time, there's a barely audible gasp and a look of alarm crosses her face.

"Oh my God..."

She's looking really concerned now, and for a second I have this awful image of my flies being undone. In a panic, I pull my hand from hers.

"What is it? What?"

"You're really..." the alarm on her face deepens to a sort of sadness "...angry. Aren't you? *Hurt*."

I wasn't expecting that. I've had a few odd encounters in my life – the worst one to date was walking in on Tony in the bath – but we now have a new reigning champion.

In all the IM/EM chaos that's going on, something in her pure, pure voice calls to a fragment of my soul that I've kept hidden for a Long Time. But I'm not about to spill my guts to a beautiful girl I've only just met.

"Isn't everyone?"

IM: *Good work. Sounds worldly-wise and is neither a confirmation nor a denial. A career in politics beckons.*

Sarah looks at me with a squint, as though trying to probe deeper, and then suddenly starts acting as though nothing has happened.

"Why were you in that shop yesterday?"

"I like the games."

"They're all about magic and stuff, aren't they?"

"Well … yeah."

"So, do you believe in magic?"

"They're role-playing games. You sort of pretend with rules." I want to die.

"But do you believe in magic?"

Whether I believe in magic or not doesn't really matter to me right now. What does matter is that Sarah is still walking with me even after my response, which was:

"I'll get back to you on that. I need to buy some milk."

Hardly a show-stopper, I know. But then, to cement my position in the world as an idiot, I add:

"But I have read *Harry Potter.*"

Sarah's reply consists of a bewildered smile and a series of blinks, which only reinforces my suspicion that I am as stupid as I look.

We retrace our steps in deafening silence, and she waits outside the shop, while I damn myself until the milk-buying is over.

IM: *WHAT THE HELL IS WRONG WITH YOU? WHY NOT JUST SHOUT "EXPELLIARMUS" AND ASK HER FOR A GAME OF QUIDDITCH?*

I think the last time I was asked if I believed in magic was when I was in the audience of a pantomime as a kid. Back then, it was just a given – of course magic was real, of course there was a Father Christmas and it was an indelible fact that something unspeakable lurked under my bed at night. However, as time passed and hairs grew, the idea of magic simply hadn't occurred to me; not as a reality, anyway.

We start walking and talking – two things I do most days, but now they seem almost impossible to do simultaneously. It takes me a moment to realize that we're walking in the direction of my old house, back towards town, and that we will soon have to go our separate ways.

But I want this to last for ever.

My EM slows the pace down to an amble. Like the ones that couples do. Throughout my pondering, fretting and self-damnation, I am now managing to explain the mechanics of role-playing games to Sarah, who wants to know how they work. And who looks confused.

"So you use dice?"

I really do want to die right now. Better still, I'd like Jason Humphries and his Pack of Grunts to reappear and for me to be suddenly possessed of the ninja skills so obviously absent from my life. *That* would be magic. Instead, I'm trying to justify playing what suddenly sound like children's games.

IM: *Pass me the Lego.*

"Yeah – there are points systems and you use the dice to accumulate or lose points, so you can learn new skills or get stronger."

"So there's a lot of maths involved?"

"Well, yeah … but it's not really about rolling dice. It's more about creating a character and trying to react the way that character would."

"What? Like acting?"

"Sort of. I s'pose it's more like narrating a story; you say what your character's doing."

"Can you die in the Game?"

IM: *I could do it right now, if you wanted.*

"Yeah."

"And what do you do? Do you dress up?" Her Antarctic eyes sparkle with mockery – but it still looks sexy.

"No! We use models. Figures."

58

"Little men?"

At this point I'm eagerly listening for the bony scrape of Death's feet behind me, almost wishing for a skeletal hand on my shoulder.

"Yeah. Little men."

"And what are they for? I mean, if you're narrating a story."

"Uh... They're more to give you an idea of where things are, like if you were in a battle or something. I'm not explaining it very well; you'd have to play it to understand."

"OK. I'd like a go. Could I?"

IM: *Oh. My. God.*

I now experience two conflicting emotions. One is a joyous lightening of my spirit: the most beautiful girl I have ever seen – with whom I have had some form of bodily contact – wants to come and play an RPG. The other feeling is as though liquid lead has been added to my soul: if I allow this, I will be vulnerable to her. She will see me for what I am: a nerd of biblical proportions. My mouth is dry and my stomach feels like it's on fire. What do I do? Rock forward on to my toes and lean into the wind or walk away from the edge?

Now or Never.

Now is quite a frightening place at the moment. Never is safe and peaceful.

"Yeah, OK."

"Great! When?"

"Well, we're having a game on Friday night. You could come to that if you want."

"Cool, it's a date."

IM: *A date? She said "date"! She said "date"! Oh my God – it's a date! You've got a date! With her! A real one! A date!*

I know that it's *not* a date, not in the official sense, but part of me is suddenly convinced that it is. It's this mad fantasy that stops me from hearing her next question, so she has to repeat herself.

"Do I have to bring a little man?"

Images of midgets flash through my mind.

"Uh … no. No. I've got one you can use." I drag to a halt; this is as far as I can go without walking her home. And much as I'd love to, I think it might be interpreted as stalking.

"Cool. I'll see you at school and we can sort it out."

"School?" I squeak. It's not a word that I usually squeak, but on this occasion it makes my heart flutter to the point that I'm wondering how long it would take a team of paramedics to get here.

"Yeah. Don't you go to the Community College?"

I nod dumbly.

"Me too! So, I'll see you there! Bye."

She goes to my school? As I surreptitiously watch her walk away, drinking in as much detail about her as possible, I find it impossible to think that I wouldn't have noticed her. Perhaps she's new. Then again, I'm a Geek and Geeks know that there are certain girls you mustn't even look at – you mustn't even acknowledge that they exist. Because if you do, your Geeky little heart will shatter in the knowledge that pretty much all girls will never, ever be in your league. Especially girls like Sarah. Sarah, who has talked to me and wants to come round to my house on Friday!

Just as my spirit spreads its wings and goes to soar, eagle-like, over the rooftops, a screech of brakes and a *honk-honk* brings me back to earth. It's Tony. He pulls up next to the kerb and the window slides down. Panic races through me like a forest fire: how much has he seen? Please, God, don't let him ruin this for me.

"Hey, Arch! Want a lift?"

I get in, my EM doing its best to appear as though I haven't just been hanging out with a real, live girl. Tony sparks up and a grin twists his face as we pull away.

"You sly old dog!"

FOUR

The car journey is a cocktail of smoke, denial and knowing nods. However much I try to tell Tony that I'm not seeing Sarah – which I'm not – it doesn't stop the worldly-wise wag of his head and the "I see through you" chuckle that accompanies each of my attempts to explain away the situation as casually as possible. I'm not helped by the fact that my EM has gone into warp-drive, causing my face to glow like a Hallowe'en pumpkin. But what's even more worrying are Tony's attempts at complimenting me on my choice of girl (like I've mail-ordered her or something). To hear the man who is living with my mother describing a teenage girl as "a cracker" does make me wish that Tony's car had an ejector seat. His or mine – I don't care. I realize that this is an attempt at bonding, but the only palpable results are my nails digging into my palms and my toes bunching up in my trainers.

"So when do we get to meet her?"

IM: *What a great idea, Tony! I'll bring her round to the house so that she can listen to your pointless comments about life and then, to round it off, we'll go and set fire to ourselves in the garden!*

"Dunno." I'm running out of energy.

"Why don't you get her round one night, after school? I'll cook dinner and we can all have a laugh."

IM: *ARE YOU MENTAL?*

"Yeah … I dunno… We'll see how it goes." I'm running perilously close to accepting his offer, which would be a disaster.

"Have you told your mum yet?"

"Told her what?"

"About your girlfriend."

"But she's not… No." I give up.

"Well, let's get back and give her the good news."

Jesus, this is getting out of hand. All I was doing was getting a pint of milk and now I seem to be the centre of some Carnival of Love! The thought of facing my mum and telling her that I've got a girlfriend – which I haven't – is too much to consider. I really need to get a grip; all it is is a girl coming round to the house. OK, it's the first time – but it had to happen eventually, even by the Law of Averages. And I'm the first to admit I'm pretty average.

"She'll be chuffed for you."

And then I see his little game. He signals it to me without knowing – a little grin to himself, a subtle change in his demeanour. Me having a girlfriend would justify *his* existence. It suddenly makes sense. People get together. If I can do it, then there's no reason why my mum can't do it. Tony's presence in my life would be entirely justified. A sneaky, shameful part of me realizes that if that were the case, I'd have nothing to rail against. I'd have to accept him. The house is getting closer and I don't want to go there right now.

IM: *Bail out! Bail out!*

"Oh! I've just remembered! I'm supposed to be meeting the guys down at the Hovel. Could you drop me there?" With a bit of luck, Tony's inherent laziness will instantly dismiss the idea of driving back into town and he'll make some excuse and stop the car. Then I can get out and the interrogation will end.

"Sure thing, partner. Don't worry – I'll prime your mum."

IM: *Partner? And so it begins. Tony's acceptance into the fold starts here.*

Ordinarily at this point, I would want to die. Today, however, I want Tony to. Even if he *has* miraculously decided to drive me into town.

We pull up outside the Hovel and I hand over the milk and get out of the car, my EM throwing a casual wave at my stepfather as he speeds off. The way this is all panning out is making me tired; I need to clear my head. The Hovel's the best place I can think of.

Although it's a Sunday, there are quite a few people in here. Some old-school metal is blazing away in the

64

background, screaming something about running to the hills.

Whoever's singing has captured my mood perfectly and the thought of just vanishing is an attractive one. I could get a little backpack together, with my trusty walking staff, and just wander into the countryside, like Frodo Baggins. But I don't have a backpack or a staff and the Black Rider that hunts me owns a BMW. Plus I couldn't do it to Mum.

Another metal song from the Dark Ages starts up – something about "You Shook Me All Night Long". Like an age-old demon answering a summons, the sex-serpent in my head uncoils and whispers an idea. And it's a good one.

I need to paint a model for Sarah.

OK, this might not be an earth-shattering idea by most people's standards, but it works for me on a number of levels. Indulgently, I picture the scene.

Sarah enters my bedroom (hereafter to be known as my Lair). Matt, Ravi and Beggsy are there, settled round my gaming table. A gentleman to the last, I pull out a chair for her and she sits – do I sense she is a little flustered? Perhaps it is the aftershave I'm wearing. Sarah looks around my Lair, her curiosity piqued by the reams of dusty tomes that line the walls. I hand her a character-sheet for the Game, all filled in and ready to go. She looks at my friends and the miniatures they are holding; dismay crosses her perfect face.

"Oh!" she exclaims. "I didn't bring my little man."

"Not to worry," I breeze with a casual smile, "here's one I knocked up for you earlier."

Sarah takes the model from my hands, barely able to suppress her delight that I've thought of her, and gushing with admiration at my masterly brushstrokes.

"Did you do this just for me?"

I take a seat and casually produce a bottle of champagne.

"The pleasure was all mine. Would anyone care for a drink?"

As I pour and my friends turn their attentions to dice and rule books, Sarah casts me a secret smile and I'm sure I can feel something brushing against my lower leg...

This is neither the time nor the place to chase that particular narrative, so I turn my attention to the rows of blister packs that adorn the walls. It is with some indignation that I am, for the first time, suddenly aware of the lack of figurines for girls. What's the matter with the company that makes them? Don't they realize that girls play too? Or do they think these games are the sole pursuit of fourteen-year-old boys who've never had a girlfriend?

IM: *And so rests the case for the prosecution.*

After some searching, I manage to find some: there's an archer(ess?), an elven witch and an elven thief(ette?).

Which one should I choose? This is more difficult than choosing a model for myself; Matt, Ravi and Beggsy will know that I have painted it for the occasion and it will be scrutinized. They will be looking for the signs of anything soppy, such as a Galadriel-type figure. The archer is quite good: she's wearing a leather jerkin and tight leggings which show off her legs, but I can't help feeling that Sarah might find it a bit boring. The other two are elves, which I've always had a penchant for. Elves are sexy: they've got good, angular bone structure, long, laconic faces and there's even something a bit kinky about those ears. The thief is clutching a leather pouch of loot in one hand and a curved dagger in the other. In her belt are bottles, which I could paint up to look like a selection of poisons. But again, it's not quite right. It's not interesting enough.

The witch, however, is possibly a bit too interesting.

This witch obviously bats for the bad guys. Not that she's an old hag with a face like a crescent moon – she's an elf, remember? *This* witch has a cruel, yet seductive smile on her elegant face. One arm is outstretched, as though casting a spell and the other cradles a crystal ball. But the problem is her outfit: thigh-high boots, elbow-length gloves and a short jerkin that is cut tantalizingly low. Add to that a few bangles and a circlet on her head and you've got the general idea.

Dare I buy it?

Admittedly, I'd get a lot of kudos from the guys for presenting this one to Sarah – but how would she take it? As a compliment? With a look of horror? Or would she look into my soul and recognize it for what it is – flirting.

I look down at the miniature and, for a moment, feel as though I'm buying a dodgy magazine – which I never have, by the way. It is with some trepidation that I approach the counter before popping the witch in front of Big Marv. He picks it up and looks through the protective bubble, giving it a quick once-over. Then he raises a knowing eyebrow.

"Good luck," he says.

Home sends me scurrying through newspaper balls and over empty cardboard boxes, up to my room. As I creep Gollum-like through the hall, strangled strains of radio from outside tell me that Mum and Tony are somewhere in the garden. Perfect. I skulk up the stairs and into my Lair, closing the bedroom door behind me as quietly as possible.

My EM drops a gear and I settle myself at my painting desk to re-examine Sarah's model. It's a bit booby. Suddenly, my idle fantasies about impressing her with my Michelangelo-like abilities seem a lot less cinematic; I feel like I've just been caught drawing a dick on a school desk. Not that I ever have, you understand.

In the safety of the Hovel, the witch looked slightly classy, had a touch of refinement. Now she looks like something that a sexually frustrated teenage boy might draw on his artist's pad at night and then rub out come the morning feeling a bit guilty.

IM: *No comment.*

Maybe an undercoat will even things out. I throw open the dormer window above my desk and spray the witch with a fine blizzard of matt white. While she dries, I take a look at the gargoyle: it sits, hunched, almost scowling at me, begging for colour. Time for a black wash.

A wash, for the uninitiated, is where you thin a colour right down, until it looks almost like dirty water. Then, using a brush, you drizzle it on to your model. The liquid runs into every nook and cranny, carrying the pigment with it, exposing all the detail. It's all in the details.

After his bath, the gargoyle is already looking more alive; I can see cracks and splits in the stone skin surrounding his mouth, grooves in the horns and sinews writhing round his chest and shoulders. I can even see his irises, which are horizontal slits, like those of a lizard.

"Hello!"

My EM takes a second to find its default setting, but I needn't have worried too much; it's only Mum.

IM: *Uh-oh.*

Uh-oh, indeed. She's wearing one of those silly grins that says she can't wait to talk about something.

IM: *And we know what it is, don't we?*

My EM throws a slightly bashful smile to my lips, which fail to catch it properly and it looks more like I'm having a bout of wind. Silly grin still on her face, Mum comes and sits on the end of my bed.

"So, then…" The smile almost cuts her face in two and her expectant eyebrows reach to the heavens in anticipation of the Glorious News.

IM: *Please. God. No.*

"Tony tells me you've got a girlfriend."

At this point, my IM is barely able to contain itself and struggles with my EM for dominance.

IM: *Aaaieee! Divert all power to the main engines! Employ the cloaking device! Detonate the reactor core! We need warp factor five or we're all dead! DO SOMETHING!*

My spine seems to melt and I slide down in my chair, my eyes rolling to one side, a world-weary sigh adding to the possibility that I might be deflating.

"She's not my girlfriend, Mum."

"Oh?" Smile gone. Look of surprise.

"No. She's just someone I met."

"Oh." Look of disappointment.

IM: *Isn't it amazing how adults can wield vowel sounds to such great effect?*

"She's just a friend."

"Tony thought there might be a bit more to it…"

I deflate a little more, this time with a groan. If this carries on, I'll be little more than a sack of skin soon. Mum half rises off the bed.

"It's OK if you don't want to talk about it…"

If magic *is* real, then you need look no further than the Power of Mums; the slightest intonation or gesture can send you back to feeling like you were still in nappies. And had probably filled them.

IM: *No! Be strong! Resist!*

I give in and take charge of my IM.

"No … no, it's fine… She's not my girlfriend, Mum… But…"

"But you like her?" There's that look of hope again, the one that prays that her son might be freed from the Shackles of Geekdom.

Despite all its attempts to retrieve my dignity, the old EM just isn't built for this sort of pounding. It gives up and floods my face with blood, which promptly lights up like a solar flare.

"Yeah … I suppose so… Yeah."

"And what's her name?"

"Sarah."

"She goes to your school?"

"I think so." I'm going redder by the moment.

Mum leans forward in a conspiratorial sort of way, excitement dancing in her eyes.

"Ask her out, Archie. Ask Sarah out on a date."

IM: *That's it, she's finally lost her mind.*

"Yeah ... great idea, Mum... But it's not that simple…"

"It *is* that simple, Archie; nothing ventured, nothing gained."

I would love to believe her, love to be able to embrace that simplistic attitude, but she just doesn't understand! The mere thought of asking Sarah "out" fills me with dread and self-loathing. Equally, I can't seem to face the ludicrous levels of excitement that telling Mum Sarah's already coming over would bring. And I don't want to jinx it; I'll tell her when it's all settled in my head.

"Tony says he wants me to get her round for dinner one night." Try as I might, I can't keep the bleating terror out of my voice.

"Don't worry. I'll have a word with him, tell him to back off. I know how awkward it can be to let someone know you like them, but he's just excited for you. So am I."

Mum's earnest little face almost makes me want

to cry. Not tears of joy, but tears prompted by the fact that she's going to end up disappointed by her socially-challenged son.

"Ask her out, Archie. It'd do you good to have a girlfriend. Lunch'll be ready soon." And then she's out of the door and gone with a discernible spring in her step.

By the time I make it down to lunch, Tony has obviously been put on a leash and the subject of Sarah is dropped. However, it's clearly been dropped from a great height, because the ripples it's made make any other topic of conversation seem forced and stilted. I restrict my answers to nods and grunts, trying to become one with my roast pork.

After lunch, I thunder back up to my Lair and get some more unpacking done, leaf through old rule books, do a bit of painting – anything except think about what I want to think about, but I know I shouldn't think about. I can't help it; I end up thinking about it. I wonder where she lives.

IM: *Stop it…*

The parade of local shops is about a five-minute walk away from the new house. Given that I saw Sarah up at the local shops, it must mean her local shops are now *my* local shops.

IM: *You'll be telling us that two plus two equals four in a minute!*

And given that she was on foot, it means her house can't be too far away, either.

IM: *How* did *you manage it, Holmes?*

I wonder what her house looks like.

IM: *Stop it…*

But, try as I might, I just can't picture the sort of house a girl that beautiful would live in; this piece of the mental jigsaw puzzle has yet to be found. It's like I want to imagine it right and nothing less will do.

IM: **Sick noises**

And I wonder what she likes? Should I take a leaf out of Tony's book and start thinking about flowers? I've never bought flowers before; I wonder which ones are her favourites?

IM: *Why don't you start planning the wedding while you're at it? It's not even a proper date, you freak!*

My IM's right. I need to put these thoughts to bed. I keep going with the unpacking, but after a few hours, a hurried sandwich, a few false starts and a bubbly "good night" from Mum, I eventually throw in the towel, crash on to the bed, and take a profound interest in the ceiling. I wonder what Sarah's doing right now?

IM: *Not expending the same amount of energy thinking about you, that's for sure…*

Sleep ought to be a blessed release from the trials and tribulations of my non-existent love life, but the

Dream is waiting for me.

I wake up with a jolt, just as I'm about to discover the identity of the menacing thing at the bottom of my bed – and realize that it's standing over me.

Wearing slippers.

"What are you doing down there? And you're still wearing the same clothes from yesterday! Come on, you've got a big day at school today."

It's Mum. I groan and roll on to my back, suddenly aware of a string of dribble that's connecting me to the floor.

"Must've fallen out of bed," I mumble, climbing to my feet. "What's happening at school?"

That excited grin again. Here it comes.

"You're going to ask that girl out."

IM: *No pressure, then.*

FIVE

I realize this will cement my position as a Geek, but I like school. I like routine, I like learning – I even like homework. I keep hearing adults say that your school years are the best years of your life and, while there are worse things to be than a bookworming virgin, I hope it's not true. But today's got a little extra shine on it – today I might see Sarah. My stomach seems to be home to a kaleidoscope of butterflies.

Me and Ravi snigger through the peaks and valleys of the female reproductive system in Biology, and Matt lends his caustic wit to a debate on the themes in *Of Mice and Men* in English. It's a regular enough day, but there's no sign of Sarah.

IM: *I tell ya, I tell ya a guy gets too lonely an' he gets sick...*

Lunchtime waves its magic wand and we're all allowed to talk to each other about the things that matter most to us. For me, Matt, Ravi and Beggsy, it's planning the Game on Friday night. I still haven't got round to mentioning that Sarah's going to be there, and each time I think I'm going to say something, there's a flurry of panic in my stomach and my brain steers the conversation away to something else. Usually Kirsty Ford – they bite at that one like fish to bait.

"Yeah, but what do you think they *look* like?" Beggsy's saying. "I mean, when they're *unbound*?"

There's a brief silence round our table. The rest of the dinner hall keeps chatting and eating, unaware of the Nest of Perversion that lurks scant feet from their packed lunches and fish fingers and chips.

"'Unbound'?" Matt mocks. "These aren't oven-ready chickens we're talking about…"

"But they could do with stuffing, just the same," Ravi pipes up and we all groan.

"A little more decorum, please, gentlemen," I interject. "If we're going to plumb these depths…" resounding sniggers from the assembly "…then let's at least show a degree of respect. Mr Beggs, you have the floor."

"I'm just asking if you think they're uppies or downies – that's all."

Another stunned silence. Beggsy tries to recover ground.

"Do they defy gravity or are we talking about a pair of spaniel's ears? It's an important question!"

More laughter from the assembly and cries of "Order! Order!" from me, seeing as I seem to have been unofficially recognized as chairman. And just as suddenly as it starts, the laughter dies off and, too late, my Grunt Detector™ goes online. It takes me a split second to read the change in my compatriots' body language: rounded shoulders, eyes down and bland, unreadable expressions all round: the Nerd version of Duck and Cover – Cower and Quake. There's someone behind me.

IM: *Uh-oh…*

My EM follows suit, doing its chameleon-best to blend in with the environment, but a hand on my shoulder calls my bluff; I have no option but to turn round. Which I do, very slowly. A muscled forehead ripples at me.

"You're that kid outside the corner shop yesterday."

Up close, Jason Humphries looks even more terrifying; his skin resembles the surface of the moon and he has visible laughter-lines forming.

IM: *Probably from the twenty-four-hour delight he experiences at being tougher than God.*

For a moment I'm not even sure that he is my age – surely no fourteen-year-old can look so grizzled. And he seems to have more than his fair share of teeth, all of them little, but glittering like knives. The smell of cigarette smoke is thick on his breath as he fixes me with his dead eyes.

"You're that kid."

IM: *Deny! Deny! Deny! Even in the face of*

photographic evidence! You weren't there! It was your twin! Anything but the truth!

"Um … yeah."

IM: *Ashes to ashes, dust to dust…*

I feel Jason's meaty hand tighten briefly on my shoulder, suddenly aware that he's wearing a ring as it presses through my sweater. He blinks like cows do when there are flies bothering them.

"Who was that girl, then?"

IM: *Sister. Go for sister.*

"Um … just a friend…"

The smell of cigarette smoke gets more intense as Jason's anvil head gets closer to mine.

"Well, you tell her that I want to meet her, got me?"

I nod feverishly and I think the word "sure" drops out of my mouth like a rabbit turd.

"Good." There's another squeeze on my shoulder and then he swings away like a shark that's just detected one part blood in a million parts water. Slowly my friends unfold, like crumpled origami animals.

"What girl?" Matt's first out of the starting gate.

IM: *Oh, great. Here we go again.*

"That girl from the Hovel. I bumped into her again. Yesterday."

"Dude!" Beggsy can do wonders with that word.

This time it conveys *Is impressed*.

"And what about Humphries?" Of all of us, Ravi is the most shaken – and he doesn't care who knows it. That powerless, fearful feeling is written all over his face.

IM: *And he's not even anything to do with it!*

"He was there. With Paul Green and Lewis Mills."

"Dude!" This one conveys *Is worried*.

"And he *likes* her."

"Yes, Matt. He does." I'm getting a little irritated by my friends pointing out the potentially fatal aspects of my situation.

IM: *Coming through! Dead man walking! Coming through!*

My IM's cheery sentiment is echoed in the faces of my friends and the cloud of silence that seems to have descended over our table.

"That girl's going to get you into trouble, dude."

I try and gain control of my breathing.

IM: *Search your feelings, Archie; you know it to be true...*

And no matter how much I don't want it to be true, it is; Jason Humphries, the Human Avalanche™, likes the girl that I like. Somehow, I don't think pistols at dawn are quite his style.

It takes the journey from lunch to my next lesson for my pulse to return to something like normal. Having said I like school, my heart sinks as Mr Cook reveals the latest dose of geography homework. Tonight – and probably for the next two nights – I'll be researching precipitation in the North-East of England. In my life, when it rains, it pours…

The bell sees us spilling like a torrent of ants into the corridor and my inherent Grunt Detector™ scans the terrain for any tracks: knuckle trails, recent kills or even fresh droppings (usually cigarette butts or crumpled worksheets). Clear so far, but Grunts, like lions, tend to watch from afar, hidden in the long grass. Or the toilets, whichever is more convenient.

Up ahead, Ravi comes out of Maths, turns to see me and waits up. He calls over to Beggsy and Matt, who are heading for the drinking fountain. But all I can see is the person who follows Ravi out of his class.

"Hello, you."

My arm is linked and, once more, I'm gazing into Sarah's ice-blue eyes.

IM: *She's in your year! Re-sult!*

Addressing a fourteen-year-old boy as "You" is a sure-fire way to grab his attention. However, precede it with an "Oi!" and drop it from the mouth of a fourteen-year-old sociopath and the promises aren't nearly so inviting.

My Grunt Detector™ does a quick sweep of the locale – so far, so good.

IM: *Here's a tricky one: your three best mates up ahead and Starshine on your arm; how're you going to juggle this one?*

But my Interior Monologue is falling on deaf inner ears at the moment. I'm currently reeling from the difference in the way Sarah looks. No wonder I didn't recognize her: a) of *course* she's new. There's no way that even I wouldn't have noticed her before, and b) being a Goth must be her weekend thing. Goth make-up has that slightly forbidden feel to it; will what's underneath reveal a shining beauty, or will it unmask a Gorgon that would put Medusa up among the World's One Hundred Sexiest Women? Thankfully, it's the former; her skin is pale and flawless and her mouth curls up slightly more at one side so that when she smiles, it's like she knows something you don't. Which, in my case, is probably true.

Bolstered by the beauty on my arm, I raise the other and call manfully after my comrades.

IM: *You're a Geek! You're not supposed to be doing this!*

But recklessly, for the first time in my life, I cast the mantle aside and stride to my open-mouthed chums with more than a hint of swagger.

"Guys," I begin in a commanding tone, asserting

myself as the Alpha Male of the group. "This is Sarah. Sarah – Beggsy, Ravi and Matt." My mates shuffle and mutter a few "Heys" and "Hiyas" – no doubt in awe of her glowing beauty and possibly unsettled by the cloud of testosterone that has transformed me into a charming, yet not-to-be-trifled-with Man of the World. I briefly consider growing a moustache.

Sarah deals with the silent adulation like an absolute professional; she greets my friends in turn, making eye contact with each of them, which, for a Geek, is the equivalent of being eye to eye with Superman when he's got his heat-vision on.

"I'm really looking forward to Friday," she beams. "Let me know if you want me to bring anything." Suddenly, she spots someone upstream. "Got to go; Caitlyn's got some notes I need. Nice to meet you – see you Friday!"

And then she's gone, taking my heart with her and leaving a puff of silence in her wake. Matt breaks it. "'See you Friday'?" There's a touch of horror in his mockery and I can feel my inner Robert Pattinson being exposed to the harsh light of Reality. But there's no time to react; a lump of wall detaches itself from the rest and reveals itself to be Jason Humphries. My Grunt Detector™ needs an upgrade. He makes straight for me, ignoring my cowering cohorts, and pushes me gently with a yellowing finger.

"Friday. What's happening Friday, then?"

My inner Robert Pattinson is replaced by my inner Shaggy Rogers.

IM: *Zoinks!*

"It's nothing really... Just me and my mates..." I wish I could keep the fear out of my voice.

"Just you and your mates what? You having a party?"

IM: *Please – just make it painless...*

"No... We're... It's just a... We're playing a game. It's a game."

Humphries has a Worf moment, then all the sinews in his head constrict to form something like a smile.

"A game?" He flicks his head after Sarah and then back to me. "You wouldn't know what to do with her!" The finger in my chest becomes the focus for a lot of untapped power and I find myself pushed to the floor, covered in precipitation from the North-East of England. "See you Friday, Geek-boy." Then he too is gone. Beggsy and Ravi help me up and gather my notes. Matt is not quite so forgiving.

"What did she mean, 'See you Friday'?"

I hadn't realized that my friends were quite so insular. Trying to explain to them that a girl wants to come and game with us is a bit like trying to explain Facebook to medieval peasants. "Temper thy thoughts, good sir! Doth Satan himself conjure up such fantasies? Go! Speak of this no more!" Perhaps I'm starting to grow up.

Perhaps this is where I truly begin the transition from youth to manhood – and maybe my friends haven't quite got there yet. I might need to buy some aftershave.

"Guys, guys – I don't see what the problem is, she's just a girl! And how often have we talked about getting girls in on the Game?"

"The point is you should've asked us first." Matt's moral streak is suddenly asserting itself.

"Why? What's the difference? Surely it's going to make the Game better if we have some new blood."

"Dude, you know the score; it's the Game. We're mates." And now Beggsy's joined the lynch mob. I can feel the foundations of my argument becoming unsteady. Ravi remains quiet and watchful.

IM: *You're in the wrong. Put your hands up and admit it.*

Instead, I resort to distraction tactics. Less generous people might call it lying.

"But I didn't actually invite her, she just sort of invited herself. And then I couldn't exactly uninvite her, could I?"

"All you had to do was tell her you needed to clear it with us."

"And what would you have said, Matt? 'No'?"

"It doesn't really matter, Archie. You've taken that option away, haven't you?"

You can always tell when an argument's starting to change up a gear – people start using each other's names with pointed clarity and statements always seem to end in questions. These are the territorial displays of Geeks. Gorillas do it by beating their chests; stags lock horns; Geeks over-emphasize each other's names and bring out the Great Swords of Rhetoric. The thing is, I'm in the wrong. I *know* I am, but I've gone too far to back down. And part of me can't understand what the problem is.

IM: *Part of you doesn't* want *to understand what the problem is…*

There's a simmering silence, which is broken by Beggsy's NATO Peacekeeping sensibilities. "Dude, you just needed to check it with us. It's not like we would've said she's not allowed."

My argument fails in the face of my mate's Vulcan-like logic. Like the straw house built by the First Little Pig, it simply blows away. However, this Little Pig's not done yet; he has the whiff of the wolf about him and can huff and puff with the best of them.

IM: *Don't do it!*

Too late.

"It's not like you could anyway, Beggsy. It's my house."

Any free-standing structures built from straw, sticks or bricks should be instantly decimated. But I have this horrible feeling, even as the words leap sneeringly from my mouth, that I've just done a big one on my own doorstep. Matt fixes me with eyes that have suddenly become unreadable.

"OK," he says, nodding slowly. "Good. It's your house. At least we know where we all stand." And then, with a barely perceptible clench of his jaws, he turns briskly on his heel and walks away, something like determination in his stride. Ravi pauses for a second and then follows him.

"Aw, Du-ude!" This one conveys *Is disappointed*.

"Well... He was being stupid."

IM: *Do not pass "Go". Do not collect two hundred pounds.*

Beggsy remains obviously unconvinced, gently shaking his head.

"Dude. You've gotta sort this out." By this point, we're both staring at the same spot on the floor.

"I know..."

"Get him on the way home. Just say you're sorry and it'll be cool."

"I know... But what about Sarah? I can't just ... you know..."

"Dude." Conveys *Isn't having any of it*.

Can't argue with that. I sigh and follow the rest of the Year Nines down the corridor.

SIX

It goes without saying that Matt wasn't at the school gates at hometime; he'd chosen a different route back to his house. Luckily, this allowed me to play my Righteous Indignation card with the rest of the gang. I started out with a disarming display of humility, followed by concern that Matt was all right. This worked like a charm and my remaining friends, concerned that I was concerned, tried to alleviate my concerns by telling me that it would all be fine and he'd cool off soon etc, etc. Once they'd started to sympathize with me, it was fairly easy to suggest that Matt had overreacted and then I played my trump card.

"You never know, if Sarah likes it, she might want to bring some friends along to another one…"

The odours produced by Fear and Excitement are remarkably similar. I detected a heady cocktail of both before we all parted company in a flurry of knowing nods and stupid grins. To my friends, I am now the man who could offer them a Passport to Normality. For probably the first time in their adolescent years, they are exposed to the dizzying possibilities offered by Hope.

So why do I feel like such a fraud?

As I take the turning that leads into my road, a flash of silver passes me; Tony's going out, no doubt to clinch another deal.

IM: *Result!*

My shields go offline and I realize that I'm exhausted after clinching deals of my own. I need to chill out; I need to paint.

I can hear the bubble of the kettle as I step inside the front door and I can smell the ghost of one of Tony's cigarettes. And there's another smell, one from my dim and distant past – a sweet, comforting smell. I amble into the kitchen, unable to help myself.

"What's cooking?"

Mum turns round from the worktop and indicates a cake cooling on a wire rack.

"Fancy a cup of tea?"

I do, and Mum cuts me a slice of moist, warm cake. She hasn't baked for what seems like for ever, not since she and Dad were together, I think. I guess she's happy. For a while, the new house feels like a home: just me, Mum and the smell of cake.

"How was school?"

IM: *Shields up, maximum strength.*

I mumble something vague and non-committal through a mouthful of tea and cake.

"And…?" There's that little twinkle again.

"What?" I want her to ask the question, rather than me volunteer the answer.

"How did it go with Sarah?"

My EM responds with the laconic charm of a Bond villain; no blushing or deflating, just a casual lean-back in my chair and a brief pantomime of appraising the day's events.

"Yeah … pretty good. I spoke to her. She's coming over with the guys on Friday night."

Mum smiles and ruffles my hair.

"See? I told you," she says, grinning and putting her face right up close, like I'm four years old and I've just had a go on the slide that I thought was too big for me.

IM: *Any minute now, she'll cap it off by giving you a Kinder Egg.*

"Good for you, Archie. You see, I said it was simple."

I take a last swig of tea and head on up to my Lair, feeling a bit better about things. I don't know what all the fuss was about; Matt'll be fine and we'll all have a good time. And Jason Humphries doesn't even know where I live.

After dedicating an hour and a half of my life that I won't get back to Precipitation in the North-East, I finally settle down at my painting desk. Sarah's witch gets a black wash and then I turn my attention to the gargoyle. Time for the Base Coat.

The Base Coat can, to the uninitiated, feel like a bit of a chore. It's the first block of colour you apply to your grizzled-looking miniature. But – and it's a big but – if you choose your Base Coat carefully, it can add a hell of a lot to the finished article. In this case, I'm doing stone. Well aware that stone isn't just grey, I crank up the laptop and search for some images. Finally, I decide to mix up a grey with a touch of ochre in it. As I start to apply it, using a medium-sized brush, I occasionally change the mix, so that the colour isn't uniform.

Absent-mindedly, I log in to Facebook and have a quick flick: Beggsy hates homework, Ravi's put a link up to some YouTube *Star Wars* mash-up and a little red box tells me I've got a Friend Request. I click on it.

IM: *OhmyGod!*

It's from Sarah.

Of *course* I accept. And suddenly I'm like a six-year-old faced with a series of presents to unwrap – do I look at her Timeline or check out her Photos first?

I go for the Timeline; I need to check out the competition. Sarah's Profile Picture smiles out at me, making me feel like I've been caught reading someone's diary, but I need to know if there's a boyfriend on the scene. Nothing in the recent posts, so I root through the older ones, feverishly searching for a whiff of male interest. Nothing; all her friends are from her last school:

St Brigidine's School for Girls. With a sigh of relief, I go back to the top of Sarah's Timeline and then my palms start to sweat.

Looking through someone else's Photo Album is, I imagine, a bit like being a Peeping Tom. As I click on the Photos tag, I feel a thrill of seedy pleasure – what will I find there; how will she look? She's got four albums on the go: Party, Christmas, Family and…

IM: *You've just hit the motherlode!*

…Holiday.

I shouldn't, but I do and the Rampant Rattlesnake in my head gives an anticipatory shudder.

Click.

IM: *Bingo. It's a swimsuit shot.*

I'm not averse to admitting that I've used Mum's Next catalogue for … how shall I put it … recreational purposes. On the rare occasions that I've been tasked to pass sentence on a shirt or some jeans, there are certain sections of that weighty tome that just seem to demand my attention.

But this is different. Ordinarily, staring at a picture like this would lead to an obvious conclusion. But I can't think of her in that way, I just can't. OK, so she's wearing a T-shirt over her bikini, but the light bouncing off the sand behind her is enough to give you a good idea of what it's hiding, even if it's only a silhouette.

It makes no difference; all I see is her beauty. It's like the dark, hormone-powered recesses of my mind have shut down.

This must be the difference between Love and Lust.

IM: *Steady…*

I go back to my own Timeline. I shouldn't have looked. Flustered and damning my weakness, I pick up the Gargoyle and mix up some more paint.

A chat window flashes up on my screen, announcing contact from the Outside World. My heart leaps and my temperature suddenly reaches the equivalent of a solar flare – could it be Sarah? Does she somehow know I've looked at a picture of her on the beach in a bikini and T-shirt? How will I explain myself?

IM: *Deny, deny, deny!*

My hot flush of guilt gives way to the cooling sweat of relief; it's only Dad.

hi son. how r u?

IM: *God and baby Jesus – he's given up on capital letters now!*

All good – you?

good thx. evry1 better now. no more chkn soup! lol!

93

IM: ....*!*

Glad to hear it. How're you doing?

good thx. u? how's school?

This is interminable; same damned questions every time. Still, got to go through the motions. I wish he would just phone the house, but he won't because he and Mum aren't quite on speaking terms yet. And as I still haven't saved enough money for a new mobile we're stuck with this for now.

Yep - still standing.

lol!

(Oh God.)

wont be around wkend. got a visit from Jane's parents. but need to talk 2 u. you around fri eve?

IM: *The Game! Sarah!*

My brain accesses my Excuse Department and settles on an unusual option: the truth. Albeit missing a vital component.

Can't on Friday – got mates coming round for a game.

what time?

I groan inwardly; I know where this is going.

7–ish.

IM: *Nice and vague – might put him off.*

what about ur mum?

She'll be out.

i'll pop round about 6. it's important.

IM: *Bollocksbollocksbollocks!*

OK.

nice 1. c u then. l u. x

Love you too.

I sag over my laptop. Just what I need: for the first time, I've got a real, live girl coming over to my house and my dad's going to be there. I'll have to work out a way of moving him on as quickly as possible. Just because my parents can't get on, why should the rest of my life have to suffer?

IM: *Parents. Meh.*

My self-pitying sag turns into a resigned slump. I guess I'm still angry at him for cocking things up with Mum.

Dinner does nothing to lighten my mood. Mum's all a-twinkle with the possibility that her son might be about to join the human race, and Tony's testing the limits of his leash, dropping in questions like "Who's coming over on Friday, then?" and "Anything happen at school today?" I imagine that this is what it felt like being on the rack. I get through my shepherd's pie as quickly as I can and then lumber back to my Lair to write about the theme of loneliness in *Of Mice and Men*.

IM: *One A* coming right up.*

That night, the Dream is upon me almost as soon as my eyes close. This time, my dream-self opens his eyes and looks around my room. All is dark and quiet.

Wait; what's that?

I look over to the corner of the room just opposite

my bed and the figure is there, sitting hunched against the wall. It seems to have taken on more form since our last encounter – this time, it appears to be made of swirling grey mist that chalks its outline in the dark. Only its lava-red eyes remain constant, as whatever passes for the creature's skin rolls and curls like cigarette smoke caught in sunlight. It just sits there, watching me.

My heart is going like a jack hammer and I feel waves of hostility coming off this thing in the corner of my room. Suddenly, I heave myself from the bed, but my limbs and muscles are like dead weights and I stagger on leaden legs to the bedroom door. Too late; it's there, waiting for me, standing in my way. This close to it, I can hear its breathing; it sounds laboured and hoarse and there are weird vowel sounds coming from behind its swirling lips. Or maybe it's me, maybe I'm trying to call for help and my mouth won't work properly – I don't know.

In a panic, I totter backwards and lurch to the basin that used to be in my old bathroom and has suddenly appeared in my new bedroom. For some reason, I think that splashing my face with water will help me out of this situation. I glance in the mirror above the basin and see that the creature has vanished. To my horror, as I turn on the taps it's not water that comes out, but the curling, twisting smog of my assailant. He flows into the basin, growing in size and shape, until he eventually puts a misty hand over my nose and mouth. Choking, I drop to my knees, swiping at the creature's arm, but my hands just pass through it. I can feel the hand cutting off my breathing and I drop to the floor, face down...

...and wake up on the floor in a heap to the sound of my alarm clock, seemingly trying to eat the pillow that has followed me from the bed.

IM: *Mor-ning!*

At this point, I think I might need professional help.

SEVEN

There's nothing like a deadline to focus the mind. But it's not Precipitation in the North-East and nor is it toiling my way through the text of *Of Mice and Men* that has my brain working overtime this particular Tuesday morning. And it's not worrying about why Matt chose a different route to school. No, my waking hours are taken up with thinking about Friday.

It's got to be Just Right.

Just Right means I've got to look at the adventure we're playing that night and find a way of worming Sarah in. I've already sketched out her Character Profile in my head and pretty much decided that she'll be a Level 3 Sorceress. I could have made her a Level 4, but that might seem a bit too much like favouritism; after all, Beggsy and the boys have been playing this campaign for a couple of months and have only just earned their Level 4 spurs. And I've got to find a way of getting her in on the Game without upsetting the balance of the story too much. The story which, I might add, was penned by my own fair hand.

For those of you new to the Game, I'll keep this simple: I'm the Dungeon Master (hereafter known as the DM) and Sarah and the rest of the merry band of adventurers will be playing the Game in their guises as Player Characters (PCs). As the DM, I decide what they can see and describe it to them. The outcomes of any encounters with monsters, traps and magic spells are determined by rolling different dice – some of which have as many as twenty sides. The score is then balanced out against certain characteristics on their Character Profile, such as Strength or Dexterity, and an outcome is determined, like they kill the monster …

IM: *Win!*

… disable the trap …

IM: *Mega win!*

… or bad things can happen, like a spell backfiring.

IM: *Fail.*

Matt's Mage has nearly died three times and had to be resuscitated by Ravi's Lazarus Potion. Ravi's an Acolyte aligned to the deity G'thraax. Beggsy's a Dwarf.

IM: *It fits.*

My problem is that Beggsy and the boys have been working their way through my adventure (Tomb of the Sleepless) and have been accruing Experience Points, which increase their abilities. Shoehorning Sarah in as a Level 4 Sorceress might cause some offence, but then I don't think she'd put up with being a less able member of the group. I think I'll make her a Level 3 and give her a Summon Greater Demon spell on the quiet.

I ought to give her a name as well; we don't want play to be held up by umming and ahing through names. It ought to be something a bit slinky – but not too slinky – something like… I rack my brains for female names. Nothing.

IM: *It'll come.*

With that thought settling in my mind and Mrs Hughes blathering away in the background about John Steinbeck's use of slang, I then consider how much time I've got to paint Sarah's figurine. I've done the black wash, so if I put the base colours on tonight, I can do highlights tomorrow, lowlights on Thursday and… D'oh! No time for embellishments. This is going to have to be a rush job. I might have to employ Mum's hairdryer to help the paint go off quicker.

Then there's the Lair. The setting's got to be Just Right. Normally with the guys, we just sit round my gaming table, stick some background music on and get gaming. But I want to evoke a feeling of something more mysterious for Sarah. I can see us all, huddled over the maps, lit only by candles. If only I had some pewter goblets; that'd be good. And some incense. I ought to buy some incense.

And I ought to sort my room out, get it properly unpacked and tidied. I suddenly do a mental itinerary of the books that line my bookshelf; not so much

101

mysterious and dusty tomes as a catalogue of escapist nonsense absorbed by a fourteen-year-old whose tenuous grip on reality is getting weaker by the day. When I left it this morning, my Lair looked like little more than a theme park for the emotionally stunted.

IM: *Tony's got books...*

He has. Some pretty impressive-looking ones too: the big, leather-bound sort. There ought to be a dictionary and perhaps an atlas – might make me look a bit more travelled. I make a mental note to siphon off some of Tony's library and supplement my own. This whole process is more complicated than I thought, but it's got to be worth the effort. The bell goes, signalling the end of a lesson I didn't hear.

As if in response, my mind gives me a brief but crystal-clear vision of Sarah's icy eyes glittering in the candlelight, as she drinks in the arcane atmosphere of the Lair, a sanctuary of forbidden knowledge, where dreams become reality and—

"Dude!"

Bloody Beggsy.

"Dude! Didn't you hear me? I was calling from way back."

"No, sorry."

As chattering students file past, through and around us, we enter into the midst of what can only be described as an uncomfortable silence. As the guilty party, I'm struggling for words. Luckily, Beggsy's unofficial position of Peace Negotiator gives him the strength to get the ball rolling.

"I spoke to Matt last night."

"OK... How's he doing?"

"Dude, he's pretty pissed."

Anyone who doesn't know Beggsy's predilection for Americanisms might assume that Matt is currently reeling around the school, out of his mind on vodka. I've never really understood the sense behind that phrase; there's a difference between being "pissed" and "pissed off" and if you're going to use expletives for effect, at least use them properly. I've said this to Beggsy in the past, but I don't think that right now is the time to resurrect that conversation.

"You've got to sort this out."

For a moment I'm hit by a real sense of injustice; why do *I* have to sort this out? Why doesn't Matt have to sort this out? Why me?

IM: *Because you're in the wrong.*

"We need him for the Game, Dude."

He's right. The Game just wouldn't flow without Matt there; for all his dry, acerbic wit and apparent pessimism, Matt's one of the driving forces in the Game. Whatever else I could say about him, his commitment to making the story and his character as real as possible is one hundred and fifty per cent. I'm not even going to mention the time he turned up in a chainmail shirt (it was one of our first games). Without Matt, the evening wouldn't be the same. We need him.

IM: *And he's your mate.*

I sigh. It's not like I haven't got enough to do, what with buying incense, stealing books and painting slinky witches. Now I've got to carve myself a big slice of Humble Pie and make things right with my friend. I'm starting to feel like a plate-spinner at the circus. And if I drop even one of them, I can kiss my paper-thin chances with Sarah goodbye.

Now would be a really bad time to discover that I can't spin plates.

"Where is he?"

I know the answer before Beggsy replies and so it is with a sense of dread that I head off to the library.

I think I could probably make a sizeable sum of money renting out my mind to drama clubs: a lot of what seems to go on in there is rehearsals. At the moment, I'm going through my possible approaches to Matt, but experience has taught me that however much you try and second-guess someone's responses, they're always going to come up with the one that wasn't in the script.

I wander into the library and find Matt poring over a

Tolkien bestiary. He doesn't seem to notice me. I sit in the chair next to him and he finally looks up.

Me: Put it there, old friend.

Matt looks at my outstretched palm and a shudder of relief works across his face; the pain of being in exile is too much for him to bear. He blinks a little too much, probably stifling tears, as a cracked smile creases his features.

Matt: Thanks, mate.

Possibly a little optimistic.

I walk into the library, obviously weighed down by the stress of the situation. I sit at a table and place my schoolbooks in front of me, but burdened by the enormity of it all, I can only stare into the middle distance. A hand on my shoulder makes me look up; it's Matt. He sits next to me.

Matt: Don't worry, Archie. I understand.

This one's got a whiff of Hollywood about it, but I like the tone. Maybe the "broken hero" stance is the one to take.

IM: *Maybe not.*

Dress rehearsals over, it's time for the real thing. I open the library door and step inside.

Libraries are wonderful things. Some people report an enormous sense of peace and well-being when they step into churches: something to do with the silence, the space and probably a feeling of unity with fellow believers.

This is what libraries are to Geeks – sanctuaries where we can all lurk, safe in the knowledge that the only other inhabitants here are fellow worshippers. The silence is misleading, though, for if you listen carefully, you can hear nerdy spirits all singing together in a yearning for Something Other – to be like the heroes in books, to win the hearts of simpering heroines, to smite mighty foes. To be anything other than a Geek. But rather than being sad or forlorn places, libraries are the temples in which Geeks can briefly attain those goals, their souls soaring in snatches of printed glory.

IM: *And there are some "well-thumbed" pages in the James Herbert books.*

Matt's not at his usual table, so I walk silently through the maze of bookshelves – like that bit where Perseus is hunting the Medusa in *Clash of the Titans*. Except Matt's hair's red and not made of snakes. Other than that, the comparison still stands.

IM: *Make sure you don't look in his eyes!*

Rounding the corner to the Sci-fi section, I see something that didn't feature in my mental rehearsals at all: Matt and Sarah.

Talking.

I duck back round the corner and try to stifle the jealousy that rises like vomit from my stomach. What's *he* doing talking to *her*? What's my mate doing talking to my...? My...? Can't say "girlfriend".

IM: *Can't even say "my". She's not "your" anything.*

Nevertheless ... is something going on that I don't know about? I pull a couple of books out from the shelf and watch them, Gollum-like, from between titles. I know I shouldn't be doing this – but I just can't help myself.

IM: *So ... The Geek wants the Precious! But we mustn't let him have it, Precious! Oh no – nasty little Geekses...*

Matt's not easy around girls and it shows in his body language. His arms are locked tight to his sides and he rocks back and forth on his heels, almost achieving full tiptoe on his forward journey – a Geek to his core.

Sarah, by contrast, is a portrait in relaxation and even touches Matt's right elbow during the course of the conversation. She's doing most of the talking; Matt's just responding in brief, jagged nods, like his neck's seized up. Although I feel bad for spying like this, I can't help but drink in Sarah's form – but not, I hasten to add, with the same slavering lust exercised by Jason Humphries and his Pack of Grunts. Mine is more of an appreciation, the way an architect might study a fine building. Honest.

Sarah finishes the conversation with one last smile and a pat to the elbow, before she turns and disappears into the maze of bookshelves. I hold my ground for a moment, watching Matt. He stands, motionless, deep in thought. *It's time to make like a baby and head out.* ©Beggsy. I round the corner.

"Hey." It's a multipurpose greeting that gives nothing away.

"Hey." A more cunning adversary than I'd expected.

"Look, mate… About yesterday…"

He doesn't give me the obvious way in I was hoping for, just silence.

"…Well, look … I'm sorry. I was just a bit…"

"Don't worry about it."

IM: *And relax.*

"Cool. So, you still coming on Friday?"

"To *your* house?" Matt lets me know that I'm still not entirely off the hook. Fair enough.

"Yeah. The Game."

"Yeah."

"Cool."

IM: *Askhimaskhimaskhim…*

I swallow.

IM: *WHAT WAS HE DOING WITH SARAH?*

"So … what you doing?"

"Looking for a book. It's a library."

His evasion tactics are spot on. He's going to force me to confront him.

"I saw Sarah a minute ago." Or maybe he's not.

"Oh, yeah?" I play it nice and cool, despite the flurry

of envy that ruffles in my stomach.

"Yeah, she told me that she was really looking forward to the Game and was asking me about what we do."

IM: *And relax.*

"I've never explained gaming to a girl before. She's nice, isn't she?" And with that, I think I've just received Matt's blessing.

"Yeah, she's cool. We'll see how she gets on; it's probably a one-night-only experience."

"In your dreams." We both snigger like fourteen-year-old virgins.

IM: *Which you are.*

The bell shatters the beautiful quiet, announcing the start of lunch. We leave the library, our friendship as strong as it ever was. Stepping into the corridor, my shoulder collides with what feels like a passing iron girder. I turn to see what it was and make dangerous eye contact with the rippling, smirking face of Jason Humphries.

"Friday," he says and then pistons away, like a hungry lion.

The colour drains from my face and I turn to Matt, looking for some weighty words of wisdom and support.

"It's your house." He shrugs.

EIGHT

Getting home and painting the gargoyle gives me release – a respite from the catalogue of problems that my life seems to be throwing at me. I'm not thinking about Jason Humphries or Dad or Matt, I'm just thinking about paint and colours. And Sarah.

I've decided that this gargoyle will be the Greater Demon that her PC can summon. When she decides to cast the spell (probably at the moment when the PCs meet the Earth Elemental I've hidden in one of the crypts), it will appear, silent and brooding, ready to do her bidding. However, with Greater Demons, there's always a price to pay for using them; I've yet to decide what that is. Some would argue that playing Dungeons & Dragons with four Geeks might be price enough.

I've also decided that her PC name will be Nox Noctis; it's the Latin for "Night". Those online Latin Translators have to be good for something.

I've already applied the base colours to Nox Noctis. The main colour of her costume – such as it is – will be an elegant purple, suggesting the mysterious shades of twilight. When it comes to the embellishment, I've got a pot of Elven Silver, to suggest moonlight and starshine.

IM: **Tosses cookies in disgust**

I must confess that, although I'm now trying to assume a little more maturity in my approach to girls, I did get a schoolboy thrill when applying the flesh tones to the area of skin between the bottom of Nox's tunic and the top of her thigh-length boots. Not to mention the cleavage bit. I wonder if those surges ever leave you? Or are all males doomed to spend the rest of their lives for ever waiting on the potential of a flash of flesh? Only time will tell.

I turn my attentions to my gargoyle, which glowers at me from its base, almost resenting me for bringing it to life. I'm going to give it a drybrushing. Drybrushing is a fantastic little trick; you create your highlight colour and dip in your brush, as per usual. But then you wipe off the majority from the bristles, using a piece of kitchen roll or toilet paper. I always have a roll of toilet paper in my room, purely for this purpose.

IM: *Yeah, yeah … tell it to the judge…*

Once your brush is almost free of pigment, you then flick the bristles lightly back and forth just over the surface of your model. The remaining paint will attach itself lightly to the most raised parts of the figure, but in a faded, patchy, scratchy way that gives an aged and worn look. It's a great way to paint armour, swords and shields.

The gargoyle smoulders back at me, now looking rugged and old, as if it has seen civilizations rise and fall.

There's a knock at the door and I know it's Mum; only she could knock in a way that apologizes for disturbing you.

"Come in!"

She pops her head round the door, briefly scanning the room and her son for, I assume, any signs of me shedding my Geekhood and joining the human race.

"You all right? What're you doing?"

"Just painting."

She smiles. Although it's a solitary pursuit, her son being a Geek does have its upsides – at least I'm not out on the streets, annoying the neighbours or pursuing a career as a costumed vigilante.

IM: *Note to self: must get bitten by radioactive arachnid.*

"There's a film on the telly tonight – one of those ones you like."

"Oh, yeah? Which one?"

Mum's face blanks for a moment; she's not that hot on films at the best of times.

"You know, that one with all the dwarves running around in the woods…"

IM: *What?*

It takes me a moment, but I finally work it out and can't help laughing as I tell her the name of probably one of the greatest films ever made.

"*Lord of the Rings!*"

Mum's laughing too at this point, as though she's somehow surprised herself with her inability to retain even the most basic information – and I love her for it.

"That's it," she manages between giggles. "The one with all the dwarves running around in the woods!"

We're both laughing now and it's beautiful in its simplicity. But it's short-lived; my shields kick into action as I resort to asking a question without actually asking it.

"You and Tony digging in, are you?"

I think I see a touch of sadness pull at Mum's eyes; she knows what I'm asking.

"No. It's only me. Tony's gone out on a business dinner."

I relax. I can see from Mum's face that she'd like nothing better than to sit with her son through a film about dwarves running around in the woods. And right now, I'd like nothing better than to watch it with her. I roll my brush round the inside of my water jar and wipe it clean.

"Go on, then; put the kettle on."

It's Wednesday morning and I awake, refreshed, from a dreamless sleep. Days like this are a rarity; you wake up and everything seems to make sense. Problems are there to be overcome, to test your resourcefulness and strength of character, rather than the impenetrable obstacles that they usually appear to be. I don't know whether it's the good night's sleep or sorting things with Matt or even watching the film with Mum, but I'm feeling sharp and confident; I'm ready for anything.

Even Tony's post-bacon-buttie cigarette doesn't blister my lungs with its usual ferocity, and the walk to school fills me with a sense of buzzing anticipation; what will happen today? What will me and Sarah talk about?

IM: *How much you wuv each uvver…*

Can I be in love? Aren't there supposed to be two people involved in the equation? I hardly know Sarah, but I *do* feel a connection – a strong one. I think back to that day when we met outside the shop and she touched my hand. What was it she said? Something about me being hurt or angry.

How could she know?

Everything seems to make sense today and it seems completely obvious that me and Sarah are destined for something: she understands me without me even having to speak to her, like there's some invisible thread that joins us together.

A thrill runs through me as I wonder whether I should ask her out properly. I know she's coming round to my house, but it's not an actual date or anything; she's coming round to see how the Game works. But it's a sign, isn't it? The way she is with me at school, the way she talks to my friends and the fact that she's interested in my Geeky little life…

IM: *She likes you…*

And I like her. "Like" is such an insufficient word for what I actually feel, just like "fancy"; you *like* a song or you *fancy* a slice of cake. Maybe "love" is too big a word, but it feels more on track than anything else. A smile seems to etch itself on to my mouth and I can't shake it. Even Ravi, possibly one of the least aware people I know, picks up on it.

"What've you been up to, then?" he asks.

"Nothing. Just feeling good, I guess."

I mustn't rush this love thing; I've got to create my chance. The best thing I can do at the moment is plough my energies into the Game and see how things go. If it all goes well, then I might make it official and ask her out.

IM: *How exactly do you do that?*

A good question and the search for a good answer occupies me for the entire morning. I barely hear what's being parlayed in French, and Maths is just a blur. How *do* you ask a girl out? This is something I've never seriously considered before. Sure, I've had daydreams about smooching with Kirsty Ford, but those fantasies have always skipped over the asking-out bit; I've already been going out with her or just been the object of her wanton desire. There's never been any asking-out going on.

The thought follows me to the toilet at lunchtime. Thankfully they're empty. Toilets hold a modicum of fear for Geeks. I know this to be true after dark confessions with Matt, Beggsy and Ravi. We've all admitted to suffering from a condition that we've christened PPS: Public Piss Syndrome.

PPS manifests itself when you are stood at the urinal, ready to relieve yourself. All systems are go and you're just about to strangle the ferret (one of Beggsy's more graphic euphemisms) when somebody walks in and stands beside you.

And the entire system shuts down.

You could have drunk a bucket of ice-cold water four hours ago and have run round the games pitch ten times, but nothing on God's earth will force even the merest drop on to the porcelain below. Your bladder could be on the verge of serious rupture, but the presence of Another in your vicinity is like putting a cork in a bottle – nothing, *rien*, zilch.

Which gives rise to another problem…

You cannot risk losing face. Under no circumstances can you communicate the fact that you have suffered a no-show from the bladder department. If it's uncovered, you risk public ridicule beyond your wildest dreams – although Matt, Beggsy, Ravi and I have also confessed that we know of no such cases in our school history. Nonetheless, who'd want to risk being the first?

In order to keep your private shame private, you've then got to mime a successful delivery. You've got to go through the whole thing: the sigh of relief, the little shake, the zipping up and then, dreading the possibility that you've been unmasked as a widdle-shy freak, you've got to go through the whole rigmarole of washing your hands while, at the same time, trying to buy yourself the opportunity for another run, without looking conspicuous. God, it's complicated. And if someone *else* comes in, you might as well forget it and resign yourself to walking like a duck for the rest of the day.

However, not today. Today, I can relieve myself at my leisure, unhurried and safe in my solitude. In celebration, I walk backwards to the sinks and spin round, a bit like that thing James Bond does in the opening titles of the early Bond films.

And then my perfect day crumbles, for looking back at me in the mirror is not the suave, sophisticated ladykiller that I've been feeling like all morning. All I can see is an awkward, badly-put-together nerd. Everything's wrong: my hair's lank, my eyes are too close together, my nose is too big and the hairs sprouting out of my chin make me look like Shaggy.

IM: *Zoinks.*

Zoinks, indeed. The cloud that forms over my head proceeds to follow me around for the rest of the day. When I came in this morning, I was excited and looking forward to maybe bumping into Sarah, maybe getting to know her a bit better and kidding myself that maybe I had a chance with her. Now, the thought of her even seeing me from a distance fills me with dread.

There's nothing attractive about me at all. I have been "beaten with the ugly stick". There is no hope.

IM: *That's the spirit! Sell yourself!*

To add insult to injury, as we're queuing in the dinner hall, I see Sarah up ahead, paying at the till. Matt's in front of me so I use his height to try and mask my hideous form, ducking down so that my head is hidden by his shoulders. Unfortunately, my sudden stoop sends an elbow into Ravi, who is standing right behind me. With a resounding "Hey!", he launches his tray, complete with Ocean Pie and Peas, up into the air. Prawns, fish and peas land with an unexpected grace on my head, left shoulder and down my left arm, with a warm, wet, sloppy splat.

IM: *Not your day, is it?*

A cheer goes up from the rest of the diners and those around me and Ravi quickly split, making us the centre of attention.

IM: *As if they've never seen anyone wearing fish pie before. As if.*

"Archie! What – what are you doing?" In the midst of all the cheering and peas, I can't help but admire Ravi's Geek-Savvy: distance yourself from any involvement by naming the culprit as soon as possible. Then Beggsy lends his oh-so-welcome wit to the situation.

"Dude!" he hollers from the sidelines. "D'you want ketchup with that?" Cue laughter from anyone within earshot. I wish I didn't exist.

As if things couldn't get any worse, I'm then overpowered by a team of dinner monitors who proceed to squirt me with squirters and scrub me with scrubbers, taking my jacket off so that they can really get it clean.

"Don't want to go home smelling of fish," one advises as I'm jostled between them.

In real time, the scrubbing is over in seconds and the squad of dinner monitors return to serving starving students. In Archie Time™, the ordeal lasts for hours, but as they move off in slow motion, I see before me Sarah, standing with her arm outstretched, clutching a paper napkin, concern etched into her beautiful face.

IM: *Heads up!*

I twist my malformed features into something that might pass for a smile, feeling uglier than ever before, and take the napkin.

Sarah smiles. "You've got some on your head."

IM: *Which one?*

"Thanks," I nod, and go at the prawn in my hair.

IM: *Salmon, actually.*

"It's a good look," Sarah giggles. "It suits you."

"Everyone'll be wearing it by tomorrow," I say with a tired smile.

Sarah blesses me with another laugh.

IM: *Way to go!*

"You are funny, Archie."

"Yeah. It's a gift I've got."

More giggles, before a girl in her class comes to whisk her away to do something more important. But, as she goes, she does something that relights the Fires of Hope in my stomach: she looks over her shoulder, smiles and does one of those waves that girls do where all their fingers waggle.

When Ron Weasley looked in the Mirror of Erised, he saw himself as Head Boy...

IM: *...When you looked in it, it cracked.*

OK, I know I'm no Orlando Bloom, but there must be something I can do to boost my chances.

IM: *Time to get thinking, Prawn Boy.*

NINE

I've never asked to have a haircut before; usually I've just been told that it's happening and have grumbled accordingly. But, pursued by the newfound awareness of my physical shortcomings, I come to the conclusion on the walk home that, barring plastic surgery, I'll just have to work with what I've got – which is hair.

The problem is that I've somehow got to plant the idea in Mum's head that I need a haircut, without it looking like I want one because Sarah's coming round on Friday. And that's the other problem: Sarah's coming round on Friday. Where am I going to find the time to squeeze in a cut in the next forty-eight hours? At least forty-seven of them are pretty much spoken for. There is a slight chance that if Mum thinks I need a trim badly enough, she might ring Jean, the lady who comes to the house to do her hair.

IM: *It's a long shot, but it just might work...*

I sneak into the house through the front door and head straight for the downstairs toilet. The mirror confirms all I need to know – my hair probably looked better with the Ocean Pie in it. A flash of inspiration and I'm wetting my hands under the taps and then running them through my fringe, which starts to droop over my eyes. Perfect. I then sneak back out of the front door, to come back in with my customary cry.

"Hello-o!"

"We're in the kitchen!" Mum's voice comes back at me.

Great! "We're" suggests that Tony is around. My shields go up and I can feel my IM whirring in anticipation, but I'm going to see this one through. I step into the kitchen; Mum's got her back to me and Tony is sat reading at the kitchen table, beneath a small, smoke-filled cumulonimbus.

I try again. "Hello?"

"Cup of tea, love?"

"Yes, please... *pffft*,"– I blow at my fringe, as though it's irritating me. "*Pffft*."

With a tinkle of spoon against mug, Mum turns round, tea in hand. She stops and frowns.

"Is it raining?"

I groan inwardly; surely it's obvious that my hair is bothering me? However, my EM is already up and running – I respond with well-practised confusion.

"No. Why? *Pffft*."

The expression that Mum wears as she comes over to me is one that takes me back about seven years. It's analytical and determined. Seven years ago it would

122

have been the precursor to having my cheek scrubbed with a handkerchief. This sense-memory is obviously stored in the Emergency Files of my EM and I instinctively flinch on her approach.

"Keep still…"

Mum runs her hand through my fringe with one hand and gives me my tea with the other. There's multitasking for you.

"Archie, what's this?" She sniffs her fingers. "You're hair's wet. And you smell of fish."

IM: *Curse her powers of observation!*

"Is it? Do I?" I affect a surprised exploration of my own head. "Oh, yeah. Accident with an Ocean Pie at lunch."

IM: …*and the nomination for worst performance under pressure goes to…*

Mum looks at me again, trying to work out what her halfwit son is up to. As if to confirm her suspicions, my EM guides me to take a sip of tea and grin gormlessly.

IM: *Genius.*

Something like recognition flickers in Mum's eyes and she chucks a quick glance at Tony, but he's still engrossed in his book and cigarette. The flicker of recognition turns into something more playful.

"Take your jacket off, it needs a wash. Go and have a look in your room."

It's my turn to look quizzical.

"Go on."

I trudge upstairs carrying my tea – half damning myself for the failure of Operation Haircut and half excited by whatever's in my room. I open the door and there on the bed is a new pair of jeans, a cool shirt and a pair of trainers. I hold the jeans up – they're skinny and black, just the way I like them. The shirt's pretty good too. It's short-sleeved with a faded red-check design. While it might have a whiff of *Glee* about it, I figure I can balance out its emo-appeal by wearing it over one of my old T-shirts.

The trainers are ones I've had my eye on for a while: proof that my mum does listen to me. Grey Converse. I try them on. Cool.

Mum's trademark knock at the door announces her arrival. Her face is a portrait of nervous anticipation.

"Everything OK?"

"Thanks, Mum. It's all great."

"You checked your bedside table?"

In response, I turn away from her and pull open the drawer. There, resting inside, is a small bottle of aftershave. I don't know the label, but with an unconscious "cool!", I open it and have a sniff.

IM: *Sarah will be powerless to resist…*

"Thanks, Mum." I give her a hug.

"That's all right," she giggles over my shoulder. "You need to thank Tony as well; the aftershave was his idea."

For a fleeting second, I feel strangely betrayed that Tony and Mum have been discussing my love life. But then I realize that there's not actually any love life to discuss, so I swallow my pride and get on with it.

"Sure. I'll come down now."

"Your hair's fine, by the way," Mum grins, ruffling my mop.

I look at her as though I don't know what she's talking about, but I suspect that even James Bond would have a hard time keeping a secret from my mum.

The cumulonimbus in the kitchen has been joined by a cirrostratus. Ordinarily, I'd perform a pointed cough on entry to such a haze, but the circumstances dictate a ceasefire in the anti-smoking campaign.

"Hey, Tony. Thanks for the aftershave."

Tony unpeels himself from his book and rolls back in his chair, a satisfied smile on his face. I bite the inside of my cheek to keep the crooked grin on my face from slipping.

IM: *Tosser.*

"Not a problem, mate. Glad to help. You've got to make an effort when there's a lady coming round."

Fearing a Tourette's-style outburst, I quickly override my EM's autopilot settings and opt for manual control;

125

in those three sentences, Tony's broken the Golden Rule of Non-Specific Conversation: You NEVER refer to the heart of the matter. I know he knows what all the clothes and aftershave are for and he knows I know that he knows what it's for – but you NEVER refer to it. Mum knows the score; we've had our earlier discussions and she's made her feelings on the matter clear, but after that point, she is honour-bound never to refer to the matter specifically. It's like talking to someone who wears an obvious wig – you know they're wearing it; they know you know they're wearing it, but you are both honour-bound not to mention it. Much as I hate to liken Sarah to a hairpiece, Tony, Tosser-like, is effectively announcing my baldness to all and sundry. I decide to opt for diversionary tactics.

"Yeah, I guess so. I was wondering if I could borrow a few of your books for a couple of days?"

"Sure. What're you looking for?"

"I've got a couple of bits of homework," I lie easily. "I've got to research natural wonders of the world, classic authors from history and…" I do a mental scan on things that girls might like "…butterflies. Have you got anything in those departments?"

"Let's go and have a look." Tony heaves himself from his perch and puffs his way to his study.

Mum's obviously been hard at work here because

most of his books are on the shelves. The one thing I will say for Tony is that his reading habits are wide and varied. His study is like a small version of what I imagine the British Library must be like and I briefly consider asking him whether I could hold the Game in here. The overflowing ashtrays and the general sense of disarray bring me to my senses. Despite his eagerness to avoid anything resembling hard work, Tony's computer has been unpacked and assembled, ready to go. I know him well enough by now to understand that this is a no-touch item. Whatever dark secrets it harbours, I'll never know about them; it's his Holy Grail, his Jewel in the Crown and his Retreat from Family Life.

While Tony stretches and inspects, I make a brief appraisal: there are some shelves that make uncomfortable reading. Not because there's anything untoward up there, but because they're not dissimilar to my own. There are plenty of pulp sci-fi books, such as *The Stainless Steel Rat* series and some obscure titles that look as if they're from the fifties or sixties. Dress it up how you want, it's escapist nonsense.

IM: *Just like all the swords and sorcery that line your bookshelves.*

The other thing is that there are loads of books here I'd love to own: huge, glossy photo-books of space, books about wildlife and even a few about UFOs.

IM: *Is Tony a secret Geek?*

Or, more to the point, is this what happens to Geeks when they get older? Me and my mates – are we destined to become overweight Tossers with no real insight into the people around us, for ever making conversational blunders and surrounded by people we don't really know how to talk to? I shudder at the thought and something like sympathy for my stepfather stirs in a long-forgotten part of my soul; are Tony and I more alike than I'm prepared to admit?

"Here you go, Arch, try these."

Tony shoves a pile of weighty tomes into my arms and I give them a quick scan: there's one on the Grand Canyon, a few classic novels – including *Nineteen Eighty-Four* and *Catch-22*, a David Attenborough book with some cool pictures of butterflies in and, right at the bottom, a small, dog-eared book about witchcraft in medieval England. I look up to see Tony grinning at me conspiratorially.

"She'll like that one, mate. Maybe you can weave some magic of your own…"

IM: *Shut up, you idiot!*

"Right." I try and smile back, but the hot flush that's spreading through my body corrupts the necessary file and I'm sure it looks like I'm gritting my teeth. Which I am. "Thanks."

After tea, I take the books up to my Lair and arrange them on my shelves. While they do make my room look a bit more impressive, I can't help but feel slightly tainted by Tony's involvement in my plans. It's like everyone knows what I'm up to – except me.

After rejigging my shelves to create a more worldly-wise aspect, I survey the rest of my Lair. It's a mess. So I tidy it. Not one of those cursory tidy-ups that I occasionally undertake to appease my mum, and not like the tidy-up I was more or less blackmailed into when Tony was coming round to the house for the first time. No, this tidy-up is in earnest. Powered by the desire to make things Just Right, I pull clothes off the floor and hang them in my wardrobe, unpack the remaining boxes, hide annuals, old action figures and the damning evidence of a Next catalogue under my bed and surreptitiously dispense with certain CDs. This bedroom now belongs to a Dude.

Next up is to finish the work on Nox Noctis. With the base colours on, I give each section of the figure a colour-wash. This is much the same as the black wash, but I use deeper tones of each base colour. What you want is for the wash to run gently into the recesses of the model, leaving just enough pigment behind it to act as shading. For the flesh, I mix a reddy-brown and a deeper purple for her clothing. While the wash dries, I turn my attentions to the Gargoyle. Having drybrushed him, I now give him a colour-wash to tone down the highlights. I mix a dark grey and drop in some ochre and green to give a weathered effect.

Ordinarily, I'd leave the witch for a few hours, but time is against me, so I go against everything I believe in and give her a once-over with the hairdryer. Next up, I decide to employ a self-developed highlighting technique I've christened "blobbing". Blobbing involves creating a slightly thicker version of a wash, but in a colour lighter than your base colour. With one brush, you apply a blob of the watered-down pigment to the most raised areas of your figurine. Then, using a dry brush, you gently draw the edges of the blob across the surface, so that it blends with the shading. The result is that you get a gradation of colour from the deep shadows of your lowlight, blending into the base colour and then lightening into the highlight colour. If you get it right, it looks pretty good. However, because it involves a lot of watered-down paint, there is always the potential for the colour to run and screw everything up. It's the Geek equivalent of white-water rafting.

Thankfully, everything goes to plan and I breathe a sigh of relief. The final part, which I'll do first thing in the morning, is the fine detail: eyes, lips, jewellery and other embellishments that will bring the model to life.

Mum sticks her head round the door, just as I'm putting my brush down. Her eyes widen as she scans the rugged landscape of my newly tidied Lair.

"I must be in the wrong house," she says in mock surprise. "I thought this was my son's room…"

"Ha, ha."

Mum looks around the room again.

"I'll give it a hoover while you're at school, if you like."

Something darkens behind my eyes and a protest hits the back of my throat.

IM: *Hang on; don't forget that she was a girl too, once. Girls notice that sort of thing.*

The cloud passes and the protest is swallowed.

"OK." It's a multipurpose answer that neither confirms nor denies my feelings on the matter; I can't appear too eager.

"Needs a dust too," she mutters to herself, before catching the sardonic glower in my eyes. "Leave it to me; I won't move anything important."

Unfortunately for my EM, my mother's enthusiastic trilling is infectious and I can't help grinning ruefully and shaking my head. She takes the cue, with a huge smile which tells me that the room will have been cleaned within an inch of its life by the time I get home.

Whether I like it or not.

IM: *Which you do, really. But don't let her know that. Give her too much approval and she'll be in here every day!*

"Love you!" she half sings. "Night night!" And the door is closed.

I give Nox Noctis and the Gargoyle a quick once-over, before setting my alarm clock an hour earlier so that I can finish the job and give myself time for any touch-ups. Thursday's going to be a long day, but the effort should be worth it. Racking my brain for shops that sell incense, I climb into bed and wait to be claimed by dreams of Sarah the Beautiful Goth.

I've never really liked Thursdays. They're just a bit lame. And thanks to a decent night's sleep with no weird dreams, I'm in Fast Forward mode. I really want to get this Thursday over with, so the countdown to the Game can begin properly. It's a bit like the day before Christmas Eve – lame.

Even lamer is the fact that I get up at Stupid o'Clock to do the embellishments on Nox Noctis. At six-thirty in the morning, I can barely see, let alone wield a paintbrush, but I give it my best shot. Last night's lowlight wash and hairdryer-aided blobbing has turned out pretty well. All that remains is to pick out the details, which will be the bits that'll be noticed.

IM: *It's all in the details.*

Using my finest brush, I pick out the witch's irises in a blue that I mix up to be as close to Sarah's as possible. Instead of the traditional scarlet-red lipstick that most witches seem to sport in movies and artwork, I go for a deeper hue of the flesh-tone; the only people who look good in bright red lipstick work in circuses. As far as I'm concerned, this is an hour of my life well spent, and it's one less thing to worry about later.

Before I head downstairs, I have a flash of inspiration and post my address up on Sarah's Facebook Timeline, complete with a Google Maps link. And then I add, "Your Quest begins at 7pm tomorrow," just to try and help get her in the mood. A quick check on my own Timeline shows up a message from Dad, which he'd left last night.

r u still gud fr fri?

I'm suspecting he may eventually resort to hieroglyphics.

After a minute's hovering over the keypad, I decide not to reply. Maybe if I don't, he'll give up.

IM: *Although he did say it was important…*

Yeah, well, "important" can wait till I get my new phone. The Game's *important*. Sarah's *important*. Making everything Just Right's *important*. I get another major lightbulb moment and search for shops in town that might sell incense.

IM: *Bingo! There's one round the corner from the Hovel!*

I close the computer down and then I try and Fast Forward the rest of the day.

Which works fine until first break. It's a warm, early summer's day and me, Matt and Beggsy are hanging out in the playground. Beggsy gives an eye-witness report of the T-shirt he glimpsed Kirsty Ford wearing in PE this morning. It's tight, apparently. Once we've all calmed down, the conversation is just turning to the Game, when Ravi appears, looking like he's been dragged through a hedge backwards. Which he might as well have been.

"Archie!" He arrives, stumbling and breathless, with fear practically spraying out of every pore.

"Rav – what is it? You OK?"

"It's Humphries! He's looking for you!"

IM: *Oh my God! We're all going to die!*

"Why? What does he want?"

Ravi's shaking. "He wanted to know where you live, Archie."

IM: *Oh, no.*

Beggsy joins in with a low, drawn-out "Du-ude." Conveys *Oh my God! We're all going to die!*. To add to the moment, his voice fluctuates, making him sound like a terrified Smurf.

"And did you tell him?"

"No, I didn't." Ravi's smile is fragile, like he's been through the torments of Hell, but kept his mouth shut. "I couldn't."

IM: *Good soldier.*

"Thanks, man. You're braver than I would've been."

"No." Ravi shrugs. "I *couldn't*; I don't know your new address."

IM: *Ah. That explains it, then.*

"OK." I nod distractedly. "Well, thanks anyway. I'll text you guys my address tonight; maybe it's better if you don't know it right now. That way, Humphries can't get it out of you." Others might take this as an insult; Geeks know the truth, so no one argues with this idea, but I'm sure we're all damning our lack of muscles at this point. "Let's try and stick together at lunch and afternoon break; we're more vulnerable if we're alone."

And that's how the rest of the day goes. We spend lunchtime in the library and afternoon break finding appropriate corners to skulk in. I don't see Sarah – and part of me's grateful. I wouldn't want her exposed to this level of cowardice.

By the time I get home, I'm tired and depressed. Tony's out, wooing some client over a pint and a frame, and Mum's obsessively trying to get more unpacking done. Eventually, I hit the hay, glad to have Thursday done with. And, despite my excitement that the countdown to the Game begins tomorrow morning, I feel uneasy – there's still plenty of time for everything to go wrong.

IM: *Cheer up! At least you can sleep without fear of being bullied!*

How wrong can you be?

I'm in bed as the Dream begins. I can feel a surge of darkness from the corner of the room and two burning coal red eyes suddenly blink into life. Unable to move or call out, I anticipate an attack. But it doesn't come; the eyes just smoulder at me from the shadows.

Suddenly, two streams of … *something* … flow out from where my assailant lurks. It's like a cross between Spider-Man's webbing and sticky tape. These gluey ropes seem to have a life of their own and they wrap themselves round me, over and over, binding me tight, arms to my side, like a crude version of mummification. The strands operate like tentacles and lift me from my bed to stand me upright in the centre of the room.

From the shadows, I can hear something like a voice. Having seen the hulking form of my dream-demon in the past, I would've expected a deep, resonant growl, but what I get is a sound like a distant shout, as though I'm hearing the fading moments of an echo.

I stand, bound and trembling, listening to these muted cries, for what seems like an eternity. I wish for a knife or something sharp to cut my bonds, but nothing comes; I'm helpless, entirely at the mercy of the thing in the corner.

The distant voice stops, fading like smoke into the darkness. The following silence is worse than the weird sounds.

The creature finally steps from its hiding place and, just before it knocks me to the ground and back into the waking world, I recognize it. Its form has solidified into a craggy, angular mass of muscles and hatred, and it spreads its wings with a gristly creak as it sends me to the floor with a distant bellow.

It's my Gargoyle.

TEN

The Glorious Day arrives and I'm knackered. Not even Mum's excited chirruping can raise my spirits; her extra fiddling with my collar and smoothing back of my hair is just annoying. Tony waves me off with a parting, "Go get her, Tiger," which sends my IM into apoplexy and it's only thanks to my well-honed EM that I'm able to stop myself shouting "TOSSER!" at the top of my voice. Although I do mutter the word to myself on the walk to school, over and over, like some sort of mantra.

It's not that the Dream scares me; I've had enough now to be able to shake them off pretty quickly. But there's something unsettling about your hobby turning on you in the middle of the night. At least Nox Noctis came out well. I give her a final appraisal before I set off for school. She's sexy, but not too sexy.

IM: *Is there such a thing?*

But I think what really makes her are the skin tones – the blobbing and the colour-wash have united almost perfectly. This model would be worth entering into the next Games Day Painting Competition, but I think I'm probably going to end up giving it to Sarah. Men usually give flowers; Geeks give miniature witches.

At school, the gang are excited, but trying not to show it – it's the Geek way. Partly it's because you don't want other people to hear you hopping up and down and saying how you're going to smite the Foes of Darkness with your Level 4 Dwarf, and partly because, secretly, we're all trying to elevate the Game from what it actually is: a game. Not that we've got any illusions that it is anything else, but we're not settling down for an evening of Ludo. So, rather than slapping each other on the back and shouting about Lazarus Potions, we give each other sly looks and coded comments, preserving what little dignity we actually have. And all the time, we're on the look-out for Humphries, who remains an unseen threat throughout the morning.

Lunchtime arrives and I head for the school gates. Beggsy intercepts me before I get there.

"Dude! Where you going?"

"Into town, mate. Just to get some stuff for tonight."

"Yeah?" Beggsy chucks me a confused look; what could I possibly need for tonight? We've got the Game, we've got the figures … we've even got the girl! Who could ask for anything more?

"Yeah. Just some stuff."

"'K, dude. Catch you later." He high-fives me and heads for the dinner hall.

This is the first time I've ever been off-premises without permission and I'm already feeling like a criminal. The feeling is enhanced by the others going in the same direction; they're of a type. This is all going to sound a bit snobby, but people judge me for being a Geek, so I think I'm allowed to pass a few sentences of my own. The people mooching away from the gates seem to be those who don't really want to be at school in the first place – the skirts are tighter, hoods cowl sloping brows and walks become struts. I'm now a lone gazelle on the Serengeti of Disaffected Youth. My EM ramps it up a notch and I opt for the head-down, hands-in-pockets approach; it's amazing how interesting your own feet can become when you're trying to go unnoticed.

Town feels safer; there are shoppers out and about and office workers grazing on sandwiches – more cover for a solitary Geek to exploit. While the strutting, cackling predators march through the crowds, signalling their approach with hoots and shrieks, I hug the walls, seeking the camouflage offered by gossiping old ladies and mothers with children.

IM: *You're a regular Conan the Barbarian.*

As I pass the Hovel, I give the window a quick look, taking temporary comfort from the colours and shapes on display. But I'm not headed there today. There's an alley, not far from the Hovel, and that's where Google has told me I need to go. If I'm to find incense anywhere this lunchtime, it'll be there.

I round the corner into the alley, unseen by the tottering troupes of two-legged baboons from my school. It's a shabby little shop, bearing the name "Manisha" in the sort of writing you see on Indian restaurants. Knowing my luck, it means something like "Shop For Unrequited Love".

IM: *There's that word again…*

An old-fashioned bell tinkles above the door as I go in and I know I'm in the right place. Apart from the rows of shelves selling crystals, oddly shaped candles and statues of Buddha, the smell of incense is overpowering. Although it's a bit flowery, it creates the feeling I was looking for – already I could be somewhere otherworldly; time seems suspended and I feel my stresses gradually diminishing. The incense is located near the back of the shop, so I wander through, briefly taking in the books about witchcraft and listening to the gentle jingles of the wind chimes that hang from the ceiling.

The incense comes in either sticks or cones and in a number of different fragrances.

IM: *Which one?*

Luckily, there's a chart on the wall giving details of the various properties of each fragrance. I opt for Patchouli cones, which, according to the chart, are "a must for all special occasions". Unfortunately, even the white paper bag the shopkeeper wraps them in doesn't completely disguise their perfume; I've got to get these into my school bag ASAP, or I'm going to smell like a temple for the rest of the day.

Fate, however, has other ideas. As I round the corner back into the town centre, I'm confronted with the sight of Jason Humphries and his Pack of Grunts propping up a shop. They don't get in my way or anything; they're too busy smoking and grunting with something that might be a girl under all that make-up. Humphries, however, clocks me straight away and while he doesn't move or speak, he fixes me with his cold, dead eyes, an alligator-smile playing on his lips.

IM: *Oh, God.*

My legs are already filling with adrenalin, readying me to run. But he doesn't come for me. Instead, the six-pack in his forehead flexes just because it can. I don't know whether to look away, which might signify disrespect, or to meet his gaze, which would signal some sort of challenge. Instead, I try to do a bit of both, blinking and nodding frantically and half whispering an "all right?" in his general direction.

IM: *That's it – you show 'em!*

Just as I'm almost out of his eyeline, he responds with a slow, measured nod and mouths a single word.

"Tonight."

IM: *Might as well start digging your grave now.*

But, as far as I know, he still doesn't know where I live.

IM: *Keep praying.*

I do. All through Maths and all through Physics.

The post-school walk home ought to be an excited babble of what's going to happen tonight. Ordinarily, my mates would be trying to get clues out of me as to what's in store in the Tomb of the Sleepless, and I'd be responding with smug teasers and chucking in the occasional red herring. And in the light of recent events, we ought to be discussing The Presence Of A Girl For The First Time. But today my mates are trying to reassure me that Jason Humphries's threat is an empty one.

"Well, so what if he does turn up?" Ravi is offering some sort of masterclass in bravado. "You just call the police."

"He *won't* turn up." Matt's been saying this in response to pretty much everything that's been said for the last ten minutes. "He doesn't know where you live."

"But s'posing he turns up and wrecks the place? What if he kicks the door in?" I've got to the putting-both-my-hands-on-the-top-of-my-head stage, convinced that Humphries will somehow smell his way to my new house.

143

"He won't turn up."

"He's not that stupid, Arch," Ravi says, ignoring Matt. "That would be breaking and entering. It's illegal. He might be an idiot, but he's not stupid."

"He won't turn up."

"But you didn't see the look on his face; he meant it!" I gabble.

"He won't turn up."

Beggsy suddenly marches ahead and turns to face us, stopping us in our tracks.

"Dudes," he says, in an imploring tone. "You're all forgetting something." There's a dramatic pause and I can feel the fires of hope kindling. What can we have possibly forgotten?

"There's *four* of us…" Beggsy holds up four fingers, just in case we've forgotten how to count. "…and only one of him." He holds up one finger on the other hand, saving us all from these mathematical gymnastics. "See what I'm saying?"

There's another pause as we stare at Beggsy. Then, as a unit, and right on cue, we all burst into laughter. We're Geeks; we know what we're capable of and what we're not.

"I'm just saying!" Beggsy protests, his voice rising an octave.

"Hey!" Ravi chimes. "Is there a window over your front door?"

"Yeah. So?"

"We could fill up some buckets of water and pour them on his head!"

More laughter and everyone joins in, coming up with more and more elaborate plans as to how we can get rid of Jason Humphries, if he turns up. Which, according to Matt, he won't.

After a lot of mutual bolstering, my friends peel off to their respective homes and I get back to mine. I check the clock.

IM: *Three hours till blast off.*

And then it hits me: in three hours, a girl will be coming round to my house.

IM: *And she's gorgeous.*

And she's gorgeous!

IM: *And you like her.*

And I like her!

IM: *Holy shit.*

Without bothering to announce my arrival, I charge up the stairs to my Lair. It looks fantastic; Mum's done a great job and, true to her word, hasn't moved anything important. The duvet has been changed, the carpet's clean and the dust is just a distant memory. Anything resembling a cardboard box has mysteriously vanished, and my bits and bobs have magically found themselves new homes. It looks perfect.

Mum knocks at the door and pops her head round. "Everything all right?"

"Thanks, Mum. It's great. I'm just going to jump in the shower."

"Go on, then, and I'll fix you some tea."

Never have I paid so much attention to my personal hygiene: hair is washed, armpits are scrubbed and those important little places are given Maximum Soapage. With my new jeans and shirt on and a dash of aftershave watering my solitary chest hair, I walk into the kitchen. Mum puts a plate of spaghetti bolognaise in front of me.

"You look nice." Perfect delivery: it's understated, so as not to cause embarrassment or self-consciousness, but the twinkle in her eye tells me that I'm looking pretty sharp. It's all I need to know.

Unfortunately, there's another opinion to be offered, and it arrives through the front door with a jangle of keys and a trail of smoke. No prizes for guessing.

"Hey, hey, hey, Casanova! Lock up your daughters, Arch is on the prowl!"

IM: *It was a mercy killing, Your Honour…*

"I picked up those paints you wanted. Are these the right ones?"

IM: *Eh…?*

Tony's lingering at the end of the hall like an inflated shadow. He furtively beckons to me, obviously trying not

146

to catch Mum's attention.

IM: *Sighs* *Might as well play along and see what the Man of Mystery is up to...*

"Let's have a look," I manage, weakly embracing the charade. As I reach the end of the hall, Tony presses himself up against a wall, keeping his eyes on the kitchen. At this point, I feel like I'm in one of those old spy movies where no one can act. My EM suppresses the urge to break into a Russian accent.

"What paint?"

Tony shoves a carrier bag under my nose.

"Thought you might need something special tonight."

There's a bottle of Cava inside.

This throws my IM into unprecedented conflict with itself. On the one hand, it's an ostentatious gesture, one that fails to take into account a) my age and b) that a few cans of lager would be more appropriate. I ought to turn it down. On the other hand, it's going to look pretty cool to Sarah when I casually whip out a bottle of something fizzy. The internal argument lasts a matter of seconds before the hopeless romantic within makes the final call.

IM: *Coooool.*

"Thanks, Tony. You didn't have to do that."

"No problem," he demurs. "But don't tell your mum; she'd kill us both if she knew. It'll need chilling, it's warm.

147

Wait till we've gone, though." Quickly stashing the bag behind the curtains that frame the front door, he bursts into a tuneless rendition of an old song about someone being once, twice, three times a lady. This unforeseen outburst sends Mum to his side and she gives him a cuddle as he lapses into a succession of wheezy chuckles and drops into a chair. I loiter in the hall for a moment, feeling a little tainted by the deception that I'm now party to.

IM: *Sometimes you've got to dance with the Devil…*

Justifying this to myself as a one-off foxtrot, I check that the illicit cargo is well out of sight and follow the trail of smoke back to my spaghetti.

"There's Coke in the fridge," Mum says, giving Tony a final squeeze and stacking two large bottles in the fridge door. "And there's crisps in the cupboard," she adds over her shoulder.

"Nice one," I say. "What time are you guys…?" I leave the question hanging.

"We're meeting at the pub first, so we'll be off around six-thirty. What time's Sarah coming?"

"Everyone'll be here about seven." I use the "everyone" to try and get the point home that this isn't a date. It's just a Game Night.

IM: *But you could consider it a date.*

Of sorts.

"We'll be gone before then," Mum says and then

checks the clock. "I'm going to have a bath. Tony, you ought to think about getting ready."

"Yep." The man's a master of repartee.

I slurp down the rest of my spaghetti, then join the exodus and scuttle up to my Lair. I've got preparations to make.

The first question is where to put the Games Table. I clear away my paints and then root through my model collection, taking out the miniatures I might need tonight. On top of Nox Noctis and the Gargoyle, I've got a selection of undead creatures: zombies, skeleton warriors, wraiths and so forth. Tomb of the Sleepless is a vampire story, but the gang haven't met the Bloodsucker-in-Chief yet; that'll happen around Level Six. Until then, they've got to gather a series of clues to work out his or her identity. It's all terribly intricate.

I move the table to a spot just in front of my bookcase. Not only will I be framed by my collection of literary marvels, but I'll also be directly under a wall-mounted spotlight, adding to my air of mystery and detachment; I will appear to be of this world, but not part of it, a loner by day and...

IM: *A twat.*

OK, so I'm just going to go for a bit of moody lighting. I set up my Dungeon Master's kit: a screen that divides the table, hiding the assorted rule books, maps, miniatures and dice that I will use to challenge, test and guide the players. Having pinched a few tealight candles from downstairs, I put them about the room, with one in the centre of the table. Next up, the incense cones. I realize I've never used these things before; how many should I light? I've bought a dozen and they smell quite strong, so I opt for three.

I nick the four kitchen chairs from downstairs and position them round the table with the one from my desk; it's going to be intimate. I also grab some crisps and put them in bowls on the table. Ordinarily, we'd just tear and share, but I'm thinking of Sarah.

Time to test: I switch on the spotlight, light the candles and turn the main light off. It looks cool; there's an unearthly glow from the table, the candles casting long, soft, flickering shapes on the walls. I'd better check out how things look from the driving seat. Sitting down at my chair, I adjust the spotlight behind me so that it spills directly over my head, but gives me a decent amount of illumination over my books and maps. Glancing up, I see a faint reflection of myself in my attic window. I am defined only by shadows.

IM: *Perfect.*

Gazing up at my reflection, I'm aware again of how nervous I am. I scrutinize the reflection a bit harder. Do I look OK? Too calculated? Just to be sure, I ruffle my hair to give that haven't-really-tried look. That's better.

"Ar-chieee!" Mum's calling up the stairs. I snuff out the candles, switch the main light on and head downstairs. Mum's there, grinning and looking all glammed-up.

"You look good," I nod sagely. Tony appears next to her, wrestling with a tie.

"Oh, come here," Mum laughs and sets to work on the knot for him. "Right, Archie," she begins, multitasking furiously. "We'll be back at eleven o'clock at the latest. I've left the restaurant's number by the phone, and if that's no good, you can always ring Tony's mobile. OK – keep still!" Tony is putting up a fight, using only his neck – which is quite impressive.

Unconsciously, I flick a glance at the clock. It's already quarter to seven.

IM: *GO, for God's sake!*

Mum catches my look and checks the time as well.

"Come on, Tony, you look fine. We're going to be late."

Tony gives his tie a last pull at the knot, straining his head upwards as if he's trying to take off. Mum leans in and gives me a hug.

"Have fun, love." She smiles and gives me another squeeze. Tony offers me a handshake.

"Good luck, mate," he says, patting me on the

151

shoulder with his other hand. I've seen scenes like this in Hollywood rites-of-passage films. And then, to cap it off, he adds, "And don't do anything I wouldn't do!" This is followed by a pointed look to the curtains and a knowing wink. And a tap on the side of the nose.

IM: *Please. Make it stop.*

To curtail this excruciating mime, I mumble some affirmation and chivvy them out of the front door. It's only when I hear the car drive off that I fully relax.

IM: *Ten minutes to go…*

I check my reflection again in the downstairs toilet, then retrieve the Cava from behind the hall curtain. There's no time to chill it now, so I gather five wine glasses and head up to my Lair. I do a double-check of the room and then a double-double-check of the position of the table, examining it from almost every possible angle.

IM: *Five to.*

How does time seem to be going so quickly? I light all the candles and the incense cones and kill the main light. And then stand on the landing, not really knowing what to do with myself.

Ding-dong!

IM: *It's showtime!*

ELEVEN

"Hello, son."

IM: *Nononononono – NOT NOW!*

What with worrying about Sarah, Jason Humphries, my room and everything else, I'd forgotten about Dad coming over – and I've a feeling that my EM isn't quick enough to mask my disappointment that he isn't someone else.

"Sorry I'm a bit late; I just wanted to make sure your mother had gone ... didn't want anything to be awkward."

I hate it when he refers to her as "your mother". It's not said with any spite, but it's not said with any love either.

IM: *Get rid of him.*

There's a moment's silence, where neither of us really knows what to say.

"Can I come in for a moment? I won't be long."

"Oh, yeah. Sure. Come in." I step back, allowing Dad into the hall. His eyes unconsciously flick around the space, looking for evidence of his ex-wife and her new partner.

"Everything OK?" I ask.

"Yeah." Dad looks uneasy and doesn't know what to do with his hands. "Listen, I've got something to tell you. I haven't said anything to your mother yet – I wanted you to be the first to know and there hasn't really been the opportunity to say anything face to face. You're a bit hard to pin down these days."

I can feel my temper rise. That's the problem with my dad – he has a great way of making you feel like everything's *your* fault. I could point out that it wasn't *me* who was making "**chkn soup**" for my surrogate family last weekend, but I don't want to get into an argument; the gang'll be here any moment.

"So, what's up?"

"Well, I've been offered a job that will mean a bit more money, which will obviously make things better all round – I'll be able to give more maintenance to your mother…"

"Congratulations." I opt for the cheery approach to diffuse my bubbling temper at the third "your mother".

"Thanks. But the problem is that I'm going to have to move away."

My temper is silenced.

"What? Where?"

"Up to York. Jane's got family there, which'll make things a bit easier, but obviously it means I won't be around."

I feel some sort of chasm open up in my chest and there's a tightness in my throat.

"When?"

"At the end of the month; only a couple of weeks. Me and Jane have discussed it and it seems like the best thing to do all round."

IM: *And where did I feature in your discussions?*

"Uh … OK."

"I know it's a bit of a bombshell, but I wanted to let you know sooner rather than later."

I feel strangely empty. I know I'm still angry at Dad for what happened between him and Mum, but this feels like a kick in the teeth. It feels like rejection.

"We'll still be able to see each other. You can come up and stay and I'll get you a new mobile."

IM: *A mobile. A consolation prize. Something to ease your guilt.*

"Right." I think I'm blinking a lot.

Voices at the end of the drive pull us both out of an awkward moment.

"You OK?"

"Yeah," I lie, and see a shadow of disappointment on my father's face.

"Good," he lies back. "I just wanted to let you know first, before I tell your mother." He turns to the approaching figures. "Looks like your guests are arriving."

"Yeah. The usual crowd." My EM has kicked into autopilot, dealing with the situation in a light and breezy manner. Inside, I'm all chaos.

"OK. Well, I'll get out of your way. I'll Facebook you tomorrow; let's try and meet next week. After school one day."

"Yeah. That'd be cool." I'm digging my nails into my palms to distract myself from the lava that is bubbling under my skin.

"OK, then. Well. Love you, son." Dad tumbles in for a hug.

"Yeah, love you too." The words come out of my mouth like hot sandpaper, but I can't crack here. Not now.

IM: *Swallow it. Bite it down.*

Dad turns and leaves, exchanging hellos with the approaching group. I turn away from the door and draw in a deep breath, which I expel with some force – trying to breathe out the pain that's burning in my chest. I wipe a hand across my eyes, just in case, and then put my EM up to its maximum setting. It's weird, but I feel wholly detached from everything, as though I'm viewing what unfolds through a film camera. I'm dead inside, coasting, not here.

"Duuuude!" Beggsy announces the group's arrival. "Look what we found!" He points at another figure in the group; it's Sarah.

Just the sight of her makes my EM want to betray me. It wants to give up and expose my hidden hurt. But that's not going to happen. I put out an emergency call to my inner Engineering Department, demanding Warp Factor Five – or we're all dead. With a bit of effort, my shields remain intact and I greet the gang with a wry smile.

"Abandon all hope, ye who enter here!" It's my customary greeting on a game night.

Sarah steps into the porch. She's wearing her Goth gear and my heart melts; she's beautiful and sexy and everything you could possibly want. It's only been two days since I saw her, but I've missed her. Her mascara-bordered eyes glitter a pale blue and her smile could unite nations. I love her.

"Hi," she says, her voice like tinsel. It's the only way I know how to describe it.

"Hi." Behind her, I can see Beggsy doing boob motions with his hands, like he's pretending to honk two old-fashioned car horns at the same time. Matt's grinning evilly and Ravi has turned away, his shoulders shaking.

IM: *Bastards.*

"Right. You'd better come in then." Not the most inviting of invitations, but I'm running on auxiliary power right now.

Sarah steps into the hallway and, while her back is turned, I scowl at my sniggering mates. Beggsy gives the air one last honk for good measure, as I close the door behind them.

"Gentlemen. And lady. If you'd like to make your way upstairs and take your places, I'll join you in a moment. Follow the stairs right to the top."

As they go, I walk casually into the downstairs toilet and lock the door behind me. Quickly, I splash my face with water and then look in the mirror. With no one to see or hear me, my EM climbs down a peg and I can see tears rimming my eyes. I grit my teeth and flare my nostrils, panting my pain. With each threat of tears, I punch the wall beside the mirror and mutter to myself like a lunatic.

"Come on, Arch. Fight it. Come on!"

I feel like a can of Coke that's been shaken, but I can't give in to it now. Dad's obviously got his own life to lead and I can't argue with that, but I feel so … *unwanted*. Daring myself to cry one last time, I splash my face with water again, towel off and get myself back into check. EM running normally. I throw a smile at the mirror, just to see if I can still carry one off.

IM: *It'll do. Focus on Sarah. Focus on the Game.*

Breathing like a boxer ready to go into the ring, I head upstairs to my Lair, where I can leave this world behind me for a few precious hours.

Outside the maelstrom in my head, the evening seems to be going rather well.

As I walk in, Matt goes into a fake coughing fit, squinting at the doorway.

"Archie? Archie? Is that you?" He waves his hands in front of his face, as though wafting smoke. "I can't see you! Talk to me, Archie!"

The others laugh, while Sarah rolls her eyes in mock exasperation. "What's the matter with you guys? Haven't you ever smelt incense before?" She turns to me, with a nod of approval. "Well I like it!"

I'm still watching everything through a camera lens, but no one seems to have noticed. I go through the motions, producing the warm Cava from under the table.

"Who's for a drink?"

"Dude!" Conveys *Is well impressed*.

Ravi just laughs and holds up a glass. Matt, as ever, takes a little swipe at me through a veneer of innocence.

"Is it a special occasion?"

But my brain's suffering a systems overload right now, and I don't take the invitation to join in the banter. Instead, I turn to the only thing that's preventing me from falling apart right now.

"Sarah?"

"No, thanks," she smiles, embarrassed. "I had too much of that at a wedding last year and spent the whole night throwing up. Just the smell makes me feel sick."

I fetch her a Coke from downstairs, feeling the smug grins from my friends on my back. The anger burning in my throat makes me curse them and I fleetingly wish they weren't here. Luckily, I find that Cava has an almost anaesthetic effect and, after downing a glass, I'm coasting on a bubbly cloud – everything seems a little brighter, everyone's a little funnier and I feel a little lighter.

It's all very well for them to mock, but I'm not the only one who's made an effort: Beggsy and Ravi look like they've walked off the set of a washing-powder commercial. Their usually crumpled shirts are pristine and their jeans have been ironed so flat that you can practically hear creaking whenever they move their legs. Only Matt has retained some sense of Geekiness through his unusually-well-turned-out appearance; unlike Beggsy and Ravi, he's tucked his shirt into his jeans and has done the buttons up all the way to his collar. And we won't even talk about the hair gel that he's used to tame his ginger 'fro. I didn't know side partings were in.

IM: *He looks like an old-time Quaker.*

Sarah's blending in perfectly, although she's

160

obviously the centre of attention; Beggsy keeps winking at me whenever he thinks she's not looking and Ravi can't take his eyes off her. Oddly, Matt, possibly the most uptight person I know, seems completely relaxed in her company. I can see that part of him can't quite believe that she's interested in the Game, and he's taking the time to explain the set-up to her in clear and simple terms. You can see that he's got his committed-to-the-game head on and wants the newcomer to feel just as enthusiastic about it as he does. It's almost as if Sarah radiates peace and Matt's usual acidity has been neutralized.

Once I'm sure that Sarah has understood the basics, I take charge. "Right, everyone, let's get down to business. The Tomb awaits."

Matt, Ravi and Beggsy bring their miniatures out from their bags, unwrapping them from various layers of bubble wrap and toilet paper. Sarah is obviously impressed.

"Wow. Did you guys paint these yourselves?" There's nothing better she could have said and we spend the next five minutes with Sarah examining Ravi's Cleric, Matt's Mage and Beggsy's Dwarf Mercenary as the guys point out little details and explain techniques with unreserved pride. I can feel myself getting nervous.

IM: *And out comes the trump card...*

From behind my Dungeon Master's screen, I pull

out Nox Noctis and hand it to Sarah with a casual "Here's yours," that masks the tickle of anticipation that worms its way through my Cava shield.

IM: *Nicely played.*

She holds the miniature up to her eyeline, turning it gently between her finger and thumb.

"Wow," she breathes. "It's amazing! Did you paint this especially for me?"

Out of anyone else's mouth that would be a cliché – an obvious flirt. Out of Sarah's mouth, it's a genuine appreciation that makes my heart skip and a warmth spread through my body. I'd paint the Sistine Chapel for another look like that. Unfortunately, her question is one I'm unprepared for and I'm suddenly aware of the wry looks from my mates.

"Yeah …"

IM: *You're blushing!*

"… well …"

IM: *You're mumbling!*

"… we've all got them. So that one's yours." Not quite the killer comeback I was hoping for.

She studies it closely. "Nice outfit…" The look that accompanies that statement would get a rise out of a corpse.

"Let's have a look." Beggsy grins, having a James Earl Jones moment. Sarah passes Nox Noctis to him and he examines her, his eyes twinkling with mischief. "Do you dress up like that often?"

"Not usually," she counters. "Maybe for the next game."

The minds of four boys all summon the same image in unison.

IM: *The trousers of four boys tighten as one.*

"OK, then," I manage. "Sarah, here's your Character Sheet; guys, here's the map of where we ended up last time." The group of adventurers place their pieces down on the map and all eyes turn to me.

"You're in a crypt," I begin. "It's dark, dank and cold. At the back of the room, straight in front of you is a door. Between you and the door is a large stone coffin… What do you want to do?"

The group look at one another, Sarah obviously unsure of how to begin. I think the guys are conscious of not wanting to look stupid. Thankfully, Matt, who is completely committed to the cause, breaks rank.

"I'll cast a Spell of Illumination; we need to see more, I think."

"OK. The end of your staff lights up and you can see scratches along the sides of the wall, perhaps as though someone's tried to escape – claw marks."

"Could be that they've imprisoned a vampire down here…" Ravi frowns. "Remember what that thief told us back in the village. It could be in the coffin."

I take another sip of Cava and smile to myself, feeling the bubbles in my head blessing me with confidence and worth.

"Should we look in the coffin?" Sarah's still a little unsure, but is having a go.

"Let's inspect it first," says Matt decisively. "I shine my staff over the lid, looking for runes or inscriptions."

"OK. The lid of the coffin is quite ornate. There are runes among the engravings, but you can only make out one word: '*Damned*'." I give the word as much gravity as I can muster.

"I get my battleaxe ready," says Beggsy, shifting in his seat and unconsciously gripping an invisible weapon.

"I'll go for my mace," concurs Ravi.

"Hang on." Sarah's looking at Ravi's Character Sheet. "You're a cleric; you've got some Holy Water and a crucifix – wouldn't that be better?"

"Nice work," Matt comments. "Ravi?"

"Yeah. I'll go for the water and the cross. No bloodsucker's going to mess with us – not on my watch!"

"I'll get my…" Sarah scans her sheet, "…my Talisman of Protection ready."

"OK. Who's going to open the coffin?"

"Better be me," Beggsy responds, "I'm the strongest." He picks up a die and rolls it. Behind my screen,

I counter-roll, using another die.

"OK. Beggsy – the lid is really heavy, so you're just able to slide it halfway off. Inside, there is a skeleton. It's dressed in decaying robes and covered in amulets that all bear the sign of the Sleepless. It's clutching an old wooden staff and you can see that its canine teeth are sharp, like fangs. It doesn't move." I put down a skeleton miniature.

The group look at each other again. "Could be a vampire," Matt speculates. "But if it is, it's obviously been dealt with."

"Could be the body of one of those fanatics – the Sons of the Sleepless," Ravi says.

"Could be, Jh'terin, could be." Matt's sounding grim now; he's in The Zone. "Do we want to inspect the body?"

I sit back and watch the group through my haze. It's wonderful. Sarah's wonderful. She's entered fully into this geeky world and hasn't so much as batted an eyelid. She's there. In *my* world.

The group decide to ignore the coffin and open the door instead. It takes a couple of goes and Matt opts to cast a Spell of Destruction. Just what I'd hoped: I've set up a magical trap triggered by that very spell. The skeleton (actually an undead warlock) rises out of the coffin and attacks them. Within moments, Beggsy is incapacitated and Ravi has taken a wound from a Cursed Blade. Panic spreads through the group like a forest fire.

"Somebody do something!" Ravi cries, as I cheerfully tell him how low his Hit Points are falling.

Beggsy groans as he rolls a die to see how much longer he's going to be out of action.

"Can I summon a demon? Would that be a good idea?" Sarah asks Matt.

"It'll take too long," he replies. "Summoning demons takes time."

"Could you buy me that time? Have you got anything that would hold him off for a bit?"

Matt looks down his Character Sheet and then nods. "You are a worthy companion, Nox Noctis," he says, in his character voice. "OK, Archie. I'm going to cast a Distortion Field between us and the skeleton."

Dice are rolled and scores calculated. Behind my screen, I can see that Matt's roll has failed against the skeleton's Resistance to Magic. But I want to give Sarah a chance to shine.

"Your Distortion Field flares into life and the undead warlock lowers his sword; it's as if he can't see you."

"Get behind the coffin," Matt orders. "There's no way of telling how long this thing's going to last. You summon and I'll hold off old Boney here."

Sarah moves her piece to the back of the map and looks at me.

"I want to..." she scans her sheet, "...Summon a Greater Demon."

"OK, but it's risky," I warn her. "These guys have a way of asking for more than they give."

"I'll take that chance," she smiles, and then holds the die up in her hands and closes her eyes. "Spirits of the Netherworld," she intones, "grant me the aid of one of your agents. Make him mine and mine alone!"

I can sense the others freezing for a second: this is role-playing at its best. In other circumstances, it would be cheesier than an Edam factory, but here, in the sanctuary of my Lair, it's perfect. She rolls the die. Behind my screen, I can see it's another failure, but rules are meant to be broken. With a dramatic flourish, I place the Gargoyle in front of her.

"What is thy bidding, Mistress?" Emboldened by bubbles, I enter the spirit of things.

"Whom do you serve?" She looks directly into my eyes.

"Only you, Mistress." I look directly into hers.

"And why are you here?"

"Only to do thy bidding."

"And what will you ask in return?"

"Only that which is in your power to grant."

I can almost feel an electric charge between us. As far as I'm concerned, there's no one else in the room; it's just us. I don't care about the others watching and I don't care what they think of it; all I can see are Sarah's ice-blue eyes and the delicate curves of her mouth.

"Then do my bidding and you will be rewarded."

A million images flash through my mind and I have to cross my legs. God help me if I need to go to the toilet.

"What do you wish, Mistress?"

I never get to hear her answer. There's a sudden bang against my bedroom window; a large stone rolls down the glass. We all sit in silence, throwing anxious glances at each other.

BANG! Another stone.

"What the…?"

BANG! Another one.

Gingerly, Matt creeps over to the window, opens it and pops his head out. Quickly, he ducks back in as another missile clatters on the roof.

"I was wrong," he scowls. "He did turn up."

TWELVE

We sit, frozen, in silence, listening to the barrage on my roof.

"He'll break the window in a minute." Ravi's retreated into his natural Geek's demeanour, cowering and afraid.

"What are we going to do?" Beggsy, too, is withdrawing into his shell, and sounds like he's been sucking on a helium balloon. "How did he find us?"

IM: *Good question.*

"That's that boy we saw at the shop – Jason Humphries. What does he want?" Sarah is watching the window, obviously nervous, while Matt paces the room, only to stop as another stone hits the glass.

IM: *What're you going to do?*

The responsibility is mine. My friends are at my home and in my Lair. I'm sick of feeling impotent and afraid. I want some control back in my life. The bubbles in my head fuse with my frustration and anger to create something like bravery.

"Sod this," I mutter darkly and go over to the window.

"Dude! Don't!"

I ignore Beggsy's plaintive protest and wrench the window open to look down on to the drive. In the soft pool of the streetlight, I can see the taut figure of Jason Humphries, preparing to launch another stone.

"Oi!" My anger darkens my voice. "What're you doing?"

Humphries looks up and a short bark of laughter slices through the night before he lobs the stone.

"Coming to the party!" he shouts.

I want to kill him. This is my home! It's not fair and it's not right.

"Stop it! There's no party!" I shout, ducking. "Get lost!"

Another laugh, another stone.

Matt's beside me. "Tell him we'll call the police if he doesn't stop." His voice is tight and urgent. Humphries responds to the idea with another bombardment. I look around my room and see a picture of fear and self-loathing; we're all too scared to do anything and we know it and we hate ourselves for it. Even Sarah looks shocked.

"What's he *doing*?" she asks, incredulous.

I can feel a hot flush rising in my chest and my breath is getting shallower.

"Pack it in!" I yell.

Humphries pauses for a moment. "You got that girl in there?" he leers.

IM: *Denydenydeny!*

But something in me has ignited, probably thanks to the Cava.

"Yeah! So what?"

"You'd better let me in, then!"

"Yeah? What if I don't?"

My answer is another volley of stones.

"Archie, this is serious."

"Shut up, Ravi. Let me think."

Sarah suddenly stands up. "I'll go and talk to him." She leaves the room.

At that instant, I feel more powerless, more worthless and more pathetic than I ever have done in my life. In a white-hot explosion, the Cava bubbles burst and fury floods my system like molten magma.

"Bastard!" I hiss and thunder down the stairs, overtaking Sarah.

"Archie! What are you—?"

"Stay there!"

I rip the front door open and stand, panting, trembling. Matt, Ravi and Beggsy join me. Humphries saunters towards us.

"*What do you want?*" My voice is shaking. "How did you know where I live?"

"Saw it on your 'girlfriend's' Facebook page. Told you I was coming."

"No, you're not. *Now get lost!*"

Humphries looks over my shoulder; by the sinister change in his face, I guess that Sarah's appeared behind me.

"Hello, Sexy. What're you doing with these losers?" He doesn't bother to hide the leer in his tone.

"Why don't you go home, Jason?" Sarah is the calmest of the lot of us.

"You playing games in there?" It's as if he hasn't heard her. He takes a step closer.

"Please go home."

"I could show you a few games." A reptilian smile reveals small, stained teeth.

"Piss off, Humphries."

IM: *Did I just say that?*

Humphries's body ripples. I've made a challenge and he's showing me what he's got. Another step closer.

"What did you say?"

There's no turning back for me now.

"Just piss off, will you?"

I can dimly hear Beggsy in the background repeating, "Oh, my God" over and over, and hissing to Ravi to call the police. Humphries's face is granite.

"I think I'm going to come in." His voice is low and cold, thick with intent. And then he does it. He puts a foot on my doorstep. My doorstep.

Something happens and Jason staggers back. My arms are outstretched and I can feel molten metal in my veins.

IM: *Oh my God! You pushed him! You pushed Jason Humphries!*

I'm panting and shaking like a leaf. A dangerous smile plays on Humphries's slit of a mouth and his eyes darken under his brow. Without a word, he comes back at me, slowly, precisely, his face full of murder.

"Wanker," he hisses. "*Geek.*"

There's a thunderclap in my head and my body is owned by rage and hate. Everything that's been dulled by the Cava suddenly finds a focus. My arms throw Humphries back into the drive and my legs launch me after him. A wild yell rolls up from my gut and into the night. My weight throws us both to the ground, me on top of him. Humphries gets his feet on the ground and slides himself out from under me. We're both up and we grab each other's arms at the shoulders. Our legs do a weird dance as we each try and trip the other over in some bad imitation of Judo. Humphries's breath stinks and the gash of a smile never leaves his face. I'm panting and making whimpering noises as our feet twist round each other's shins, losing and regaining balance in milliseconds.

Suddenly, we're apart; he must have thrown me

because I'm staggering back. Instinctively my arms come up above my head and are answered by a hail of piston punches. It's a mess; this whole thing is a mess. Not like those fights you see in films where guys are slugging at each other with long, clean punches; this is a tight, coiled, frenetic spasm of lashes and noise. But Jason's a fighter and I'm not. With my arms protecting my head, my ribs are exposed and I feel the impact of his fist just under my armpit. It knocks the breath out of my lungs and I double over, my hands flailing above me. More blows rain on my shoulders and back. Blindly, I flail about, throwing my fists outward, hitting air, scuffing his hoodie, whimpering and yelling. Somewhere, I can hear Sarah shouting for us to stop it.

And then I connect. My unguided knuckles meet something that crunches. The blows stop for a second as Humphries reels back, a hand to his face. He stands for a moment, then looks in his palm with something like disgust. Blood rolls down from his nose, black in the half-light. A decision flashes across his face and he looks at me.

I'm already taking shaky steps backwards, but it's too late; he comes at me like a bull, his arms swinging. I feel an impact to my cheek and the grind of gravel under my heel as I fall, Humphries on top of me. He growls, grunts and swears, getting in his shots wherever he can.

IM: *I'm going to be killed.*

174

And for a moment, I think I have been. Everything goes white and I can't feel anything. When I open my eyes, I see that the drive has been lit up by car headlights and Tony is hurling Jason out on to the street. Mum pulls me to my feet, a look on her face that I've never seen before.

"Get inside. Now."

Sitting holding a packet of frozen peas to my face and listening to my mother scold me about the dangers of fighting, I've never felt less like James Bond. It may have been a tenuous fantasy to begin with, but my sore face, sore ribs and severely dented ego do nothing to build it back up. Despite the twenty minutes of my friends and Sarah explaining to my mother what happened and how it wasn't my fault, my mum seems to think that right now is the best time to make sure that I don't do it again – like I'm about to go pounding the streets in search of vengeance. And I think I'm having a premature hangover.

IM: *But you did plant one on him.*

That thought does fill me with a little pride, I admit, but it also fills me with more than a little dread – my life at school's not going to be worth living. Every step I take is going to be haunted by the psychotic figure of Jason Humphries.

"Well? Aren't you going to say something?"

I look up into my mother's eyes. I could tell her about Dad leaving, but it would sound like an excuse.

IM: *Just do the apology and get it over with.*

"Sorry. It just happened."

Mum's lips purse and she lets out a long breath through her nose.

"But you're all right? How's your cheek?"

IM: *She can't help herself.*

"It's a bit sore, but it's OK. Sorry, Mum."

She nods and straightens up, asking who wants a cup of tea. It's her subliminal way of letting me know that I'm off the hook. Tea solves everything.

"Well, I'm going to have a beer," Tony huffs, heaving himself to the fridge. "I think I've earned it." He clenches and unclenches his hand, wincing at some strain or bruise. "That kid was heavy."

"I know!" I laugh ruefully. "I was under him! Thanks for getting him off."

"No problem. Looked like you had it all under control, anyway…"

I raise an eyebrow wryly. My friends chuckle. Only Sarah remains quiet, staring at me intently, almost as if she's trying to figure something out.

IM: *It could just be grateful awe.*

I think not. Mum doles out mugs of sweet tea and offers round a few biscuits.

"Drink up," she says. "And then I think I'd better take you all home. We've had quite a shock."

"Yeah," Beggsy manages through a biscuit. "But not as big a shock as Jason Humphries got."

With the adrenalin having subsided and tea coursing through our veins, we all start to relive the whole thing, comfortable and safe in our surroundings. This is a moment of camaraderie that we've never really experienced before – because for once in our submissive little lives – something has *happened*. For once, we're part of our own story, instead of living out our fantasies with maps and miniatures. I listen to my friends recounting the various threads of the evening. It turns out that Ravi did try to call the police, but kept dialling 911 instead of 999. He watches too much television. But he did spot Tony's mobile number on the pad and rang it, so hats off to him. Matt had been trying to work out whether to jump in on the fight or not and Beggsy comes up with some story about putting himself between the action and Sarah. Only Sarah and I have nothing to say.

IM: *What's she thinking?*

In all the fantasies I've entertained about protecting Sarah from danger, her reaction has been profoundly different to this. Usually, I've been battered within an inch of my life …

IM: *Check.*

… but have emerged victorious …

IM: *Check.*

… possibly with a dramatic wound that trickles a trail of blood from my forehead and down the side of my face …

IM: *Bruised eye and sore ribs … we'll call it a check.*

… that *she* tends …

IM: *Mum. Peas. Scolding. Uh-uh.*

… before falling helplessly into my arms.

IM: *Tea. Biscuits. Silence. Nope.*

Perhaps she's disappointed in me; perhaps my Cava-fuelled display was too animalistic or even too *pathetic* to have won her adoration.

"Everyone ready?" Mum says, surveying the collection of empty mugs. "Come on, then." My friends get up and say their goodbyes to me. Ravi opts for a high-five, Matt shakes my hand and Beggsy stands motionless for a second, pointing at me meaningfully. It's all a bit solemn. Sarah stands in front of me, then sits gracefully on her heels and puts a hand on mine. She looks straight into my eyes.

"I'm going to call you tomorrow."

My EM, unable to cope with anything, allows a

178

glowing blush to slip through the net.

IM: *Makes trumpet noises*

"'K."

She puts my number into her phone, and then they leave. I see Tony look towards the front door, listening for the revs of the car. It fires up and disappears into the night, delivering my friends and the girl who's going to call me tomorrow to their homes.

With the car gone, Tony turns to me, a conspirator's grin on his face.

"Well, well, well," he smirks. "I didn't know you had it in you, Arch, defending your lady's honour. And against a thug like that. I'd have done the same in your shoes, though. She's a cracker."

My EM smiles and nods. My IM groans and sighs.

"Must've been the Cava," I shrug.

Tony stops and looks up, as though listening for something.

"Lose the bottle before your mum gets back," he says evenly. "We don't need any more grief tonight."

"Yeah, OK."

As I trudge painfully upstairs to retrieve the bottle, I silently resolve never to foxtrot with Tony again.

IM: *He'll only tread on your toes.*

The Dream is different tonight. The Gargoyle is waiting and I'm dragged out of bed and left to stand motionless in the middle of my room. For a while, it just circles, staring at me with its glowing eyes, its canonball muscles rolling under its stony carapace with every step.

Then it stops and regards me with a snarl. Slowly, it begins to walk towards me. Again, I'm paralyzed and brimming with fear, but suddenly, there's a flash of purple light between us and another figure appears.

It's Sarah, dressed in her Nox Noctis outfit. She extends one gloved hand and the Gargoyle responds, retreating slowly into the shadows. Although I can still see its eyes burning corrosively from the darkness, I feel safe now.

Sarah turns to me and her ice-blue eyes fix on mine as a soft smile plays on her lips. Her other hand goes to the back of my neck and she pulls me forward for a deep, lingering kiss. I feel a pulse of fire from my stomach and wake up.

I'm going to have to change my pyjamas.

THIRTEEN

When I finally reawaken the next day, everything decides to kick off on the wrong foot. Firstly, there's the issue of my pyjamas. The most obvious thing to do would be to try and slip the incriminating evidence into the washing machine. However, as much as my mum knows me, I know her too; when it comes to washing, she's like a border-patrol guard. Nothing gets past unnoticed and anything she's unsure about gets severely questioned. Instead, I opt to begin my day by standing at the bathroom sink with a sponge and some shower gel, hoping to scrub my DNA from the scene of the crime. By the time I've finished, the circumstantial evidence suggests that I've wet myself during the night. Strangely, I'm happier for the court to draw this conclusion than for them to discover the Awful Truth.

Once I've stashed the wet pyjama bottoms discreetly on the radiator, I chuck on last night's clothes and inspect my war wound in the mirror. I have got a shiner, but it doesn't look as heroic or as casual as the ones they get in the films. My black eye isn't so much black, as a clash of colours, ranging from blood-red and nicotine-yellow to a dirty blue. The damaged skin looks waxy and, as I find out when I practise a smile, hurts. Rather than looking like a devil-may-care swashbuckler, I look like a bruised fruit.

I enter the kitchen to the fading smell of bacon and the growing smell of cigarettes. Tony's sat at the table, poring over a newspaper. As I appear, he looks up and starts singing something about "The Eye of the Tiger" and making strange noises that I take to be an electric guitar, whilst doing little jabbing actions with his fists. Which are a bit girly.

IM: *What with you being the heavyweight champion of the world and all.*

Mum reprimands him with a disapproving look and sets about sorting me out a bacon sandwich.

"We thought we'd let you sleep in," she says, placing some rashers into a pan.

I look at the clock: it's half-past ten. I must have been more tired than I thought.

"Cup of tea?"

"Yes, please. Sorry about last night, Mum."

"Well, it's done now. But I'm going to be seeing the head about that boy; we don't want anything like that happening again."

My hearts sinks. Mum's tone pre-empts my unborn protest and tells me that it's going to happen, whether I like it or not. Which I don't. I understand her concern, but it's tantamount to putting a bounty on my head. Schools work a bit like prisons – Jason doesn't have to touch me to get me back. All he has to do is let the right word out to the wrong people and I stand about as much chance as a kitten in a piranha tank.

"How's your eye?" The question arrives with a cuppa and a bacon sandwich, ketchup already applied.

"Yeah, it hurts a bit. But I'll be OK."

Mum tuts to herself and starts to clear away the pans. Then she turns to me with a look as though she's just remembered something. She couldn't be more fake if she tried.

"Oh! Sarah called for you this morning."

My EM goes from nought to sixty in about three seconds, sending a flush to my face and tightening my throat round the food that I've just swallowed.

The options available to me are questions that should convey little or nothing about the fairground thrill I feel because Sarah has called, and the ghastly horror that my mum has spoken to her while I was asleep. I could go for the casual "Oh, yeah?", the gentlemanly "How was she?" or even the non-committal "Uh-huh?" Instead, my IM takes charge and leaps out through my mouth like a laryngitic express train.

"What did she say?"

IM: *Oops.*

Mum smiles her "I can see through you" smile and sits down opposite me.

"She said," she begins, as though she was reading a story to a four-year-old, "that *she* wanted to know if *you* wanted to go over and see her."

"What? Today?"

"Today."

IM: *Her house! You'll be going to HER house!*

While I try and create some cool and blasé response, the Greek Chorus at the end of the table contributes with a jackpot-style noise: "Ker-ching!". Mum and I both scowl in unison.

IM: *Tosser.*

"Her number's by the phone. I said you'd call her back."

I don't need telling twice, but I can't look too obvious; don't want to wear my heart on my sleeve. I wait a few seconds. Mum and Tony are looking at me and the silence that follows is thick with anticipation. I wait a few more. Beneath my cool, calm exterior, I'm riddled with panic. What the hell am I going to say? Unfortunately, Mum doesn't allow me the time to consider this fully.

"Well, go on, then!" she splutters. "Don't keep the poor girl waiting!"

Fighting the rising urge to go and hide under my bed until it's all over, I go to the phone. There, in Mum's handwriting, are the glorious numbers that will connect me with the most beautiful girl in the world.

IM: *Well? What are you waiting for?*

What I'm waiting for is for my senses to get back into line: the phone suddenly looks like a piece of alien technology. The beeps it makes as I dial the Hallowed Numbers sound off-key and the ringing tone seems ridiculously loud. And there's a strong possibility that my heart will flatline in the next thirty seconds.

"Hello?"

IM: *Oh, God. It's her.*

I cough nervously, trying to clear my throat before I speak. For some reason, my body – which may as well belong to somebody else right now – decides it's a good idea to bring a little bit of bacon sandwich up with the cough. The result: more coughing. In fact, it's one of those coughs that just won't stop and gets your eyes watering with it. Between racking hacks, I manage to choke out a word or two.

"Hell—*Cough*—o?" I think I might be dying.

IM: *From shame or oxygen deficiency. Either'll do.*

"Hello? Who's that?" Sarah sounds a little worried. And after last night, that's pretty understandable.

"Sarah!" I splutter, before gaining control of the cough. "It's Archie!" Unfortunately, these last two words come out as a hoarse, post-cough wheeze.

"Archie? Are you OK?"

"Yeah," I manage to say, whilst clearing my throat for what I hope is the last time in my life.

"You sound awful."

"No, no," I say, in my normal voice. "Had something stuck in my throat."

IM: *Well, at least that's the awkward hello taken care of…*

"How are you?" I throw the spotlight back at her, hoping to make my phone-retching a distant memory as soon as possible.

"I'm fine," she says. "It was a really fun evening and thanks for my figure. It's on my bedside table."

IM: …*!*

"I'm sorry Jason saw my Facebook page, I've blocked him now. And I've changed my privacy settings. What a creep!"

"Well, he obviously likes you…"

IM: *Attempt at comedy! Abort! Abort!*

"He needs to work on his chat-up lines!" Sarah giggles. "But I was really starting to enjoy the Game. I'd love to do it again sometime."

IM: **Sound of wedding bells**

"Yeah, sure, yeah," I rattle off. "That'd be cool."

"So. D'you want to come round? We could just hang out."

I can think of nothing in the world that I'd like to do more, but I don't want to frighten her off with what might sound like desperation.

IM: *Best keep your mouth shut, then.*

"Yeah. That'd be cool."

"Great. I live on Davenport Road. Number seventy-eight."

"Oh, I know – the road just down from the shops."

"Yeah. D'you want me to post it on Facebook?" There's a tease in her voice that sends the butterflies in my stomach into a multicoloured flurry.

"Maybe next time," I quip, planting the seeds that there might even be a next time.

"See you in about half an hour?"

"'K." I don't want to be the one to put the phone down first.

"Cool. Bye."

IM: *She obviously doesn't have the same problem...*

"Bye." I stand, looking at the receiver for a second, perhaps hoping that she'll come back on the line.

IM: *That wasn't too bad, was it?*

Surprisingly, it wasn't. Talking to a girl I'm hopelessly attracted to wasn't too bad at all. It was almost like talking to a mate.

IM: *Weird.*

Mum appears in the hallway, no doubt having

heard every word.

IM: *You really need that mobile phone.*

"Perhaps you'd better go and get changed. You can't turn up in the same clothes you wore yesterday."

I dumbly agree and head to my Lair, clutching my bacon sandwich. As I climb the stairs, I hear Mum saying something to Tony about it being nice to see me so happy.

"Packing my pants" would be more accurate.

Rather than accepting Tony's offer of a lift in "the Beemer", I decide to walk to Sarah's. It's not too far and, after last night's debacle, I'm done with being ostentatious; now it's a case of what you see is what you get. Having said that, I did submit to Mum's orders in choosing what to wear. I'm currently sporting jeans, the new trainers and a black shirt. All of which were ironed at Mum's insistence – just after she'd noticed my sodden pyjamas on the radiator. I explained it away as a toothbrushing incident where I'd turned the tap on too hard, but I'm not sure whether my mother, the human polygraph, bought it.

My Grunt Detector™ is on overdrive; everyone who appears round a corner or out of their house or on the horizon is marked out as a potential threat. But there's no sign of Humphries. Which is sort of more worrying than seeing him; it gives my already over-active imagination plenty of time to think about what he might do next.

IM: *Don't fancy your chances in a rematch?*

I don't. Maybe Mum talking to Mrs Holly will keep him off me for a while, but no matter how much of an eye the school says they'll keep on him, he'll be back, I just know he will. His is the Way of the Warrior.

IM: *Yours is the Way of the Worrier.*

After chasing a few scenarios round in my head – all of which involve my untimely death – I decide to try and forget about it. I've got other things to think about; I've walked along Davenport Road many a time, usually on my way to Matt's. But today, it looks different. Even the air feels different.

IM: *SHE lives here.*

As I walk along the pavement, I'm suddenly aware that these are the sights she sees every day – the parked cars, the lines of trees, the other houses – this is her environment. This must be how Frodo felt when he was walking through Lothlórien to meet the Queen of the Elves. Everything seems brighter and more profound; every leaf, every padding cat, every child on a bike – they're all somehow inextricably linked to Sarah, and have some meaning in her life, no matter how small. I soak it all up, sensing the differences between her life and mine, trying to figure out a bit more about her. And, like Frodo, while I'm aware of the sense of supernatural beauty of my surroundings, I'm also apprehensive of meeting my Queen, feeling unworthy of her presence.

IM: *And thank God that she can't read minds like Galadriel could.*

Number seventy-eight appears on my right and I take a moment to drink it in, scouring it for any clues that might tell me more about the girl who, whether she knows it or not, has captured my heart. Number seventy-eight is a modestly-sized, semi-detached house with a small gravel path leading to the green front door. Some sort of climbing plant has swathed the brickwork in purple blooms, giving it the appearance of a country cottage.

IM: *And it was the colour you chose for Nox Noctis. Maybe it's a sign…*

Maybe there is some sort of link between us. Again I think back to our meeting outside the shop.

I push open the gate. A fluffy black and white cat bowls over to me from the small front lawn. I crouch down and give it a stroke, feeling it push its head against my fingers. Could this be Sarah's cat? It seems appropriate that it would be.

IM: *Only one way to find out – brace yourself!*

I stand, take in a deep breath and crunch my way to

the front door. The cat does figures of eight between my legs as I walk, meaning that I have to stride with my legs apart in case it trips me up. But it likes me; could *this* be a sign?

IM: *Here goes...*

For a second, I stand on the doorstep like an idiot until I realize that the iron door knocker right in front of me probably wasn't put there for decorative purposes only.

IM: *Take two.*

With my heart pulsing in my throat, I knock on the door. Only twice. And trying to make it sound as casual as possible.

A moment passes and nothing happens. Then, through the front door's frosted glass, I see a distorted shadow moving and hear the scuff of feet on floorboards. The door opens and I'm given a glimpse of the future.

My dad always used to say that he knew that Mum would always "be a looker" because of the way her mum, my nan, aged.

I am confronted with what Beggsy would describe as a MILF. Crude, I know, but Sarah's mum definitely falls into that category: the same crystal-blue eyes, Cupid's bow lips and midnight hair. A leak in the old EM allows a little blush through the net and all the moisture leaves my mouth.

"Hello," she smiles. "You must be Archie."

"I am. Yes. Hello. I'm Archie."

IM: *Right words. Wrong order.*

For some reason, I offer my hand out in a handshake which Sarah's mum takes. She then responds with another melting smile and I counter-respond with another hello. For fear of being stuck in some sort of vocal loop, I manage to throw in a "How are you?"

"Very well, thanks. Come in, Archie. I'll call Sarah down."

I step into the house and my senses go into overdrive, taking in pictures on the wall, the sage-green paint and the vase of flowers on the hall table. Something else hits me: a smell, a faint smell, which takes me a moment to search through my memory banks and identify.

IM: *Incense!*

Incense. I've never been so grateful for a smell in my life. It tells me that I got something right last night; that I've edged a little closer to finding out what it is that makes Sarah Sarah.

Sarah's mum goes to the bottom of the carpeted stairs and calls her daughter's name. There's a vague thunder of activity from somewhere upstairs, which Sarah's mum pretends not to notice.

"Would you like a cup of tea, or a cold drink?" she asks.

My IM flips through its underused Etiquette Files and I go for a cup of tea; it feels a bit like having a security blanket with me. Just as she turns to the kitchen, Sarah's mum looks intently at my face.

"That's a nasty bruise," she says. "Have you put anything on it?"

"Peas." I blurt out, embarrassed. "I mean cold ones. Frozen ones."

IM: *The name's Bond. James Bond.*

"Have you tried arnica?"

My memory banks are unfamiliar with this, so I respond in the negative.

"It's a cream; very good for bruising. And it's all natural – no chemicals. Would you like some?"

IM: *OhChristwhatdoIsay?*

"Um… Yeah. OK. Thanks."

Sarah's mum takes me into a small, quaintly decorated kitchen and tells me to sit on one of the chairs. Once again, vampire-like, I suck as much detail from the surroundings as I can: photos of Sarah when she was younger, small knick-knacks lining the window sill and a cat flap in the back door. Sarah's mum reaches into a cupboard behind her and produces a small tube of cream.

"This won't hurt," she says, squeezing a blob on to her middle finger. "It'll bring the bruise out quicker."

She leans in close to me and rubs the cream on to my cheekbone in gentle, soothing circles. My EM has a complete power failure and my IM has taken a brief vow of silence; all I can do is stare ahead, like a broken android.

"Look up." The soothing circles go under my eye.

"Look down for me." The soothing circles go under my eyebrow.

IM: *Eep.*

Eep indeed. I can see right down the front of Sarah's mum's loose jumper.

IM: *Bra alert! Bra alert!*

Quickly, I shut my eyes.

"Sorry, did that hurt?"

"No, no. I'm fine." I manage, still with my eyes closed, trying to force the image of Sarah's mum's bra out of my mind. "I think I can feel it working."

IM: *Well covered.*

"Mum! What're you doing?"

Sarah's voice snaps me back into reality and I open my eyes to see her standing in the kitchen doorway, wearing a punk-style T-shirt and black jeans. I try and ignore the flash of black bra strap on her left shoulder. I'm surrounded by bras. It's a bra carnival.

IM: *A Mardi Bra.*

"Just treating Archie's bruise," Sarah's mum trills. "It's a nasty one."

"Yes, well I'm sure Archie doesn't want you poking about with it," Sarah replies tersely.

"No… It's fine… I'm OK…" I mutter, like I've just learned how to talk.

"There, you see." Sarah's mum smiles, triumphant. "Why don't you two go on up and I'll bring you some tea in a minute. Do you take sugar, Archie?"

"Two, thanks."

"Come on, Archie. Let's go."

With a feeble smile and a muttered thanks to Sarah's mum, I begin the ascent to A Girl's Bedroom.

As we approach the landing, I half expect to see Gandalf leap out, shouting "You shall not pass!". Instead, the black and white cat appears from nowhere and starts figure of eighting round my legs again. I half stumble up the final stair.

"Oh, Aslan; leave him alone!"

"Aslan?" I try to keep a chuckle out of my voice.

"Yeah, *The Lion, the Witch and the Wardrobe*. It was one of my favourite films when I was little."

With some horror, I realize that she's just named one of the few sword and sorcery films that I don't actually like.

IM: *It could be worth re-watching…*

"Yeah. It wasn't bad. Hello, Aslan." I give the cat another stroke, hoping that my action will be taken as some sign of approval. The smell of incense beckons like an invisible finger from behind a door at the end of the long landing. As we walk towards it, I'm transported back to the Shop of Unrequited Love, experiencing that strange, otherworldly feeling. It's as though I'm experiencing things for the first time; everything seems unfamiliar, no matter how ordinary it might be: the pale landing carpet seems to absorb our footsteps, the walls seem almost to be watching us and the closed doors hint at parts of Sarah's life that I have yet to see. Only the smell of incense is familiar, although not necessarily comforting.

"Come in." Sarah pushes open the door and steps inside. I give the cat one last pat – just for luck – and follow.

Sarah's bedroom somehow isn't what I expected – although I'm not sure *what* I expected. The walls are a sunshine yellow and adorned with a few framed pictures. A star-shaped crystal on a chain, which I presume to be a rainbow maker, hangs in front of an old-fashioned, criss-cross window, below which is a small dressing table and chair. Her bed is white and there's a delightful absence of cuddly toys from it; TV and stepsisters tell you that all girls have cuddly toys on their beds. On one wall is a freestanding bookshelf, quite tall, and crammed with books of all sorts: big ones, small ones, hardbacks, paperbacks – it's amazing what you can take in when your future depends on it. And there, on the bedside table, is Nox Noctis. I try not to announce that I've noticed by not doing anything.

IM: *Do something! Say something!*

"Nice room." I stand, jamming my hands in my pockets and turn slowly on my heel, like I'm in an art gallery. "Yeah. Nice." I throw in a sage nod or two for good measure.

"It's OK." She smiles. "Not as nice as yours, though."

An alert runs through my system as my brain tries desperately to figure out whether there is any hidden meaning to this statement. Does she like my room because of its size, its decor, because it's mine, because she'd like to be in it? A thousand possible meanings present themselves in an instant – is it a compliment just about my room or is it somehow about me as well? Thankfully, Sarah's mum walks in with a tray carrying tea and biscuits, otherwise I'm sure her daughter would be able to hear the page-flipping going on in my head as I mentally scour my copy of the *Female Phrasebook*. There appear to be a few crucial pages missing.

"Tea?" Sarah's mum asks, as though I might have changed my mind in the minutes since I last looked down her top.

"Thanks, that's lovely."

IM: *You sound like a plumber.*

"I gather you're a bit of an artist, Archie. Have you seen Sarah's paintings?"

IM: *So – she's spoken about you.*

"Mu-um…" Sarah's voice is enough, but her beautifully arched eyebrow sends her mum out of the room, apologies echoing in her wake.

"Paintings?"

"Oh, I like to paint a bit in my spare time. They're silly, really."

"Let's have a look." I've got that coy, slightly teasing tone in my voice that I hate when I hear other people do it.

Sarah gestures casually to the pictures on the wall, but I'm sure I can see the beginnings of a smile on her face, almost as if she's pleased that I'm showing an interest. I decide to pursue it.

"These? Here?" It's a fairly fatuous question, but helps propel me across the room, tea in hand, to look at the pictures in question.

IM: *Zoinks!*

They are pictures of fairies. But not your common or garden, tutu-wearing fairies. These are Sexy Fairies. Once I get past the fact that most of them appear to have little or nothing on, I can see that she's used the paint with stunning ease, creating an effect that suggests that each fairy is luminous, so bright in fact that their light obscures any of the really naughty bits. They're all in different poses, and each is a different colour, but all of them have the same knowing look on their faces. It's a gallery of erotic Tinker Bells.

Whilst my EM has a stiff word with the Blush Department and puts extra sandbags round the pores, I realize that I've got a slight problem on my hands.

IM: *What do I say?*

If I show too much appreciation, it might suggest a pervert in sheep's clothing. Too little and I'm going to come across as arrogant.

IM: *Go for "nebulous".*

"I've never seen fairies like these before!" I accompany the statement with a little laugh that could be interpreted as both surprised and/or cheeky.

"I've always thought that fairies were too girly in books. I always thought they'd be a bit sexier."

"Well… They are. They're really good."

A bit too good, actually. My own painting skills suddenly feel a bit primitive.

"Thanks."

Fearing an awkward silence, I take a little tour of her bookshelf and see that it's lined with lots of different-coloured crystals of varying shapes and sizes. Being a Geek, I've got a vague knowledge about such things and pick one up that I recognize.

"Amethyst," I announce, confidently. "I like amethyst."

"Interesting you should be drawn to that one."

"Is it? Why?" My EM is caught off guard and I look up too quickly, feeling like I'm under the microscope.

"Amethyst is a healing stone. You can use it to help you sleep or cure headaches, but its greatest power is to heal emotional wounds."

"Oh. OK."

IM: *We are now entering uncharted space. Please remain calm.*

I sip my tea and then grin inanely.

"Well. I like amethyst."

IM: *There's only so many times you can say this before you start to sound like a madman.*

"You're hurting, Archie."

"No, I'm fine. Honestly. Your mum put some cream on it."

Sarah laughs; a delicate, silvery sound, which only adds to my feeling of unease and confusion.

"Not your eye." She smiles. "You. You're hurting *inside*."

IM: *Eh?*

"Eh?"

"Come and sit down."

200

Another problem and another absent page in the *Female Phrasebook*. Does "Come and sit down" mean "Come and sit down by *me*" or "Feel free to be seated anywhere in this room, but not necessarily by my side"?

IM: *Maintain standard orbit.*

I opt for the chair.

"Do you remember when we met outside the shop?"

Although the scenario is branded into my memory, I go through a very amateur pantomime of trying to remember.

"Yeah, Jason Humphries was giving you some hassle."

IM: *Which is no longer a problem, ma'am.*

"I could tell you were hurting then. Do you remember I said so?"

"Yeah. Sort of."

"I knew it when I touched your hand. It felt like an electric shock."

Sarah looks at me very intently and then a decision works its way across her face.

"Archie, have you ever had your aura read?"

IM: *Man battle stations! We are under attack!*

FOURTEEN

Sarah gets up from her bed and closes the curtains.

IM: *Doors to manual…*

"Put your tea down and come and sit on the floor."

I oblige, trying not to show fear. I've heard that girls can smell it.

"Do you know what an aura is, Archie?"

"Uh… Isn't it a light or something that surrounds you?"

That gossamer laugh floats through the darkened room.

"Sort of." Sarah settles, cross-legged in front of me, fixing me with her eyes, which look almost translucent in the half-light. "Everything living has an aura. They're energy fields and they can reflect how you're feeling."

"So – how am I feeling?"

IM: *You want to start praying that this is inaccurate…*

Sarah laughs again; I seem to be good at making her do that.

"It's not *that* easy! Shall I read yours? Mum says I've got a gift for it. She's taught me loads."

"What is she? A witch or something?"

"No! She's a psychic practitioner! Come on – are we going to do it or not?"

IM: *If only.*

The earnest expression on her face and the want in her voice are impossible to resist. This is one of those "Now or Never" moments.

"Yeah, OK."

Whether I believe in this or not, I still feel a thrill of excitement, coupled with a sense of dread. What if she *is* able to read my aura? She'll know just how deeply I feel about her. Is there any way I can hide it? Should I push those thoughts to the back of my head or focus on them, in the hope that she gets the message loud and clear?

IM: *It would save you having to ask her out.*

"OK, then. First I need you to relax. Close your eyes."

I do, but am unable to prevent a self-conscious grin from escaping.

"Come on, Archie. Stop messing about. Just relax."

IM: *In for a penny…*

I take a deep breath and try to relax. While my body seems to welcome the opportunity, I can feel my mental shutters going up as a just-in-case and all my other senses kick into overdrive. There's a scent of whatever soap or shampoo she uses; I can practically feel her presence and her voice seems to melt through me.

"Breathe in, Archie. And out. And in. And out. Now focus on your muscles and try and relax them. Let's start with your toes; feel them relax and go limp…"

Sarah takes a tour of my body, so to speak, telling me to concentrate on each area and let the tension go. Everything's fine, until she says the word "buttocks". At that precise moment in time, I become convinced that if I relax that particular region, I might fart. To cover the fact that my buttocks are now rock solid with tension, I expel another deep breath – in keeping with the spirit of things. Finally, we reach my shoulders, neck and head and I allow my cast-iron backside to sink a little deeper into the carpet.

"Good, Archie. That's really good. Now I want you to rock gently from side to side."

IM: *You know how stupid you look, don't you?*

As I rock, I can hear Sarah breathing in and out deeply. It's horribly sexy, but the fact that I'm wobbling like a nodding dog seems to take the erotic charge out of it for me.

I wobble and she breathes for what seems like an eternity, until finally Sarah tells me to open my eyes. When I do, it's to find her staring at the space round my head, heartbreaking concern written all over her face. I raise my eyebrows in a silent query.

"Well," she says, looking a little brighter, "you're very healthy, physically – although the Cava has dulled your psychic abilities. You should be careful of drinking too much; you're a little out of alignment."

Feeling a little out of alignment, I nod. Slowly.

IM: *I think you're being told off for last night's fisticuffs.*

"But it's obvious that you do have some psychic abilities. The yellow colouring tells me that you're a perfectionist and too self-critical. You should cut yourself some slack. There's a lot of red, which says that you have a great inner strength and that you're very passionate."

IM: *Ker-ching!*

"You're sympathetic and reliable. But there's a lot of dark blue, which tells me that you feel misunderstood. You don't communicate easily with the rest of the world."

IM: *OK, this is getting weird.*

"But there's a lot of black, Archie. Almost all of your colours are surrounded by this black…" She searches for a word. "…halo."

For a moment, my ego awards itself a series of medals; I like my newfound position as a Dark Angel. It feels cool. But the expression on her face tells me that that's not a good thing, so I break my silence.

"What does that mean?"

Sarah searches my halo before answering. When she

does, she looks straight into my eyes.

"It means you're hurting, Archie. That you've developed a protective shield against the world – like a mask, or armour. It means that you don't really show your true feelings to people because you don't want to get hurt any more. But you're paying a very high psychic price for that shield."

This is starting to feel a little too close for comfort. On one level, I'm really enjoying being so close to Sarah and getting a foot inside her world, but something in her words is appealing to something inside me that I'd rather not think about.

IM: *Because she's right. You are hurting.*

My EM gets the fidgets and I start scratching behind my ear, even though there's no itch. It's like she's pressed the button marked "Do Not Press". The one that sets everything off. The one that opens doors that ought to remain shut. I can feel an unfamiliar pressure building up in my head and chest and my EM fidgets more; I sit back, resting on my hands and breathing hard.

IM: *You're losing control…!*

I grit my teeth together and force another breath out through my nose, like a poor impression of a hunted dragon.

"What is it, Archie? Why are you hurting?"

I scowl at the floor, trying to pull my EM back into

alignment, but it's no good; my fingers clench into fists and back again.

"It's … uh… It's nothing." But my voice is thick with yearning confession. Sarah's hand on my ankle does nothing to draw me out of my scaled-down breakdance.

"It's OK, Archie. It really is." Her voice is heartbreakingly soft. "Is it your stepfather?"

IM: *Self-destruct sequence initiated: Five – Four – Three – Two…*

In a final act of betrayal, my EM shuts down completely, leaving my face to tremble and crack into tears. Instinctively, I lurch forward and wrap my arms round my shins and thrust my head between my knees, silent, seething sobs escaping between ragged breaths.

And then it all comes out.

I tell her everything: Tony, the divorce, my dad leaving, how much I love my mum, how I'm a Geek, Tony, how weak I am, how I don't really talk to anyone, my IM, the Gargoyle, the Dream; the whole lot comes out in a big, wet, snotty, snivelling mess. And then I'm silent, exhausted, plagued only by trembling, weepy sighs. I don't even notice Sarah's arm round my shoulders until I've managed to regain some sort of control over my spasming lungs.

"It's OK," she says gently. "I can help you."

"Can you?" I moan hopelessly from between my legs.

"Yes. But you've got to trust me."

Sarah helps me to my feet and points me in the direction of the bathroom, where she leaves me to splash my face with water. I look in the oval mirror above the white, glistening basin to see my mismatched eyes rimmed with red and a nose that wouldn't look out of place on a certain reindeer. I can't believe I've done this. I've wept like a snivelling child in front of the girl I love. Any chance I had with her is now melting like a snowball in Hell.

But I'm tired. Too tired to be cross with myself for breaking like I did. Too tired to try and get my shields back online. Too tired to try and plug my IM back into the grid.

I feel empty and exposed, but too tired to care.

After a final splash, I go back into Sarah's room with an apologetic half-smile on my face. The curtains are open and she's sat on the end of her bed, a bright smile glittering in the light.

"OK?"

"Yeah," I mumble. "Sorry about all that."

"Stop being sorry!" I can't tell if she's cross or putting it on. I feel like I'm back in primary school. "You've been strong for too long, Archie – it's time to stop."

"OK. So… What do we do?"

"We talk. Properly."

Because I seem to have nothing left to say, Sarah takes the reins.

"Have you ever wondered why you were drawn to that Gargoyle in the first place?"

"I just liked it," I manage dumbly.

"Just like you liked the amethyst. It goes a bit deeper than that, Archie. When I read your aura, I could tell that you've got psychic abilities, but they're being suppressed by your shield – your armour. Yet they're still trying to find a way to leak out – to communicate with you. Your dream is your subconscious trying to make contact, but you keep pushing it away; you don't want to hear what it has to say."

"Which is what?"

"That you're far more powerful than you think. You can change things, Archie – you can make your life what you want it to be."

"Can I? How?"

"The Gargoyle in your dream represents your subconscious. It's your Psychic Self trying to talk to you. You have to embrace it. Your Internal Monologue is part of your shield; you need to shut it out because it's made up of fear and hurt. You need to start listening to your Psychic Self."

Despite the fog that has descended over my senses, this seems to make sense. My IM has always been the voice of doubt; that thing that has stopped me from taking any uncertain steps. Perhaps Sarah's right, perhaps there is more to me than meets the eye.

"What do I do?"

"We need to give you some exercises to help you develop your psychic awareness."

We spend the next half an hour going through some "alternative" books that Sarah's got on her bookshelf. Right now, I wouldn't really care if she told me to go and boil my own head. She really seems to understand me and she gives me a series of exercises that she says will help me embrace my Psychic Self, something to do with Positive Visualization and chatting to myself in the mirror. My IM remains in exile; I trust her. I have no doubts. I can change.

"Take this – it'll help." She presses a thin, dog-eared paperback into my hands.

"Thanks." I smile. "I guess I need all the help I can get." I'm sitting next to her on the bed and we enter one of those silences where I don't know if I should be doing something or not. I guess I've got a lot to learn. I think it might be time to make a graceful exit; I don't want to make any more of a fool of myself than I already have.

"I'd better go," I say, looking at my watch. "Stuff to do." It's a generic answer that suggests I won't be sitting around thinking about her and nothing else for the rest of the day.

"I'll see you out."

As we walk downstairs, I check my reflection in any surface that will bear it; I think I look OK. In fact, I look considerably better than the blonde lady that Sarah's mum is helping out of the room opposite the kitchen. Judging by her puffy eyes and her luminous hooter, I reckon it's fairly safe to assume she's just had her aura read too. What have I stumbled upon? A suburban coven? Sarah opens the door and I step out of the sanctuary of her home.

"OK ... well ... thanks. And sorry about earlier..."

"Stop it!" Sarah scolds, before joining me on the path and fixing me with a determined stare. "It's all going to be OK, Archie."

And then she kisses me on the cheek.

My head detonates with pure, crystal-clear joy. I am flooded with energy, bright, fizzing power, and I want to laugh out loud. Instead, I hang on to what's left of my self-control and walk to the gate.

"See you Monday," I say, grinning, and head for home, ten foot tall and bulletproof.

PS

FIFTEEN

Even running the last five minutes back to my house doesn't help me get rid of the superhuman feeling that has flooded my system. But I don't want to wear it like a badge; for the moment, this is my secret. Not that it's going to become a major concern for the FBI or anything. It just feels that talking about it will somehow diminish it. There's a warm glow in my stomach and I want to keep it that way.

But I'm also determined not to suffer any more of Tony's insensitive cracks. I can still hear my IM chattering away in the back of my head, but I'm pushing it away, ignoring its self-conscious babble. I'm going to find a new voice and I'm going to start now – strike while the iron's hot.

Mum's in the kitchen, making a cup of the predictable.

"Tea?" she asks.

"Yeah, please. Where's Tony?"

"He's just nipped out. Be back in a bit."

There's a lull while Mum presses a teabag against the inside of the cup, getting the most for her money. In goes the milk and sugar, and then I'm presented with my tea and a twinkling smile.

"So. How'd it go?"

IM: *With a snivel and a kiss.*

Mum's excitement is almost palpable and, ordinarily, I'd feel pressed into giving some immediate answer. But this time, I take a moment to consider how I want to play this. I don't *have* to tell anyone anything; I can make my life what I want it to be.

"Yeah. It was cool. She's a nice girl."

"Good." The subtext in that one word tells me that she wants more information. She tries a different tack. "And? Do you like her?"

I allow the silence that would usually make me so uncomfortable. Instead of looking for the answer that suits everyone else, I look for the answer that suits me.

"Yeah. She's cool."

Even the way Mum sips her tea is riddled with frustration; it's all lemon-sucking lips and a tightening round the eyes. But I maintain my Zen-like composure. She's got to let me grow up.

"And does she *like* you?"

My mind does a slow-motion action replay of the kiss and I purse my lips, as if in contemplation.

"We'll see."

Mum mock-glowers at me; I haven't delivered the goods – but I'm not going to feel guilty about it. For the first time in my life, I'm starting to do things *my* way.

"I'm going upstairs," I announce. "Stuff to do. When's lunch?"

"We'll see," comes the wry answer, but we both laugh knowingly; there's a game being played and we're both playing by the rules. "Five minutes."

IM: *And she just lost.*

In the hallway, I bump into Tony as he squeezes in through the front door.

"Aha!" he declares, pulling a cigarette out of his mouth. "The wanderer returns!"

With no IM to muddy the waters for me, I trust in my instincts. And it's an interesting experience.

"I do live here, Tony. In case you hadn't noticed." My delivery is perfect; it's not aggressive, just a clear statement of fact, delivered with a non-committal smile. I can virtually hear Tony's certainty crack beneath his nervous chuckle.

"Yeah. So – how was Sarah?"

"She's fine."

"Great. You want to get her round for dinner one night?"

"Maybe. We'll see."

I leave him, wreathed in smoke and obviously confused, and walk calmly upstairs to my Lair.

Dumping myself on the bed, I pull out Sarah's book from my back pocket. It's entitled *We Are All Our Souls* and has a picture of a feather and an egg on the front.

IM: *Puh-lease!*

I make a conscious effort to ignore the cynical rantings of my underdeveloped psyche and give the pages a cursory flip: there are various chapter headings along the lines of "Allowing Yourself to Be You", "The Higher Resonance of Intention" and "Awakening to Grace".

IM: *Depends if Grace is worth waking up to...*

"Shut up!"

Great – I'm talking to myself now. Out loud. I obviously need this book more than I thought.

But Mum's got other ideas and I hear the Summons for Physical Nourishment. Once in a blue moon, Mum decides to get all creative in the kitchen and pulls out a recipe book she'd forgotten she owned. Today is that day. While the food's always great – and today's curry is no exception – it does mean that me and Tony are subject to a long description of what ingredients are used and how they work together, peppered with the intermittent question: "So, what do you think?" At this point, we both know that a simple "yeah, it's great" isn't enough and we have to qualify our approval. But, today, this suits my needs; I don't really have to fully engage with Tony or discuss what's going on in Archie World™. Between mouthfuls, I offer up my theories about the taste of fresh herbs, go *"mmmm"* a lot, and then leave the table to continue my spiritual journey.

I go back to the book and rattle through the pages until I hit on the heading "Dreams and their Meanings". There's a list of subjects in alphabetical order and under the letter "G", I find the word "Gargoyle". A quick read reveals that, apparently, I'm suffering from "hidden and embarrassing fears over secrets you have not shared with anyone". Page thirty-three of the Next catalogue springs to mind. Chugging through the list of dream topics, the word "Beard" catches my eye. It seems that dreaming of growing a beard signifies "growing spiritual awareness".

Caught by a sudden flash of inspiration – or perhaps a message from what Sarah calls my Psychic Self – I charge to the bathroom mirror: there on my chin are a few straggly hairs, whilst my upper lip coyly displays something that could be mistaken for a shadow.

What if I grow a beard?

IM: *Please remain seated, everyone. Do not panic. We'll let you know what the problem is as soon as we have identified it.*

My IM is trying to gain ground, but I'm already seeing a pattern; it kicks off in moments of self-doubt and uncertainty, feeding on my insecurity like a vampire.

"Shut UP!"

Using my mental Photoshop, I replace my teenage

tufts with a thick, blond beard – probably a bit pointy to highlight my rakish charm. It'll make me look older. It'll make me look more devilish, give me a certain edge. I'll look more intelligent.

IM: *You'll look like a gnome crawling out of a bear's arse.*

And it'll make me more attractive to Sarah. If she's into all this spiritual stuff, then what could communicate my buying into it more than a lustrous piece of face furniture? A touch of the warrior, a touch of the wizard and a prime example of my spiritual development.

If I'm going to grow some proper facial hair, I'm going to need a shave.

IM: *What you need is a psychiatrist.*

But I've got no razors and no money with which to further my spiritual quest. I charge downstairs as casually as possible.

I breeze into the kitchen, my Tosser Tracker™ on full power, sweeping the terrain for any indication of Tosserish activity. No signs of life; Tony's either hunkering down in his study or disappeared off to his other favourite place in the world: the toilet. The length of time that man can spend in there beggars belief. With no danger of my plans being scuppered by his inane trumpeting, I mask my designs with an air of innocence and creep up behind Mum, giving her a hug.

"Oh, hello, love! What was that for?"

IM: *The dance begins.*

"Nothing. Just wanted to give you a hug. What time's tea tonight?" It's a poor attempt at a smoke screen, but it's all I've got.

"Not for a while." She cocks her head slightly; she knows me too well. "Why?"

"Just wondered. Have I got time to nip to the shop?"

"I should think so." Another flash of her probe. "What d'you need?"

I could lie at this point and come up with something about pens or something to do with school, but she'd see through that; Mum knows that the only shop I've got any interest in is the Hovel. A better option is to tamper with the truth and hope that she doesn't know too much about the effects of testosterone on teenage boys' facial hair.

"My face is itching." I back this up with a scratch to the chin and neck. "It started a few days ago. I think I need a shave."

I can virtually see Mum's brain weighing up this information with what she knows about young males. She fixes me with a stare that's trying to search out a lie, but is obviously confused by the symptoms I've thrown at her.

"Let's have a look." My neck and chin undergo the sort of intense examination that only a mother can give. "Well … it *is* a bit red…"

IM: *She's buckling…!*

"Hmmm…"

IM: *… buckling…*

"You might be right. D'you need some money?"

IM: *And down she comes! Bingo!*

"Thanks, Mum." I throw in another dig at the chin for good measure. "How much are razors?"

"Take a tenner. You'll need some shaving foam."

How did she know that? More to the point: why didn't I know that? Shamelessly, I raid her purse and set off for the shop, the wind blowing through my childish whiskers for the last time.

Fast-forward a love-powered trot to the shop and I am gazing, slack-jawed, at rows of Male Grooming Products. I had never considered that buying razors could be so difficult. How am I supposed to know if I want disposables, triple blades, quadruple blades, aloe vera strips, swivel-headed or fixed? And then there's the foam: moisturizing, protecting, razor-rash reducing; I only want to shave off my bumfluff so I can grow something a bit more butch! In the end, I go for the foam that has the coolest-looking logo and the razor with the most sharp bits.

IM: *What could possibly go wrong?*

Ten minutes later, I'm back in front of the bathroom mirror and feeling a little nervous: I realize I've got no idea what to do. Getting the razor out of its packaging was hard enough – I suppose I could give Dad a shout and get some *hombre* to *hombre* advice, but I'm just not ready to talk to him at the moment. My chin hairs laugh at me from the mirror, daring me to cut them off. I wish there was someone I could talk to. A concerned knock at the door and my mum appears with all the timing of a genie.

"How's it going?"

"It's not at the moment. I don't … really…"

"Hang on, I'll get Tony."

The "NO!" doesn't even make it to the back of my throat before Mum has bellowed his name across the landing. There's a moment of silence, followed by the muffled flush of the downstairs toilet and Tony lumbers upstairs and appears in the doorway.

"What's up?"

"Can you give Archie a hand?" Mum might think I don't notice the little elbow to the ribs she gives him, but I do.

"What? Oh, yeah … yeah … right … OK."

As Tony manfully enters, Mum tactfully exits; she's engineered the perfect bonding moment and, judging by the tension in the air, it's one that neither Tony nor I are thankful for. In the absence of any spiritual enlightenment, my EM takes over and plasters a loose impression of a smile on my face. My IM cheerfully comments from the back seat.

IM: *Tosser.*

And Tony lives up to my expectations.

"Oho! Shaving, eh? The Big Day! Right then, let's get stuck in!"

"Thanks."

He then lurches into some flannel about how the razor's going to be my best friend, as long as I treat it with respect. Like a woman, apparently. A beautiful one. Like my mother. It's a wonder my teeth don't impact with the pressure I'm putting on them. Finally, we get to the point where it looks like we're going to do something.

"OK, you want to fill the basin with hot water…"

I do so and am subject to another Wikipedia-style monologue about opening up my pores and getting my oils flowing. After an instructed splash of my face, it's time to put foam in my palms and stick it on my face.

I look like Santa. With a black eye.

Tony's reaction is to fall into a series of wheezing laughs that culminate in a long, rattling cough. Despite the protestations of his lungs, Tony continues to wheeze/laugh until there are tears in his eyes and he has to hang on to the basin for support. All I can do is stare back at my reflection, which seems to make him laugh all the more.

"Sorry, Arch," he gasps, slapping a hand on my shoulder, "but I think you've put a bit too much on there!" More steam-train laughter.

IM: *Tosser.*

Once he's calmed down, we get round to the razor. Downstrokes and don't be afraid of putting pressure on the skin. With more than a little apprehension, I put the razor to my cheek. It practically disappears along with most of my hand into the thick layer of foam that's hiding half my head. Within five minutes my face looks like I've had a terrible accident with a Victoria sponge; I am a mass of blood and foam. Needless to say, Tony is as hysterical as a man of his limited lung capacity can be. Mum, who's obviously been hovering outside the door, comes in.

"Oh, Tony!" she scolds, "Get out! Go on! Go and put the kettle on!" As he exits, sniggering, I hold a towel to my face, but the nicks on my skin just won't stop bleeding. What am I going to do? Sarah's never going to look at me again!

IM: *Meet my boyfriend: Freddy Krueger…*

"Shut UP!"

"What?" Mum looks suddenly startled.

"Sorry – not you."

"Right … let's have a look at those cuts."

It turns out that there's only four or five, but they're

running like rivers. Mum grabs the toilet roll and starts ripping up toilet paper like a demented hamster, then wets a bit and glues it over a cut. Pretty soon, I'm covered in pieces of red-stained bog roll.

"Let them dry out before you take them off. I'll go and make you a cup of tea."

"Thanks, Mum."

IM: *You're practically an advert for razor blades. "Hi! My name's Archie! When I'm trying to impress a girl, I like to lacerate my face with razors made from barbed wire!"*

Alone at last, I survey the damage in the mirror. My euphoric state has finally been crushed. Too drained to do anything else, I head up to my Lair and hurl myself on to the bed, only to have something smack me on the forehead. It's Sarah's book. It could just be coincidence, but it has fallen open at a chapter called, "How to Silence Your Inner Critic".

Time to start reading…

This book is weird. The way it's written is like being told off by someone in a syrupy American accent. My IM is hurling derision from the sidelines, but I need to focus. According to the author, my IM has "morphed from a protector into a destroyer, leading to self-punishment". Apart from being told that I need to love myself rather a lot (he obviously doesn't know the nocturnal habits of twenty-first century teenagers),

Dr E. P. Hughes gives me "ten ways to tell the Universe that you are worthy of love and positive outcomes", under the title of "Attracting Abundance".

IM: *Attracting a kicking, more like…*

My IM is the "manifestation of all my doubts and fears". Reading between the lines, Dr Hughes is telling me that the reason I'm a Geek is because I'm too scared not to be one. Sort of makes sense. I chug on. I don't know what "Affirmations" are yet, or how to "Make My Mind More Beautiful" and I think I'll "Learn to Forgive Myself" another time, but Step Five catches my eye.

"Talk Back: When your Inner Critic remains unchallenged, you have no choice but to listen. Focus on developing the voice of your True Self, your Psychic Self. This voice is the voice of your untapped potential and is only isolated from the Universe by your own fear of just how powerful you can be."

Blimey. This must be how Luke Skywalker felt when he found out that he could be a Jedi. *I* could be a Jedi, I've just got to stop being scared of it. An image of me standing on my head, levitating rocks with the power of my spiritually-aligned mind lingers just out of reach.

IM: *You're a Geek. And this isn't about spiritual enlightenment. It's about Sarah. Remember her? The girl who kissed you…*

Right. I've had enough. It's time to take charge.

Following the book's instructions, I sit on the floor, try to clear my mind and access my Psychic Self. I visualize myself as a bearded mystic, dispensing wisdom and holding Jason Humphries up in the air with my telepathic abilities. Maybe even doing that choking thing on him like Darth Vader.

IM: *The farce is strong in this one...*

I focus harder, imagining the effect my blinding transformation will have on those around me: Tony cowers in the face of my towering intellect, Dad weeps into his **chkn soup** in York, regretting his decision, and Sarah looks on, awestruck. I am the eye of the storm and she walks towards me, helpless in my presence. She takes her hand in mine slowly and says—

"How's your face, love. Are you OK?"

I open one eye towards the sound of Mum's voice and see her poking her head round the door.

"I'm fine. Just ... thinking."

"OK. Tea'll be ready in a minute."

Bloody hell, it's hard trying to achieve spiritual fulfilment sometimes. As soon as she's gone, I get back to my visualizations and try and concentrate on finding the voice that represents the psychic colossus I've hidden away. Instead, all I tap into is the voice of my doubts, fears and general insecurities. It's a bit like trying to throw away a comfort blanket.

IM: *I'm still here, Geekboy.*

Concentrate. Lose the negative.

IM: *Still here! *Whistles a random tune**

Concentrate! Focus on all that's positive about you!

IM: *We're one and the same, Archie. Stop trying to be what you're not.*

And then it happens. I hear the voice that's been lurking at the back of my head all my life. It's the voice of self-confidence and doubt-free reason. All I had to do was let it through, instead of hiding it beneath a jumble of fear and insecurity. My IM's cheerful babbling is suddenly cut short by a commanding, assertive voice. Complete with American accent.

PS: *Silence! You are the voice of doubt and fear! Begone!*

IM: *Eh? Who said that?*

PS: *I am Archie's true voice, the voice of what he can truly become: powerful, worthy and able to attract abundance!*

IM: *Yeah, yeah, Obi-Wan – whatever.*

I've been so used to talking to myself in this voice that it's hard to let it go. Dr Hughes has a point: I'm scared of my potential. I've lived for years on a diet of self-criticism. Time to change the psychic calories. I take a deep breath and force myself to banish the voice of self-doubt and give the voice of self-worth a bit of room to breathe.

PS: *You are not welcome here!*

IM: *And what are you going to do about it? Meditate me to death?*

PS: *Your mockery betrays your fear! And it shall be your undoing!*

IM: *You and whose army?*

PS: *I need no army! I can access the Power of … THE UNIVERSE!*

And then it's as if my PS swells in my head, taking over every corner and dispelling the shadows of insecurity, filling them with the bright, almost incandescent light of absolute certainty. It's amazing what giving yourself a good talking-to can do.

IM: *I'll be baaaack!*

And then my IM is gone. I do feel different; I believe in myself at last. I feel ready, poised to take the life-affirming steps that will lead me into Sarah's arms. I can almost feel the ghost of her lips on mine…

PS: *Stop! There is no room for base lust on the road to spiritual enlightenment! From this moment on, Archie, you will learn to see the world with new eyes! You are shedding your old psychic skin!*

And bits of toilet paper. A piece falls off just as Mum calls me for tea. With a quick pit stop at the bathroom, I remove the rest from my face. I look like a pizza, with one big, black olive on it. Great.

Habit drags me from the table and back up to my painting desk. I sit there for a while, just staring at the paints and brushes, aware of a slight weight behind my eyes. It takes a little effort to choose a model to paint until I eventually settle on one I'd been saving for a rainy day. This ogre was going to be a treat; it's larger than the rest, with more scope for detail and embellishment. I pick it up and give it a once-over, trying to take in all its features and looking for the bits that I can use to show off some serious paint-slinging.

And then I put it down.

I can't seem to get it together; the enthusiasm's gone. The magic's gone. What's wrong with me?

PS: *You are seeing these models for what they really are: physical totems of your fear of truly living.*

Could this be right? By locking myself away in my room and daubing metal men with paint, have I just been avoiding life? And there was me thinking it was art.

PS: *Art is found in the heart.*

I slump back in my chair and down tools. A long period of time passes with me just staring at my desk, not even a thought for company. The sound of Tony's Beemer roaring down the road brings me back to the present. I've got to *do something*!

PS: *You must continue with your studies.*

The book is waiting for me on the bed and I go through the list of things I can do to unlock my potential. It might be jumping the gun a bit, but Step Nine looks like something I can do without too much trouble: "Project Your Positive Energy Through the Clothes You Wear".

So far, so good; Dr Hughes gives me a description of the effects that different colours of clothing can have "on the wearer and those around them". Unconsciously, I run my fingertips over the lumps and bumps that have formed on my face since my near-death experience at the hands of a razor. It might just be "razor-rash" to Tony, but this level of disfigurement could seriously scupper my chances with Sarah. Maybe changing the way I dress would be distraction enough that she wouldn't notice. And maybe it's a better way of communicating my advances in the spiritual realm.

Red could be a winner: it's the "colour of excitement and people surrounded by red often feel their hearts beating a little faster and find themselves short of breath". While the thought of inducing a lust-driven cardiac-arrest in Sarah is appealing, I suddenly realize that I'm going to be on Jason Humphries's hit list for the foreseeable future. And we all know about red rags and bulls. Perhaps not.

According to Dr Hughes, green is "associated with

masculinity and wealth" and is also a "powerful bringer of good luck". I'm just wondering what I've got that's green in the wardrobe department, when my eye hits the final paragraph and the colour that's going to help solve all my problems at once.

Believe it or not – and in my situation I'll believe anything right now – "often our most dangerous criminals are housed in pink cells as studies show that this colour calms aggression and drains energy". On top of that, it's "the colour of true love". From where I'm standing, it's also the colour of two birds with one stone. A quick root through my wardrobe confirms the horrific thought that crashes through my mind: I've got no pink clothes, whatsoever.

Time to consult the Oracle, in case she knows something I don't.

"Mu-um!"

"Yes?"

"Have I got any pink clothes?" I can't be expected to keep track of *every*thing in my life.

Her head appears at the bottom of the stairs.

"What?"

"Pink clothes; have I got any?"

OK, as questions go, it's not the one you expect to hear from your teenage son's mouth. It's also not one *I* expect to hear from my mouth. I'm running several risks here, that a) this might not work, b) Jason Humphries will kill me on sight and c) that my already tenuous social standing at school will crumble into outright ridicule.

PS: *Trust in your sense of self! Worry not what others may think! Yours is the Path to Enlightenment!*

"Like what?" There's more than a hint of concern in her voice.

"Like *clothes!*" I wonder if getting ratty with your mother hampers your spiritual development, but it irritates me that I've got to ask my stupid question again.

"I don't think so. Why?"

Good question. I could opt for the bog-standard "Oh, God!" and shut the door, but I'm in need of some serious pink in my life.

"It's a school thing for Monday: wear something pink for charity."

"Oh." More cogs turn. "Which charity?"

My mother would have been a phenomenal asset to the Spanish Inquisition.

It's all in the details, but the only charity I can think of that has anything to do with pink is one for breast cancer, and the thought of saying the word "breast" to my mother sends my EM supernova, generating a glow on my face that would keep a solar-powered house in energy for a year.

I huff and puff before wheedling, "Does it matter? Is there anything pink I could wear or not?" I don't think I sound sane at this point.

With a dark "Hold on," Mum climbs the stairs and scuttles into her bedroom. God help me if she brings out a nightie.

"This is all you've got."

"What is it?"

"It's out of your Baby Box. Your Great-aunt Bertha was convinced you were going to be a girl."

In my hand is a pink handkerchief. Complete with lacy edges.

"A handkerchief?" A half-decent shirt is obviously not on the menu.

"Well, if you'd let me know a little sooner..." I can feel a huff coming on, so I give her a hug and tell her it's great.

Back in my Lair, I examine my frilly heirloom. A pink bloody handkerchief.

Fifteen minutes later, I've worked out that I can fold it enough that I can hide the frills and tuck it into the top pocket of my shirt. I look like a waiter. With cuts and a black eye.

PS: *Vanity is a sign of spiritual blindness. You must look beyond your physical self and see what lies within.*

What lies within right now is someone who is very

tired. But if I'm to win Sarah's heart, I will have to draw on all the psychic energy that Dr Hughes tells me is at my disposal.

And probably have an early night.

I spend Sunday waiting for the phone to ring.

PS: *To learn patience, you must first be patient!*

It doesn't.

SIXTEEN

Monday begins with a small object smacking me on the forehead and the all-too-familiar aroma of cigarette smoke.

"Hey, Arch! You alive in there?"

Tony is standing in the doorway, puffing on his early-morning heart-starter. He points to a tiny box that has rolled off my forehead and on to the pillow.

"What d'you think of that?"

With all the enthusiasm of a sedated bear, I open it up to see what can only be described as a very showy diamond ring. My brain can't quite process this information; have I forgotten Mum's birthday or something? It's not Valentine's Day; what's the occasion?

"I'm going to propose to your mother."

I am then subject to a split-second montage in my head that depicts Mum in a Cinderella-style wedding gown, my father gatecrashing the ceremony and shouting "Nooooo!" as he chases them up the aisle, and me having to call Tony "Dad". In the midst of this, I just manage to croak out an "Uh … OK," when a final, apocalyptic thought detonates inside my mind: what if they have children?

What if they have children? What does that make me? Where do I belong? Which family is mine?

"So what d'you think?" Tony's nodding at the box again.

PS: *Read the signs. Use your powers of psychic perception.*

The only immediate signs are that my world is starting to crumble around me, but I try and dig a bit deeper. Looking at Tony with my PS coaxing me in the background, I can see that he's nervous – he keeps shifting his weight from foot to foot and is sucking on his cigarette with a little more than his usual ferocity. And then it dawns: in his own weird way he's asking my permission to ask Mum to marry him. If the idea wasn't like looking into a crystal ball and watching yourself being torn apart by rabid wolves, the notion might be quite touching.

PS: *He has his own path to walk. Show him the way.*

"Good luck," I manage, and chuck the box back his way. "When're you doing it?"

Tony obviously relaxes and, now that permission has been granted, takes charge.

"I thought I'd wait until you'd gone to school. Take her by surprise sort of thing."

I take the hint.

"I'll make myself scarce."

"Nice one." He disappears in a puff of smoke. I wish the thoughts in my head would do the same. Once Mum slips that ring on, I'm not going to belong anywhere.

At least the mirror's showing a degree of sympathy: my lacerations have calmed down and are barely noticeable, although there's no sign of a beard on the horizon. I chuck my uniform on, tucking my pink handkerchief into my shirt pocket, and wolf down a bowl of cereal before heading on out.

The walk to school affords plenty of time for thought. Unfortunately, all I can think about is how Jason Humphries is going to kill me. Suddenly, my handkerchief looks less like a protective talisman and more like a handwritten invitation to beat me to death. All I can do is try and keep a low profile. Not so easy when you're wearing a Bully Beacon™ in your top pocket. I pull Sarah's book out of my school bag and wonder if Dr Hughes has got anything up his sleeve for disturbances in the Force of this magnitude.

The closest thing I can find is his advice on "How to Avoid Negative Energy". Reading between the lines, criticism, pessimism and teasing are like a "poison that can permeate and damage your ego". All I've got to do is work out who in my life generates these negative energies and cut them out of it. And I've got to "get into the psychic orbit of those that generate positive energies". Sounds simple enough.

Cutting Tony out of my life is going to be a hard one, especially as he's liable to be my Official Stepfather sometime soon. And, if I'm being honest, he doesn't particularly criticize me – he's just a Tosser.

"Dude! How's your eye? What's with the pink hanky? You looking to get your ass kicked?"

Beggsy arrives.

PS: *And with him, the acrid stench of criticism.*

"Ha, ha, you're a funny guy. It's called *fashion*."

"Dude!" Conveys *Is disapproving*. Up in the distance, he spots Ravi and Matt. I brace myself for the onslaught.

"Dudes! Check this out! Archie's turned into a fashion icon!"

"Yeah, I hear bruises are gonna be big this year. Anyone who's anyone is gonna be wearing them!" True to form, Ravi's missed the blindingly obvious.

PS: *But not the opportunity for teasing...*

And Matt completes the unholy trinity.

"At least it'll be useful for mopping up the blood when Humphries gets hold of you."

PS: *The pathetic poison of pessimism.*

"Jesus, guys!" I explode. "It's only a hanky, for crying out loud!" And with that, I march on ahead of them, getting lost in the swelling crowds of teenagers approaching the school gates. There's a dull nagging in the back of my head that I've let loose on my mates – not about the hanky, but about everything else that's going wrong in my life. Perhaps I should stop and apologize.

PS: *Those are the words of someone whose ego has been weakened by negative energy. Stay strong and true. Avoid them.*

Even the harshest advice sounds right in an American accent; maybe the PS has a point. All we ever do is take the mick out of each other and I don't need that in my life right now. But I can't shake the feeling that I'm in a spade shop, looking for a bigger shovel.

"Hey, Archie!"

Positive energy almost sweeps me off my feet in the shimmering physical form of Sarah. Suddenly, my negative friends are little more than a foggy memory.

"Hey, yourself!" Damn, I sound almost cool!

"Nice handkerchief. Going somewhere special?"

My heart leaps – Dr Hughes was right! I don't think I've ever felt so pleased about anything in my whole life. My handkerchief *is* nice – it's the nicest damn handkerchief I've ever had. God bless Great-aunt Bertha! And God bless whoever invented handkerchiefs! Especially pink ones.

"Oh, you know," I reply airily, "thought I'd give this

place a try – I hear the food's quite good."

My reward is a bounty of beautiful laughter and a squeeze on my upper arm; it's like being touched by an angel.

"There's Caitlyn – I've got to go. See you later? Maybe lunchtime?"

"I'll reserve the best table in the house. The chef's a personal friend." I think I can feel my beard starting to grow.

More laughter and another squeeze before she runs off to meet her friend. Life doesn't get any better than this. The truth of that thought is reinforced by something like a battering ram thudding into my lower back. I swallow the retort that's forming on my lips as I turn to face the hardened, thundercloud visage of Jason Humphries complete with Battle Damage. I guess Mum's already rung Mrs Holly this morning to report him; he's angrier than ever. But due to the presence of the occasional wandering teacher, all he can do is draw a finger across his muscular throat and leer darkly at me.

Perhaps pink isn't his colour.

Learning goes out of the window for the rest of the morning. Even basking in the whispered glory of being in

242

a fight with Jason Humphries goes out of the window; the pats on the back, thumbs-ups and furtive compliments I'm paid are overshadowed by desperately sneaking peeks at Dr Hughes's words of wisdom. More specifically, I'm trying to find out what Dr Hughes thinks are the best methods of dealing with an overgrown Grunt who is doubtless going to want to use me as a punchbag. The closest he gets is in dealing with "negative energy that is aimed directly at you". As far as I'm concerned, a smack in the face is pretty negative and it takes some energy to do it, so it's as good a place to start as any.

Unfortunately, this is where the first shreds of doubt creep in. So far, Dr Hughes has had it all pretty much spot on: I've managed to silence my inner critic, developed a more positive outlook and enticed Sarah into my psychic orbit with the criminal-quelling powers of my pink hanky. But I don't think that "denying these negative forces" is going to stop Humphries's fist from connecting with my nose. Dr Hughes's advice is to imagine the negative energy flowing from me like a jet of water. The only jet of water flowing from me I can imagine in the whole scenario is the one that is likely to be expelled by my treacherous bladder if Humphries comes anywhere near me.

PS: *Ask the Universe and the Universe will answer.*

Rather than asking, I offer up a quick prayer.

The lunch bell sends me scurrying through corridors, trying to be as invisible as possible. Which doesn't seem to be that easy when you're sporting a pink handkerchief. Who'd have thought that such an innocuous item could cause so much of a stir? One minute I'm a folk hero, the next my sexuality seems to be in question and the amount of people who call me a twat has got to be some sort of world record. Fame can be so fickle.

PS: *Dare to be different!*

Jason Humphries is thankfully absent from the slavering hordes who gossip, cackle and trudge their way to the canteen. Just as I think I can breathe easy, Ravi rounds a corner and we literally bump into each other.

"Hey, Archie – you OK?"

"Yeah, I'm cool." I can almost feel his psychic probes sounding me out, but I'm giving nothing away.

"You seemed pretty hacked off this morning. You know – the hanky thing."

PS: *Let him know that you will not be the recipient of his negative energy!*

"I'm just tired of all the piss-taking, Rav. I don't need it in my life."

"Oh. OK. I'm gonna hang for the guys." There's a question in his statement: he wants to know if I'll wait with him. Once I would have been drawn into his gravitational field, but my recently installed psychic thrusters give me all the power I need to break free; I need to be around positive energy. I need to be around Sarah.

"I'm not. See you." Simple as that.

PS: *Your strength is growing!*

I'll have to reserve judgement on that, but Dr Hughes's advice to avoid negativity has opened up another window of opportunity for me: I can see Sarah's hair shining like an ebony flare through the heads and shoulders up ahead. With a bit of squeezing and diplomatic shoving, I finally make it next to her.

"Going my way?"

"Well, hello, stranger!" There's enough sauce in her voice to start up a ketchup factory.

PS: *You must dispense with lustful thoughts!*

I take a quick mental cold shower.

"You going in?" I jerk a casual thumb to the canteen doors.

"Yeah. Just waiting for someone. You go ahead."

There's a slight whooshing sound as the rug is pulled from under my feet. Suddenly, I'm not quite so cocksure, and the skin on my chin feels naked and hairless. I'm just about to suggest pathetically that I'll wait, when a loud American voice cuts through my self-doubt.

PS: *Channel your positive energy!*

"OK. I'll go and check our table's ready."

"I'll see you in a minute."

I award myself a mental medal.

All this positivity has made me hungry and I plump for my favourite on today's menu: Spicy Beef with Rice. After a moment's hovering by the till, a group of girls leave their table and I jump on it: perfect. Actually, on closer inspection, it's not quite that perfect and I clear the trays and plates that the girls have left behind.

"Dude!" Beggsy barges one of the chairs with his backside and starts to slide into it. I can see Matt and Ravi leaving the till; I'm going to have to work fast.

"Uh… It's taken."

"Ha, ha."

"No, really; it's taken."

Matt looms over the table, his Geek-sense obviously having detected that thing that Geeks fear most: change.

"What's going on?"

"Archie's saving this seat for someone, apparently." Beggsy's butt still hasn't made contact with the seat, but he maintains his half-squat as though he's waiting for orders to either sit or stand. There's a moment as the three of them test the tension.

"Fair enough," Matt decides and moves to sit in one of the other chairs. If his tray touches the table, he'll have staked his claim and the deal's done.

"So's that one," I gabble. "They all are."

There's another freeze-frame as this information burrows its way into their brains. This is like a stand-off in those old westerns, but instead of hands hovering over guns, I've got trays and butts hovering over tables and chairs. The only movement between us is from our eyes as they flick between one another, trying to see who's going to give first.

It's Matt. But he doesn't say anything; he doesn't have to. He just flicks me a look that says it all. Then he walks deliberately away, followed by the others.

PS: *They are not enlightened! They do not understand!*

Safe in my solitude, I quickly rearrange the chairs, putting the one I hope Sarah will sit in just a tad closer to mine than maybe it should be. She arrives within seconds of me sitting down.

"Aren't your friends going to come over?" she asks, taking a seat opposite.

"No. They're working on a project together. I'll catch them later." This positive energy is certainly improving my ability to lie.

"Oh, that's a shame. Matt's really funny."

Note to self: maybe I need to patch things up with Matt.

PS: *Stay true! Be firm!*

"Yeah, he is funny. Where's Caitlyn? I thought you

were waiting for her?"

"No, I'm meeting her later."

"Oh. Who were you waiting for, then?"

"Chris."

I tense slightly.

"Oh, yeah?" I manage, with as much psychic positivity as I can muster. "Chris who?"

"Oh, I don't know his surname. He's a new friend; we got talking in Chemistry. He's over by the till now."

I look and wish I hadn't. Chris is none other than Chris Jackson, the tall, blue-eyed athletic type whose name alone inspires giggling and flustered flapping in girls throughout the school. He pays for his salad and charms his way through the rabble to our table. And sits across from me. Next to Sarah. Right next to her. Where I should be sitting.

"All right?" His perfect chin glitters with shards of real live, genuine stubble.

No. I'm not all right. Right now I'd like to trade my pink handkerchief for a phaser. Or a beard.

The next forty-five minutes are spent with me trying to choke down my Spicy Beef and Rice – made all the more difficult on discovering that Sarah is a vegetarian; every meaty mouthful feels like betrayal. Chris, meanwhile, crunches through his salad with all the affability of a masticating cow, his stubble glistening in the convenient spotlight created by the sun shining through a neighbouring window.

I think I hate him.

PS: *Positivity is the key!*

The trouble is, no matter how many rictus-grins I beam across the table and no matter how many witty or edgy comments I throw into the arena, Chris just seems to command the conversation. Sarah is entranced by him and is more tactile than I think she needs to be: every one of Chris's rib-tickling funnies is met with a playful touch to the arm or a coquettish flick of the hair. I'm really trying not to notice, but each occasion her hand goes near him, it's as if time slows down and there's a zoom lens in my eyes that follows every movement in heart-tugging detail.

To cap it off, Chris is manfully ignoring the bandage on his right hand. Sarah's attention is piqued and it's all I can do to stop myself throwing up when it's revealed as a "rugby injury". When she asks to see his other hand, I have to bite the inside of my cheek to retain a modicum of self-control. I throw a wayward glance across the tables; Matt's watching me with a dark look on his face.

"Now *that's* interesting," Sarah purrs, tracing a delicate finger across Chris's palm. My own palms itch jealously.

"What?" Chris leans back in his chair, obviously entirely at ease with female contact. The git.

"Well, this is your love line…" Sarah feathers a line on his hand, "…and it looks like you've got a secret ad*mi*rer…" She draws out the middle syllable in a teasing, sexy drawl, precisely at the moment that I can hear my heart shatter.

"Yes," she continues, lowering her head to get a closer look at his weathered hand. "Someone close to you … a friend…"

The chair beneath me seems to have disappeared and I can feel myself falling into the deep, dark hole that could only have been made by the Demons of Despair.

"Oh, yes?" Chris replies, with a Hollywood arch of one of his incredibly dashing eyebrows. "Who?"

"Well!" Sarah counters, unaware of the small crowd that seems to be gathering to watch, "I couldn't possibly say. All I know is that the person may be closer than you think!"

The urge to put my face into my Spicy Beef and try and die there is overwhelming.

"OK," Chris grins. "I'd better keep a lookout! Thanks for the tip. See you later." And then, taking his tray, he sweeps majestically out of the room. I look at where his tray was; not so much as a crumb on the table.

Some of the crowd are asking Sarah if she'll

read their palms and, within seconds, she's drummed up a queue.

"Well, I'd better get going," I announce, dragging my pointless form out of the chair.

"OK," Sarah beams, as her first customer settles into Chris's place. "See you after school?"

In a parallel Universe, another Archie is telling her to get stuffed and emptying Spicy Beef all over her head. In this one, he agrees, pathetically grateful for the chance to be near her just one more time.

SEVENTEEN

The afternoon doesn't pass so easily. I just can't seem to soak up Precipitation in the North-East; my mind is too busy playing and replaying the trailer for a new film: *The Courtship of Chris and Sarah*.

I don't know why I'm surprised. With people like Chris in the world, did I really think I stood a chance? He's even got those little muscles in the corner of his jaws that flex like little walnuts as he speaks. A lifetime in the gym couldn't give me those.

My PS remains silent, no doubt swamped by the wave of self-loathing that crashes through my head. Even my doubt-riddled IM doesn't bother to reclaim its territory; my mind is devoid of anything except depressing reruns of *Sarah and Chris's Most Intimate Lunchtime Moments*.

The end-of-school bell sounds, but I remain seated, staring into space, serenaded by the squeak and scrape of chairs as they are pushed back under desks. Even Beggsy leaves without saying anything. But I barely notice that the room is empty until Mr Cook pipes up.

"Everything all right, Archie? Haven't you got a home to go to?"

I have. But I don't want to go back there. All that waits for me at home is the news that my mum will have allied herself with a Tosser and I will no longer belong to any family in particular. Even the thought of walking back with Sarah has lost its appeal. For a split second, I consider unburdening myself and telling Mr Cook everything that's going on in my life. He's my form tutor as well as my Geography teacher and he's always letting us know that we can talk to him if we can't talk to anyone else about stuff. But I already did that with Sarah and look where it got me: no friends, no girlfriend, an appointment with Certain Death at the hands of Jason Humphries, and a pink handkerchief in my top pocket. It's not good.

"Sorry, sir. Daydreaming, I guess."

"Well, as long as everything's OK…?"

There's the Gift Horse again, and I give it a full oral examination, coward that I am.

"Yeah, everything's fine." The words tumble out of my mouth a little too fast and I get my stuff together as quickly as I can. "See you tomorrow."

"See you, then."

The corridors are emptying of students, much like a bath draining of water. My misery is so profound that my Grunt Detector™ fails to spot two Neanderthal figures lurking by the school gates and before I know what's what, Paul Green and Lewis Mills have got me by the arms and have dragged me down the little alley behind the History loft. Jason Humphries appears, swathed in smoke, like some creature of the Netherworld. Where my fist connected with his nose, there are now two bruises ringing his eyes, upping his Fear Factor into six figures.

"Bet you think you're something special, don't you?" he hisses out of the side of his mouth that doesn't have a cigarette dangling from it. "Think you're hard."

Strangely, I'm too miserable to be frightened; I've got too much else on my plate at the moment. Instead of the familiar scream of adrenalin, there's only the tired sigh of resignation.

"Not really. No."

"What?" The tendons in his rippling face work together to create an ugly mask of confusion. "Are you taking the piss, Geekboy? From what I've heard, everyone thinks you gave me a kicking."

"No, I'm not taking the piss," I reply dejectedly. "I got lucky. I'm no fighter. I'm not anything."

For some reason, this admission unsettles him even more and he cocks his head, either trying to size me up or let a stray thought roll out of one ear.

"Think squealing to Mrs Holly's going to help, do you? Gonna get your mummy to ring her up again?"

But I'm beyond being goaded and just about manage a feeble shrug.

Finally, Jason reaches some Olympian decision in his head.

"Pathetic!" he spits. "Hold him."

With that, Mills and Green pull my jacket down over my arms as Humphries primes one of his fists for action. I always thought left-handers were supposed to be the artistic sort.

I wait for the inevitable.

"What's that?"

I open my eyes and follow Humphries's battered gaze to my chest.

"My hanky."

"What? What you wearing that for?" Without waiting for my answer, Humphries pulls it out of my top pocket and it opens, flower-like, in all its pink, frilly glory.

"A pink hanky? Are you gay?" he sneers, a nasty laugh forming on his lips as he shoves it under my nose. "What's this for? Mopping up the blood after I've done with you?" I dimly recall Matt saying something similar; perhaps he's got psychic powers.

"It's for calming criminals," I reply without any thought or irony. But right now, it's hardly the lump of kryptonite I was hoping for.

"What?" This information causes some sort of

systems overload in my attacker and he starts to laugh, waving my hanky around like some sort of Satanic morris dancer. Green and Mills start laughing too and soon the air is thick with murderous mirth.

"Oi! What're you boys up to?" Mr Cook's voice cuts through the braying. Humphries stops stone dead and rubs the hanky in my face.

"You'll keep!" he hisses and the trio of bullies scatters.

"Archie? What's going on?" Mr Cook appears in the alley.

"Nothing, sir."

"Well get home, then!"

"Sir."

Pocketing my handkerchief and shakily shrugging my jacket on, I leave the school premises, slightly unsure as to what's just happened. I think I've just been saved by a pink hanky.

"I wondered where you'd got to." Sarah is waiting for me on the pavement. "I thought you'd stood me up!"

The irony isn't lost on me and, despite feeling grateful about my narrow escape, the Fog of Unrequited Love falls on me once again. It's going to be a long walk home.

Every step I take feels inadequate. My chin is as naked as a baby's backside and I am a Geek. And each word Sarah speaks hardens to form a knife that strikes straight at my heart. Not even her reassurances that Humphries will probably leave me alone offer me any comfort.

"What's up, Archie? You're a bit quiet. And you were very quiet at lunch. Everything OK? You're not embarrassed by what you told me at the weekend, are you?"

What do I say? That thanks to her thinly disguised flirting with Chris Jackson, my life has no meaning? Instead, I offer up a rough approximation of my concerns about Tony's proposal to Mum. It's a futile, last-ditch sympathy card, but I play it anyway.

"I don't think you need to worry too much about it, Archie. It's only a piece of paper. It doesn't really change anything."

"Yeah, I guess you're right," I lie. "It just feels a bit weird."

"It's only as big a problem as you choose to make it, Archie. Everything'll turn out for the best."

"I s'pose."

"Hey – did you like my trick with Chris at lunchtime?"

She's obviously completely unaware of how I feel. But who am I to stand in the way of True Love? No one, that's who.

"Yeah… You had me fooled!"

"Sorry it had to be over lunch, but I didn't think I was going to get another opportunity."

I know how she feels.

"Yeah. So, it was a trick? You can't read palms?"

"Oh, I can a bit, but I just told him what he needed to hear."

Her self-confidence is chilling. This is more what I'd have expected from the White Witch of Narnia; perhaps she's watched that film a bit too often.

"OK…" I dread the answer as the words leave my lips. "So, what happens next?"

"That's up to him and Caitlyn, I guess."

"Caitlyn?" I've never seen a guppy, but I think I might look like one now.

"Yeah. She's fancied him for ages. I couldn't tell you, but that's why she wasn't there at lunch."

"What – you were…"

"…pointing him in the right direction, yeah. They both like each other, but neither of them's had the nerve to do anything about it."

Within the blink of an eye, the world is suddenly a brighter place. My positively-charged batteries fire up and my PS has enough power to start up again.

PS: *The power of positivity cannot be denied!*

I think my denial days are over. For fear of opening

my mouth and saying the wrong thing, I change the subject and tell Sarah about the protective powers of my pink handkerchief. Pearls of laughter rain down on me, soothing my troubled soul.

"I'm not sure I buy into all that colour stuff," she giggles. "Not to the point where I'd trust my life to a pink hanky."

"Yeah," I laugh in agreement, comfortable in my role as court jester and happy to betray my beliefs at the drop of a hat.

PS: *She is the source of positive energy! See how much better you feel in her company!*

Once the giggling subsides, the conversation turns to psychic stuff and I find myself telling Sarah just how different I'm feeling; like I'm coming out of my shell and discovering the real me.

"Well, I think the thing is not to rush it, Archie. It's powerful stuff and you need to give each phase the weight it deserves."

"How d'you mean?"

"Everything you're discovering is new; you're in a transitional stage, like a butterfly coming out of its chrysalis."

"One step at a time, sort of thing?"

"Definitely. The way we think and feel is down to years of learned behaviour. You can't just unlearn it overnight. It's not a competition; you should just go at the speed that's right for you."

Eventually, the time comes for her to peel off and I'm left with a feeling like sunshine in my stomach as I walk the remainder of the journey home. I'm still in with a chance; all I've got to do is try and plug into her mindset and the rest will follow. But even the sun has to set: the feeling lasts until I see my house at the end of the street and I stand for a while, just looking at it.

I don't want to go in.

I don't want Mum and Tony to be engaged.

But I live there.

With a deep breath and a sinking heart, I head inside.

I walk through the front door and straight into Tony descending the stairs – no doubt from another sortie to the toilet. The newspaper under his arm kind of gives the game away.

"All right, Arch?" He's either playing his cards close to his chest or suffering from some strain-induced form of amnesia.

"Yeah… How'd it go?"

"What?"

"You know … the ring thing…"

From a normal human being you'd either expect a few "hoorays" to be thrown about or a face like a bulldog chewing a wasp. Tony gives me nothing to work with but a few chuckles and the instruction to "Go and ask your mother". This must be what it feels like to be on Death Row.

I follow the sound of the radio to the kitchen, to find Mum on her hands and knees with her head in a cupboard. Despite the burden on my shoulders, this sight makes me smile – especially when she swears to the clatter of pans. Mum has a special way of swearing: it's not offensive, probably because her favourite curse sounds like it was made up by a Victorian spinster.

"Buggeration!" Clatter, clatter.

"OK down there?"

Mum extracts her head from the cupboard and hauls herself to her feet.

"God, I'm getting old!" she half mutters. "Hello, love – how was your day? Cup of tea?" She can rattle off questions faster than a Gatling gun.

"Good, thanks. Yes, please."

"How did your hanky go down?"

"Yeah, it was good. What about you?"

"Oh, you know, the usual."

The usual? Have I missed something? Are marriage proposals a part of my mother's everyday life? I'm starting

261

to wonder whether I've imagined the whole thing, or whether some rogue brain surgeon has been hard at work on Mum while I was at school, when she suddenly remembers the vital part of her day.

"Oh, yes! Tony asked me to marry him today." It's casual and non-committal enough to stretch me on the rack just a little bit further.

"And…?" Trying to keep the frustration out of my voice puts a strain on my psychic reserves.

"I said no."

Anticipation of an entirely different answer makes my eyes widen; it's like tensing yourself for a blow that never comes. Perhaps there's more to this pink hanky malarkey than Sarah gives it credit for.

"What? Why?"

"I've been married, Archie," Mum says a bit sadly, but still managing to supply me with a cup of the Holy Brew. "I don't need to do it again. I think it was marriage that finished off my relationship with your dad."

When I actually come round to understanding that statement, I'm sure I'll have to concede that I've become an adult.

"Oh. How's Tony?"

"He's fine."

"Really? He's not upset?" Despite the fact that I was dreading an impending marriage, part of me is morally outraged that Tony could take this rejection so casually.

"Go and see for yourself."

I lumber into the lounge on autopilot, as I struggle to try and make sense of all this: no one seems that bothered. It's not that I want to kick up a hornets' nest or anything, but everyone seems to be handling this so … positively.

"All right, Tony?"

"Yes, mate." He doesn't even bother to put down the paper he's reading.

"I heard about … you know … the ring thing."

"Oh, yeah!" Another sofa-bound chuckle from behind *The Times*.

"Are you… Are you OK?"

The paper goes down at this, with all the majesty of a drawbridge being lowered.

"Yeah. Why shouldn't I be?"

"Well … she said no…"

"Yeah."

"Isn't that bad?"

More chuckling, which, quite frankly, is starting to get on my nerves. If there's some secret at the heart of all this, somebody'd better tell me soon.

"Let me tell you something, Arch…" (I hate it when grown-ups talk like this) "…it wasn't that she said 'no', it's *why* she said it." He knows that this statement demands qualification and I know that I'm going to have to ask for it.

"OK. Why?"

"She said she was happy enough and she doesn't need a ring to make her any happier. If she's happy, I'm happy."

"Oh. Right. OK."

Either I've been party to an incredibly Zen-like approach to relationships or somebody's been spiking the tea. If he could just leave it there, I might have some respect for him, but Tony being Tony and, therefore, a Tosser, can't.

"And how's it going with your little lady?"

"I don't need to borrow the ring yet, if that's what you're asking."

A final round of chuckling from Tony's crisp-packet lungs sends me up to my Lair. I flip open my laptop and head straight for Facebook. Matt still doesn't exist and Ravi's uploaded a picture of a figure he's just completed, possibly trying to get my attention. Beggsy, however, is still trumpeting the news of my tussle with Jason Humphries as loudly as possible. His status reads: **"GUESS WHO GOT THEIR ASS KICKED BY ARCHIE?"** There are a few guesses from friends, including "**Miley Cyrus**", which makes me smile. But at the end, he can't help himself and puts Jason's name, with an unnecessary number of exclamation marks. Not the best idea he's ever had, especially given how Jason found out where I live. I'm just about to message him when I see that Dad's been trying to get in touch; there are a number of unanswered chat attempts.

ru u there No question mark.

where r u Same.

need to talk 2 u Numbers for words: meh.

call me plse Fail.

But even these don't pop the bubble of serenity that seems to have formed around me. I check out Sarah's page: her list of friends is growing rapidly and her status reads "**Peaceful**".

I know what she means.

EIGHTEEN

The rest of the week is spent getting to grips with my Psychic Self, courtesy of Dr Hughes. The only hassle is that I'm having to stay up late to keep up with my homework, but Mum thinks I'm tired because I'm on Teenage Time.

This whole positivity thing is a bit like learning to fly; I'm learning to distance myself from my problems and look at them from a higher perspective. But flying tends to be a solitary pursuit, and when Sarah's not around for lunch or break, I'm alone. Matt, Ravi and Beggsy aren't avoiding me as such, but they're keeping out of my way; maybe they think she's my girlfriend. Maybe I ought to apologize, but to be honest, when Sarah's around I kind of forget about them. I kind of forget about everything. I haven't even replied to my dad's frantic Facebooking yet.

PS: *You are spreading your wings and leaving your old life behind!*

There's a lot of truth in that. Even the new Next catalogue that arrived has remained unthumbed, thanks to my recently discovered purity. The weird thing is that I can't even begin to think of Sarah in a sexy way. I think I've reached greater heights of spiritual development.

But I'm realizing there's a lot of work to do and I'm trying to work through the book from the top. "Give everything the weight it deserves," as Sarah said.

Humphries is biding his time. He occasionally surfaces on the horizon like the fin of a Great White Shark, only to disappear silently into the crowds. But he's letting me know that he's still there. Even though I've stopped wearing the pink hanky, he seems to be able to sense where I am. Maybe *he's* got psychic powers.

Friday arrives like a breath of fresh air and at three-fifteen, I find myself waiting at the school gates once more. Sarah arrives, saying goodbye to her growing throng of friends/admirers/palmistry clients.

"Hey, you! How's things?"

I love it when she calls me that. Strangely, for such a generic term, it sounds incredibly personal coming out of her mouth. Especially when she's a little breathless, like she is right now.

"Hey, yourself! They're fine!" I've got this down pat.

"What about your mum and Tony? The dreaded proposal. I didn't know whether to say anything before."

"False alarm."

"Told you!" she teases. "Your friends still working on that project?"

"Yeah. Still at it." This "project" is going to be the

longest project in school history. "What's the goss?"

"Chris and Caitlyn split up. She's been crying all afternoon."

"But they've only been going out two days! What happened? I mean, I've heard of speed-dating…"

"Well, I spoke to him and he fancies someone else."

I can see this one coming a mile off, but I brace myself just the same.

"Oh, yeah? Who?"

"Me! He told me he was only pretending to like her so he could get closer to me! Can you believe it?" The outrage in her voice gives me more than a little hope.

"So what did you say?"

"I told him to get lost!"

And relax. But not too much.

"How come? Every girl in the school wants to go out with him."

"Well, I don't! He's not my type."

"No?"

"No. I like my men with a bit more depth. Besides, I'm off men at the moment. Apart from you, of course."

What the hell is that supposed to mean? Does that mean she wouldn't go out with anyone except me – or that I'm "safe" because we're friends? I ask the Universe for some guidance, but the Universe is busy answering other calls.

We lapse into comfortable conversation about nothing in particular, with Sarah showing no signs of having said anything that I ought to be concerned about. Should I just throw caution to the wind and ask her out? Even the thought of it causes a flipping sensation in my stomach and a faint blush. But the American in my head won't entertain cowardice. It's just not an option.

PS: *You can achieve anything through the powers of positive thinking!*

Maybe I can. Maybe I should.

PS: *Step forward or step back. There is no middle ground.*

I think I've heard that before somewhere. But it makes sense; the longer I fluff about in Maybe Land, the less chance I've got of getting anywhere. Should I do it? My stomach flips again. Once for yes, twice for no. I count about six in as many seconds.

PS: *Lean into the wind! It is Now or Never!*

As the idea threatens to become a reality, my body kicks into fight or flight mode.

"Archie? Are you OK? You look a bit pale!"

I silently and not very positively damn my treacherous skin.

"No, I'm fine. Can I ask you something?"

PS: *Spread your wings and FLY!*

This is all very well, but I think I've just discovered I'm scared of heights.

"Sure. Is everything all right?" The concern on her face just seems to be making this all the more difficult.

"Yeah… I … yeah… Sarah, would you…?"

"Archie!"

Bloody Tony pulls up in the Beemer and shouts out of the window.

"Fancy a lift?"

Sarah looks at me expectantly. But my courage withers and dies.

"Uh… Yeah, thanks, Tony."

"What about your girlfriend?"

My eyelids drop like stones. I want the world to swallow me up, take me deep into its core and never, ever let me see the light of day again. Ever. Only Sarah's giggling pulls me out of my horror.

"Sorry," I grin through my burning shame. "Sorry. D'you want a lift?" I don't know why I'm asking; she's nearly home. My face hurts. I think it's the stress on my muscles as they try and keep a smile in place.

"Don't worry," she demurs. "No, thanks, Tony!" She gives my shoulder a quick squeeze and walks off, taking all my hopes and dreams with her.

I get into the car, seething in silence.

"All right, Arch?"

"No," I manage, through gritted teeth.

Nobody says anything for a bit.

"Have I screwed up?" Tony asks, as we pull into the drive.

All I can do is sigh.

It's Friday night and I sit, dejected and depressed, alone and with no game to look forward to or friends to see, at my painting desk, surveying my room: the bed, the books, my miniature collection. It suddenly looks different.

My Lair was my sanctuary, the place where I could escape from reality and walk upright. But now that I'm finding my feet in the real world, it looks like what it is: a safety net. I've never really faced up to anything in this room, it's all been fantasy, imagination and cowardice. It looks childish.

There's a knock at the door and Tony sticks his head in.

"All right, Arch?"

"Yeah. You?"

"Yeah. Sorry about the 'girlfriend' thing."

I can smell Mum's hand in this. I think this is the first time I've ever had an apology from Tony. But there's no point dragging it out. There's no real harm done; I can deny everything at a later date and then ask her out in my own good time.

"It's OK. I guess I just overreacted."

"What you doing? Painting?"

"No, actually," I reply, standing. "I was just thinking of getting rid of a few things."

"What about going to a boot sale tomorrow?"

"Hey, yeah…" I mutter to myself. "A boot sale…"

"Get some cash for your trash…"

"No. It's not about the money." But I think Tony's provided me with the answer I was looking for. Dr Hughes is always saying that I should "ask and the Universe will answer". Perhaps the Universe has finally got off the phone.

"Well, we've got a load of stuff we should've got rid of before the move. How about it?"

"A boot sale?"

"Yeah. We'll leave your mum in bed and go and flog some stuff. A boys' day out."

This is another one of those bonding attempts, but right now, it suits my needs.

"OK."

"Nice one."

Tony thunders downstairs, no doubt to report to Mum just what great mates we are now. I'll give him his moment of glory.

As I start to clear my desk, putting miniatures in bubble wrap and snapping lids on my paints for the final time, I feel like I'm doing the right thing. I'm going to be brutal in the cull of my personal belongings – I can't afford to hang on to the past if I'm going to fulfil my inner potential. Miniatures, books – they're all going.

I'm just raking through my books when I notice a Facebook message window popping up. My stomach does a quick backflip in the hope that it's Sarah. But it's Dad.

off 2 york next fri pls call urgent

Doesn't even bother with punctuation, full stop.

I stare at the screen for a while, wondering what to put. I ought to see him, I know, but right now I can't be bothered to sort it out.

PS: *Do it in your own time. It's his decision to leave. Not yours.*

It takes me a moment, but I uncheck the "Available to chat" option. No other messages come through and I finally turn the laptop off.

PS: *That wasn't so hard.*

I like this feeling. I like feeling worth something. Fuelled by making my own decisions, I plough back into the task at hand and pretty soon I'm staring at a pile of boxes that are ready to go. My room looks strange and unfamiliar, but I'm not frightened by it. The new Archie embraces change; this is just a blank canvas for me to start a new picture on. If I play my cards right, I might be able to paint a Sexy Fairy into it.

Mum knocks at the door with a cup of tea, her face full of surprise as she sees what's left of my Lair.

"Are you sure about this? That's a lot of stuff to get rid of. And what about your paints and your models? I thought you loved doing that."

"Yeah … it's just time for a change. I can't sit in my room for ever, can I?"

"I suppose." Mum looks wistful.

PS: *There's probably a montage of her little boy's greatest moments playing in her head. She'll get over it. Her little boy's turning into a man.*

After me 'n' Mum have packed the last of what I'm going to sell into more boxes, Tony – ever the creative chef – orders pizzas and a couple of films. Ordinarily, I'd do my best to avoid sitting through his accompanying narrative, but I want to see one of the films. Of course, he can't help himself and within fifteen minutes there are a succession of "Uh-oh"s, "Behind you"s and

"Shouldn't have done that"'s being barked at the screen.

PS: *You don't have to put up with this.*

I lean forward in my chair and chuck a look over at the sofa where Tony's sitting with Mum.

"Tony."

"Yes, mate."

"D'you mind?" I gesture at the TV. Tony responds like someone who's just understood Einstein's Theory of Relativity for the first time.

"Oh. Yeah." He does a big stage whisper on the last word: "Sorry." Mum, sensing a disturbance in the Force, cuddles up to him. But it can't last – and it doesn't. Within about half an hour, he's resumed his role as Commentator-in-Chief. But this time, Mum gives *him* a warning pat on the shoulder and makes a gentle, "Shhh," which acts like a dummy on a baby.

Until my newfound psychic revelations, I would have felt guilty about putting Mum in the position of peacemaker.

PS: *Why should you? You live here too. He needs to remember that.*

The rest of the film passes with little interruption and I'm actually able to almost enjoy it.

PS: *You see. You do have the power to change things. All it takes is speaking your mind.*

This is all slightly new to me – but I enjoy the feeling

that I'm being taken notice of. I've got to maintain this frame of mind – and that's going to take a bit of work.

As the credits roll, Tony gets out the other film.

"Fancy this one, Arch?"

"No, thanks. Not my scene. I think I'll call it a night."

"OK. I'll wake you up around six-thirty – boot sale starts at nine, but we need to be there early."

"Don't worry. I'll set my alarm."

"Night, love." Mum is picking through the remaining pizza crusts, looking for a good one.

"Night."

I leave them to it, feeling a strange sense of satisfaction wash over me.

PS: *You're starting to call the shots now. Starting to fulfil your potential.*

My Lair looks weird. With all the boxes packed, it looks like I'm about to move out.

PS: *Part of you is. The part that's been holding you back.*

After turning the main light off, I climb under the cool, crisp duvet and glance towards my bedside table. The Gargoyle is there, hunched beneath my bedside lamp and scowling fiercely. I look closely at him.

PS: *He doesn't need shields, he's made of sterner stuff than that. And so are you.*

I am. I decide I don't need him any more and put him in one of the boxes at the end of my bed. I kill the light, sink back into the pillow and try to relax by going through every part of my body, just like Sarah did when I was at her house. In my mind's eye, I picture the Gargoyle and focus on the qualities that make it the imposing creature that it is: its strength, its demeanour, its weathered wisdom – all attributes that I need. It's difficult at first; my mind keeps bubbling up with other things, like Dad and Tony and, of course, Sarah and the kiss. But as Sarah suggested, I try and blot everything else from my thoughts, until all I can see are the craggy features of my totem.

Without knowing it, I fall asleep and the Dream begins. I'm lying in my bed and my gaze turns to the corner of the room. The red eyes are there, burning at me from the darker shadows. Then the Gargoyle unfolds itself and stands in a square of moonlight that is shining through my attic window.

Instead of the usual fear, I feel only awe and respect for this monster in my room. And instead of the usual paralysis, I get out of my bed and stand before it, the two of us bathed in silver light. The Gargoyle towers over me and could crush me with a single blow. But I know why I'm here. I put out a hand and place it flat on the creature's chest.

And then it vanishes.

I stand in the moonlight, looking at the space in front of me. It takes me a moment to notice my hand, how it has changed, how the soft pink skin has been replaced by weathered, craggy stone. I *am* the Gargoyle. I feel powerful.

I feel like a force of nature. The feeling lasts as I wake, although I'm slightly disappointed to see that I am returned to flesh and bone and lying in my bed. Quickly flicking my bedside lamp on, I pull the Gargoyle out from the box and put it back on my bedside table.

NINETEEN

All too soon, my alarm goes and I drag myself out of bed. I don't think I've ever been up this early on a Saturday.

After yesterday's highs and lows, I seem to have lost a little of my swagger. I can almost hear my IM in the background, telling me that the Dream was just a dream and that I'm being stupid.

PS: *But you're prepared.*

Sarah told me this might happen. She said that until I've fully embraced my Psychic Self, I'll experience peaks and troughs in my self-confidence, but it's all part of my transformation.

PS: *From Geek into something more significant.*

It's time for my Affirmations. Clutching the book, I stand in front of the mirror, hardly a portrait of significance in my crumpled pyjamas.

PS: *Put that from your mind. Concentrate on your inner self.*

"I am confident and strong." It feels weird saying these things to myself.

"I am supported by the Universe."

"I have high self-esteem." I'm still not convinced, but I'm trying hard to believe what I'm saying. On to the next one – which gives me a little thrill as I say it.

"I am worthy of true love."

"I can handle anything that happens to me today."

"Who da man?!" I can see Tony, grinning like a goon in the mirror, poking his head round the door like some overweight jack-in-the box. He does a few pale imitations of kung-fu moves and chuckles.

PS: *Ignore him. His insecurities are not your concern.*

"Bacon butty, Arch? We need to be moving soon."

"No, thanks. I'll be having fruit." Sarah said I must balance my body as well as my spirit. It's a break with Saturday-morning tradition, but I'm going to see this through.

Although it's not going to be easy. The smell of bacon drifts up the stairs as I get dressed and by the time I go into the kitchen, my mouth is watering. Tony is poking at a few rashers in the pan, trademark cigarette dangling from his lips.

"Sure you don't want one, Arch? There's enough here."

PS: *Control your petty desires!*

In response, I grab a pear from the fruit bowl and with a self-congratulatory smile, defiantly crunch into it. As a counter-attack, Tony slaps three rashers on to a slice of crusty tiger bread, adds a liberal squirt of tomato ketchup and finishes it off with another slice of bread.

A pear has never tasted so bland.

PS: *He is testing your psychic constitution. Be strong.*

While on the face of it this only appears to be two people eating their respective breakfasts, my new insight allows me to see that this is more than that. What's occurring beneath this apparently domestic situation is more akin to the first battle between Darth Vader and Luke Skywalker – Tony takes a bite and sighs with satisfaction; I munch and try and look smug. Each bite is a blow; each grunt of pleasure is like that blue lightning the Emperor could shoot out of his fingers. And Tony breathes a bit like Darth Vader as well – what with all the smoking.

After our foodstuff face-off, we load our gear into the Beemer and set out for the local rugby club, which is playing host to the boot sale. Sarah's house flashes past with no signs of life. It's only a ten-minute drive, but Tony seems to think that it warrants another cigarette. Within seconds, the front of the car is filled with choking, blue smoke.

PS: *You don't have to tolerate this.*

I open the window on my side, but that just creates a slipstream of fumes that rush across my face.

PS: *You can embrace the challenge or recoil from it!*

"Tony," I rasp. "Could you either put that out or open your window?"

This must touch a nerve because he hits his window control in silence. Other than pointed coughing, I've never really commented on his nicotine habit, so it feels a bit odd, but bolstered by my new inner strength, I decide to pursue it a bit further.

"You should quit."

"Yeah, yeah. One day." His words have the hollow resonance of an addict.

PS: *Don't let him off the hook.*

"When?"

"When what?"

"When are you going to quit?"

"I don't know, Arch." His reply is tetchy and curt. "When I'm ready, OK?"

PS: *Not good enough.*

"When will you be ready?"

"Bloody hell – I don't know! Not today!"

The best course of action here is to let it go, but my PS has other ideas.

PS: *Not good enough. Spread the word.*

"Why not? It's easy. All you have to do is get in touch with your inner strength and you can do anything. Smoking is only a symptom of your psychic disharmony."

Tony chucks me a look that suggests I might have grown an extra head and we finish the rest of the journey in silence.

We arrive at the rugby ground and find our spot. It's early, but there are already quite a few cars parked up and the early-bird bargain-hunters are eyeing up the trestle tables as they begin to fill. It's a bit unnerving; Tony turns down the potential sale of a picture within two minutes of opening the boot and his customer walks away, scowling.

"Blimey," he mutters. "Give a guy a chance."

We unload our table and start to unpack our wares. I take one half and Tony takes the other. While he just dumps stuff on his side, I take the time to arrange my miniatures, books and CDs neatly in a way that I think shows them off to their best advantage.

PS: *Take a look. This is a physical manifestation of the differences between you. He is cluttered and unfocused. You are organized and direct. You are learning.*

Despite my directness, Tony makes five sales in the first hour and cheerfully jangles the coins and notes in his pockets. It's another unspoken showdown; I can hear the light sabres buzzing again. He even wields a fresh cigarette with a certain Jedi calm.

While Tony gets into some hardcore haggling with a group of bargain-hungry punters, I end up poring over one of my gaming rule books, marvelling at just how much I've changed in so short a time. Once these pages would have set my mind tumbling with images of all sorts of childish fantasy: monsters, heroes and magical spells.

Now, I see them for what they are: a trap for the weak-minded. I need to start reading newspapers.

"Archie! What're you doing?"

I look up and see Ravi standing in front of the table.

"Hey, Ravi." OK, this is awkward; there ought to have been some apologies before now. From me. "Just selling my stuff." I spot his parents at another stall, a little way away.

"Just selling your stuff? But your figures, your games – are you nuts?"

PS: *Another who must be enlightened.*

This is going to be a hard sell; Ravi's looking at me like I've just announced my intention to go on *The X Factor*.

"It's no biggie, Ravi. I'm just moving on, that's all."

"'Moving on'? What are you talking about?"

This feels too weird. Ravi's one of my best mates. Over our years as friends, we've battled demons, ransacked temples and conquered evil wizards. In the real world, we've discussed the Ample Assets of Kirsty Ford, confessed our mutual Geekhood and generally looked out for one another.

PS: *But what does he really know about you?*

I have to think about that one; I've never really told him how I feel about stuff. Sure, he knew when my folks were splitting up, but I never really spoke about it.

I haven't told him about Sarah. It's not that I don't trust him, but that's just not what guys do. Is it?

PS: *Look harder. He is a reflection of what you once were...*

Ravi's a Geek. Like Matt and Beggsy, he's a fully-qualified Geek. From his ill-fitting jacket to his scuffed-up trainers. From what he wears to what he reads to what he watches. And I'm changing. I don't want to be that any more.

"It's just time..." The words don't come easily.

"But why? What about the Game? What about Games Nights? The Hovel? Don't you like it any more?"

PS: *Show him how you are evolving.*

"But what's it for, Ravi? What does it do? Yeah – great – it's a game, but why do we do it? We should be out there, being what we can be, but for real!"

"Out where?"

"There!"

"Where? Where's that?"

PS: *Do not get distracted by details!*

"Wherever! Just not sat in our bedrooms, rolling dice and painting little men!"

"Why not?"

"I don't know – it's just – well – it's silly!"

This is a low card from a low deck, but my PS advises me that it's warranted. All Geeks have a terrible, sneaking suspicion that their chosen distraction is "silly". It's a word that belittles everything the Game stands for and says it's pathetic and childish. As Geeks, we know that; we just don't like to talk about it. I see Ravi's little bubble begin to sag beneath the weight of the Awful Truth. There's no real comeback to the word "silly" and Ravi just stands there, looking it. I feel bad.

PS: *Feel no guilt. You have chosen your path. He has chosen his.*

"The next Game was going to be at my house." His voice is wistful and distant.

"You're never going to meet girls that way."

At this, Ravi takes an uncertain step back and looks at me, as though there's a light shining in his eyes.

PS: *He can see you are changing. He feels your power.*

"Man," he mutters, shaking his head. "I guess I'll tell the guys."

"Yeah."

"OK, then."

"K."

As Ravi is swallowed up by the swelling crowds of bargain-hunters, I try and work out how I feel about this. I know it's the end of something – not just the end of gaming. My IM kicks at the back door of my head, but I'm trying to listen to my PS now. It tells me that I've done the right thing.

PS: *The Path to Enlightenment can be a lonely one and you cannot choose who will walk with you. And who will not.*

A little kid is holding up my Fire Dragon and pretending to make it fly. I feel a stab of anger at the lack of awe that he seems to have for what is one of my finest efforts. A man, whom I presume to be his father, steps forward, takes it off him and shoves it under my nose.

"How much for this?"

"This" cost me about a fiver and several long hours of concentration and precision-painting. Part of me doesn't want to let it go.

"Three pounds?" I venture.

"I'll give you a quid for it." The money is in my hand and the father and his spawn are gone before I can agree or not.

PS: *You must let go of the past. There is only "now".*

"First sale of the day!" Tony has a unique talent for stating the obvious. "Drinks are on you tonight!"

My EM produces a smile that would wither a cactus, but Tony's too preoccupied with selling a ceramic plant pot to notice.

Within a couple of hours, most of my Geekhood has been sold – primarily to people who don't really know what it's for. Each sale has been a little wound, but I try and comfort myself with the thought that Sarah was probably just being kind when she said she enjoyed the Game; she really doesn't deserve to go out with a Geek and this is my chance to make a fresh start. I want to become worthy of her.

"Fancy a cuppa?" Tony manages through a fresh cloud of smoke. "I think I saw a tea wagon over there."

"I'll have a water, thanks."

"OK. You be all right here for a minute?"

"I think I can handle it."

Tony chuckles in a patronizing way and barges off in search of our drinks. There's a lull in the crowd, so I take a moment to look around the field; perhaps Sarah'll be here. But, then again, why would she? This isn't the sort of place I'd expect her to hang out. She's more likely painting in her room or aligning herself with the Universe. Maybe she's thinking about me. I wish I could call her, just to let her know that I'm really embracing this Psychic Self stuff.

PS: *You have money. You earned it. You can decide what to do with it. You are your own master now.*

I could buy a mobile! Then I can call Sarah whenever I want. Maybe this psychic stuff really does work!

As I start to count the shrapnel in my pocket, a voice snaps me from my reverie.

"Hello, son. What're you doing here?"

There is a long and awkward silence. I know the

rule: you break it, you lose.

"I've got a stall further back; getting rid of stuff before we move," Dad continues.

I say nothing.

"I sent you a few messages on Facebook." Although Dad has technically lost, I seem to be missing a prize of any description. The Archie of old would quickly be ransacking his mental collection of lies, falsehoods and half-truths in order to control the situation.

PS: *Lies diminish you. They corrupt your psychic alignment.*

"I know."

"OK." I can hear the frustration that he's trying to get a handle on. "When were you thinking of getting back to me? I've got a time limit, Archie. I'm leaving next weekend."

"I hadn't decided."

"You hadn't *decided*? What's going on here, Archie? This is important. I'm moving away; I want to spend some time with you before I go."

There's nothing in my head at all. In the space of two minutes, I seem to have achieved a state that takes Buddhist monks a lifetime of meditation to get anywhere near. I am empty. Dad sighs and rethinks his strategy.

"Look… I can understand that you might be angry…"

My PS authorizes a full-frontal assault.

PS: *Now it is time to embrace your fears!*

"Angry?" I take a step back, as though I've been hit. It also seems to be to give my arms more space to wave around. "What do you know about it? You don't know what I'm feeling! You don't know what I'm thinking!"

"Son…"

"Don't 'son' me! This isn't your problem, is it? It's mine!" Despite the volume I'm achieving, I feel strangely calm and, for once, completely right. "You've got your new family! Good for you! Go with them; see if I care!"

"Archie!" Dad hisses, mindful of the vultures circling the tables in search of a bargain. "It's not like that…"

"Isn't it? Looks that way from where I'm standing!"

"Archie!" he steps forward and puts his hands on my shoulders tightly, like he's trying to prevent me launching myself into orbit.

"I'm your father, for goodness' sake! You're my son!"

"Hey! What's going on here?"

As if to create a Conga-line of Conflict, Tony has appeared behind my dad and placed a hand on his shoulder. Considering he's also carrying a cup of tea, a bottle of water and two hot dogs, that's no mean feat. It's also a Big Mistake. Dad swings round, wearing what I call "The Face". The Face is when my dad's features seem to solidify and take on all the appeal of a tombstone.

It's firmly in residence now.

"And who are you?" Dad's not a big guy, but what he lacks in stature he makes up for in attitude.

"Let's all just calm down, shall we?" Tony starts to put his purchases down on the trestle table. Although they've never met, Tony's seen photographs of my father. And I think Dad's just worked out who Tony is.

"Why don't you just *piss off*? I'm talking to my son!"

PS: *Truth is freedom.*

"Why don't you *both* piss off?" I bellow, exhilarated by the strength that is now at my disposal. "You heard me! Both of you! Piss off!" With that, I launch a kick at the trestle that knocks it over and into my dad's legs. He tumbles backwards and catches Tony, who yelps as hot tea splashes into his shirt.

"Archie!" Dad pleads, trying to untangle himself from Tony's sodden embrace.

But I don't care who's calling after me; I'm already running, chanting *Truth is freedom* over and over in my head. It was a line from *We Are All Our Souls* and, right now, it's the only thing in the world that makes sense. I dodge and weave in between parked cars and just keep running, not caring where I end up.

I need to see Sarah.

TWENTY

My legs finally pack up as I reach town. Buying a phone seems like a really good idea; I can call Sarah and get her to meet me somewhere, instead of going round to her house. I couldn't face another trip down her mother's jumper today.

I crash on to a bench beneath the clock tower and sit, panting. For a moment, I just watch people going about their business: a few Saturday-morning shoppers and couples going for a walk. Everything has a certain dream-like quality to it, like I'm not really here, but watching from somewhere else.

PS: *This is part of your psychic transformation.*

Passages from Sarah's book come back to me, but they're incomplete; I can't remember how I'm supposed to feel right now, so I guess I'll just wing it. "Your life can change in powerful new ways." I can remember that and, so far this morning, I'm ticking all the boxes:

Gutted room – check.

Upset mate – check.

Upset stepfather – check.

Upset Dad – check.

Kicked over trestle table as an added extra – check.

But I don't feel particularly happy just yet. I don't feel particularly anything.

PS: *To achieve happiness, you must first untangle the knots of your life.*

Trouble is, my life seems to have more knots than a Scout jamboree. But I'm determined to see this through. I count up the money in my pocket to discover that the sum of my Geekhood amounts to twenty-seven pounds and sixty-five pence; all those hours painting and concentrating haven't even earned me thirty quid. Still, it's better than a poke in the eye. My quickly-setting legs just about carry me into a phone shop.

Unfortunately, my psychic abilities don't seem to have much effect on the shop assistant, who doesn't quite have a grasp on the urgency of my situation. I briefly consider fanning my fingers and telling him "You will get a move on," in my best Obi-Wan Kenobi voice, but think better of it.

PS: *He is unevolved. His dissatisfaction in his job reflects his dissatisfaction in himself.*

"Got some ID?"

My psychic dignity flounders for a second; I didn't realize you needed ID for a pay-as-you-go. Unfortunately, the only thing in my wallet with my name and address on is a membership card to the Young Role-players Association.

Ten agonizing minutes later, I am the proud owner of a new mobile phone, complete with ten pounds of credit. Sarah's number is already burned into my mind. I can see it, looking back at me from the pad by the phone at home. Just as I'm about to dial, I hear voices calling my name. For a moment I wonder if I'm now so psychically attuned that I'm having my first experience of telepathy, but I'm not. In front of me are Matt, Ravi and Beggsy, standing outside the Hovel. They're wearing looks on their faces that suggest distrust and suspicion – to be expected, really; when a Geek leaves the fold, the remaining Geeks close ranks. As I walk towards them, they start to walk towards me. The only thing missing is the chink of spurs.

It's a showdown. Geek-style.

Things could get messy.

"Dude! What's going on, man?"

"Nothing. I'm just walking through town."

We are now entering a sort of conversational Jenga; the slightest wrong move and the whole thing could fall apart.

"But, dude. What's this about you quitting the Game?"

PS: *Be strong. Be true.*

"Yeah, I'm quitting. So what?" I try and make this seem as inconsequential as possible.

PS: *It is their world that shakes. Not yours.*

"Told you," Ravi mutters.

So far, Matt hasn't said anything; he's the one I've got to watch for. He's obviously their sharpshooter. It makes sense – of all my friends, Matt is probably the one I'm closest to; in the past we've both acknowledged the problems that come with being Geeks. By admitting that to each other, we've also silently conceded that there is a life beyond the Game – a life where we might fit in and become just part of the crowd.

PS: *Perhaps you can use this knowledge to your advantage. Perhaps he can be convinced to join you on your quest.*

"So what's the problem?" I shrug. "It's not like you guys can't carry on without me."

"Dude! The Game is the Game, man!" One of Beggsy's favourite sayings, designed to be a blanket statement that covers all arguments. Not this time.

"But that's all it is, Beggsy. A game. It's not *real*, is it?"

"Du-uh!" Another one of Beggsy's favourite sayings.

"We know it's not real, Archie." At last, Matt speaks. "That's not the point. What we're really asking is why you've suddenly decided to quit." His face is blank and impassive, but his eyes burn with an intensity that speaks volumes.

PS: *They are frightened. Frightened of the truth.*

I take a deep breath.

"Look, I'm quitting the Game because I've finally realized I don't want to sit in my room every night painting miniatures or playing 'Let's pretend' every Friday."

"Why?" Matt looks like he's genuinely trying to understand me, so I plough on.

"Because it doesn't *do* anything! We're like ostriches, sticking our heads in the sand and avoiding life – but pretending we're not! We're not *achieving* anything; we're just going through the motions!"

"I disagree." A short, sharp shot that disarms me quickly.

"What?"

"I think you're wrong."

My PS, seemingly unfamiliar with being told it's wrong, is now having a minor psychic crisis. It looks like I'm going to have to fly blind for a moment.

"OK, Matt," I nod, using the old "I'm using your name so you know I'm serious" tactic. "What, then? What are we doing when we play those games that's so life-changing? Tell me."

"We create things, Archie. We create things out of nothing. We're like alchemists." Matt's obviously been practising his shooting skills.

PS: *Don't listen to him. He is seeking to unbalance your psychic alignment.*

"'Alchemists'? What are you talking about? We're people who don't fit in and have no hope of fitting in while we're locked in our bedrooms, playing the Game! We should be out there – taking risks!" I think I've fired off a good one, but Matt just stands there, blinking.

"And fitting in is taking a risk, is it?" I can almost feel the bullets whizzing past my ears. My own incisive aim seems to be a little bit off.

PS: *His argument is rooted in fear. He is not truly in tune with himself.*

"You know what I mean! What're you going to do: spend the rest of your life in your bedroom, playing with models?"

"Probably not, no. But I don't need to fit in to be happy."

PS: *Show him his own fears. See how strong he is.*

"Are you happy being a Geek?" I've said the dreaded "G" word – that which must never be spoken. Like saying "Voldemort" or "Sauron". My developing senses discern a change in the atmosphere, as though a dark cloud has gathered over the group. On the face of it, Matt seems unfazed by the accusation. He rocks back on his heels, considering what's just been said. Ravi and Beggsy look to their leader, tarred with the same ghastly, geeky brush.

"The way I see it, Archie," he begins, "everyone's a Geek of some sort. Football, films, music – it doesn't matter what the interest is; if you're fascinated by it, then you're a Geek. Simple as that."

My PS falters. Has Matt got a point? As if sensing my hesitation, he continues.

"In fact, the people who are the best at what they do are all Geeks. Scientists, sportsmen, actors, musicians – the best ones are *Super*-Geeks; they've turned their obsession into a career, doing things they love. What's wrong with that?"

My PS has nothing left but cruelty. While this goes against the whole psychic-alignment theory, it does get me out of a big hole, very fast.

"And what are you going to be? The world's biggest *loser*?"

Matt smiles, but it's a sad one.

"See you around, Archie." Then he turns on his heel and walks back towards the Hovel, Ravi and Beggsy trailing in his wake.

PS: *See how he crumbles in the face of the truth!*

But all I really see are three guys, who used to be my friends, walking off to go and do something they love.

"…so leave a message after the tone and we'll get back to you as soon as we can. *Beep!*"

"Uh… Hi, Sarah… It's Archie… Could you give me a ring back on this number…?"

After leaving my new number, I bravely hang up.

This psychic transformation stuff's getting difficult to handle. All I seem to be doing is creating a bigger mess than I was in in the first place.

PS: *Do not waver from the path of the Gargoyle.*

For lack of anything that resembles an intelligent thought, I start to wander in the direction of Sarah's house. Perhaps this is what it feels like to be a Gargoyle: friendless and alone. Perhaps this is all you get for your affirmations and meditations. Perhaps I *am* a Gargoyle.

With this image in mind, I lumber along the pavement, feeling more and more like I've been carved from stone. I feel ugly and desolate. The only hope I've got is Sarah. I round the corner to her road and stop outside her house. The black and white cat appears and loop the loops round my ankles, but I can't be bothered to stroke it. Aslan's a shit name anyway.

The door knocker might as well be made of plasticine for all the effect it has. Sarah's out. Perhaps I should meditate and try and summon her, using my psychic abilities? Even my PS has the dignity not to respond to that one. An unpleasant feeling is bubbling inside me and I sit down on the pavement with my back against Sarah's garden wall, to try and figure out what it is. For some reason, it feels like I've been trying to wear a hat that wasn't designed for my head. Before this train of thought gets a chance to pull out from the station, a car slams to a halt in front of me.

It's Dad. Here we go again.

But instead of the expected Face, Dad looks flustered and winds down the passenger window.

"Archie! Get in the car!"

Something's wrong.

"What is it?"

"It's Tony – he's had to go to hospital."

TWENTY-ONE

Fear is a wonderful focus for the untidy mind, and right now, I am as nervous as a cat in a room full of rocking chairs. The smell of air freshener in my dad's car threatens to choke me.

"What happened?" I ask, in a voice that doesn't sound like mine.

Dad's face is tight and stressed, but he's trying not to show it.

"I don't know. After you … left … he just sort of turned white and collapsed. I called an ambulance, called your mum and waited with him until they arrived. She's at the hospital now."

"Jesus."

"Yeah, I know."

"How'd you know where to find me?"

"I didn't. I was on my way to your house to see if you were there. What were you doing on the pavement? Whose house is that?"

"Just waiting for a friend who wasn't in." I avoid the use of gender to head off further questions.

We drive in silence for a few minutes. I don't know what's going through Dad's head, but I know what's going through mine: this is my fault. If I hadn't lost my rag, if I hadn't run off, if I hadn't been such an almighty jerk – none of this would have happened.

Dad senses something in my silence and pulls over. "Are you all right, Arch?"

"I don't know."

"I know what you're thinking – and it's not true. If it was going to happen, it was going to happen. I don't mean to sound harsh, but he doesn't look as though he takes care of himself." Dad isn't saying exactly what's happened to Tony, but it wouldn't take Dr McCoy to figure it out.

"No … no, he doesn't."

"He'll be fine, I'm sure he will. But what about you? What's going on?"

This is unfamiliar terrain for me; me and my dad don't really talk about anything important and I've no idea how to respond. I'd love to be able to come out with something deep and profound, probably with a hint of mysticism about it, but my PS seems to have packed up and moved out. And I can't say that I'm sorry about it. However, there is a voice in my head and while it's very, very familiar and very, very welcome, it seems to have altered a little bit.

IM: *Just tell him how you feel.*

It seems to have grown up a bit. I take a deep, much-needed breath and don't bother to relax my buttocks.

"I guess I've been angry, Dad."

IM: *Not bad. A bit non-specific. But it's a start.*

"Because I'm moving?"

"Yeah."

Dad shifts in his seat and with my peripheral vision I can see him leaning in and trying to make eye contact with me. When I turn to look at him, he's wearing a smile, but it's one of those that people put on when they're trying to fight back tears.

"I'm sorry, son," he says in a thick voice. "It was a bloody hard decision. Really it was. And I thought of you every step of the way."

"It didn't feel like it."

"No, I s'pose not. I should have spoken to you about it right from the beginning, but I didn't want to worry you; I didn't know if it was going to happen or not. But I should have spoken to you about it. I'm sorry."

IM: *Your turn.*

"Yeah. Me too. I just felt sort of … left out, I think." There's a hand on my shoulder, but it's gentle and earnest this time, much like the look in Dad's eyes.

"I'm so, so sorry, Archie. So sorry." He breathes deep and reaches inside for something he's hidden away. "*You're* my son, Archie. No one else. Much as I love Jane and much as I care for her kids – *you're* my son and no

303

one can take that away. *No one.* I will be there for you whenever you need me and I will do whatever is humanly possible to make your life a good one. I know I'm a pain in the arse and I don't always say the right thing, but I'm your dad and I love you more than you will ever know." A rogue tear is making a break for it down his cheek.

IM: *Time to let him off the hook.*

"I'll still see you, though?"

Dad answers with a noise that is a mixture of relief and pain, but the smile that comes with it is full of hope.

"Of course you will! Jesus! With the money I'll be on, we can take holidays, I'll get you train tickets! I'll have a bigger house – you can have your own room. You'll be driving in three years, Archie – we'll make it work!"

"OK."

IM: *And cue the orchestra…*

Hugging isn't easy when you're in the front of a car, but we manage it.

"Right, then!" Dad wipes his eye in that way that men do when they don't want to acknowledge they've been a bit teary. "You OK? Good. Let's get to the hospital, your mum needs you right now."

IM: *And so does Tony.*

TWENTY-TWO

I don't like hospitals. They give me The Fear. Even children's wards; try as they might to make them friendly with poor imitations of cartoon characters painted on the walls, they reek of anxiety and shepherd's pie. Don't get me wrong, I like a shepherd's pie, but a helping of mince and mash seems to smell different in the comfort of your own home.

IM: *Especially without some mutant version of Mickey Mouse leering down at you.*

There are no such monsters painted on the corridors that lead to the Cardiac Ward – which is probably a good job, considering the state of most of the patients that are intermittently wheeled past us.

Dad and I walk in silence, following a set of yellow lines on the floor to our destination.

IM: *Not quite the Emerald City.*

And not quite the time for jokes. We arrive at a small waiting room with a busy reception desk and are told to wait; we can't see Tony yet – we're not family and he's being "worked on". Just that simple phrase ignites a pocket of fear inside me that I didn't know existed.

"What does that mean, Dad? Is he going to die?"

305

I can't help myself. Tony might be a Tosser, but I suddenly don't want to lose him. Whether it's through guilt that I might be responsible or finally realizing that he makes Mum happy, I don't know. Maybe it's both. Or maybe it's because underneath all the Tosser Talk, I know that he cares about me too.

"Let's sit down," Dad whispers, putting an arm round me. "You're here for him; that's all you can do right now."

IM: *Hang in there, Tony, you ... Tosser.*

Half an hour later, I've exhausted the problem pages in a number of women's magazines and start counting how many strip lights there are in the corridor behind us.

IM: *There's psychic evolvement for you!*

Suddenly, there's a noise that sounds like a heart monitor gone mad. Me and Dad look around, as do the nurses behind the reception desk.

IM: *It's your phone!*

I quickly root through my pockets until I find it. There's a number on the screen that it takes me a moment to register, but there's also a nurse on top of me in seconds, telling me with no uncertainty to turn it off, please. With my EM kicking back into touch and routing every possible red blood cell to my cheeks, I search for the power button and kill it as quickly as possible.

IM: *Let's hope you didn't do the same for any of the patients...*

I smile apologetically at all the staring faces and sink as low as possible into my chair. Dad leans over to me, whispering in that way you feel you ought to in a hospital, despite the fact that there are bleeps, moans and the click-clack of heels echoing all around.

"I thought you didn't have a phone." There's an accusation lurking in there, somewhere.

"I didn't. I just bought it."

"Oh. Right." There's a silence, during which he changes tack. "Who called? Anyone I know?" Even though he's whispering, I can hear the telltale tones of someone fishing for information.

"Not really…"

IM: *Go on – build the bridge!*

"It was the girl who came round the other night. To the Game night."

"Oh! What – as in girl*friend*?" The last syllable is heavy with pre-emptive approval. Here my EM takes an unexpected stance and reveals my irritation at being placed under the microscope yet again; I sigh and roll my eyes. Dad gets the message.

"Don't want to talk about it?"

IM: *No shit, Sherlock!*

"Not really."

"Fair enough. Hope you have better luck than I did, though…"

"What do you mean?" If he's including Mum in his nebulous statement, then I'm coming up fighting this time.

IM: *Rolls up sleeves*

"What? Oh, God, no – not your mother! No, sorry – I just meant generally. I was always hopeless with girls."

My IM and I have the same thought at the same time, so it just sort of trips off the tongue.

"It must run in the family." I grin ruefully.

"Like that, eh? Well, for what it's worth, just be yourself. That's the only advice I can give."

IM: *Might be worth listening to.*

Before I can respond, the door to the ward opens and Mum walks through. She looks tired, old and like her tear ducts have been working overtime. Dad stands awkwardly then takes a few steps back, giving me and Mum a bit of space. She half trots over to me and gives me a hug; one of those ones that tells you the other person needs it more than you do. I squeeze her back and let her decide when enough's enough.

"Archie," she sniffs, "what's been going on? Where were you?"

"How's Tony? Is he going to be OK?"

Mum seems to remember that the Cardiac Ward waiting room isn't quite the place to grill her son and pulls herself into a more together state.

"Yes, I've just had a chat with the doctors and they think he's going to be OK. It was a warning. I don't think he'll be smoking when he gets out."

"Can I see him?"

"Not now. He's very tired. I'm going to come back later, but I think it might be a good idea if you left it until tomorrow."

"Couldn't I just nip in for a couple of minutes?"

"No, Archie. Best not."

IM: *It's not about you. It's about Tony. "Sorry" will wait till he's ready to hear it.*

"OK."

Mum glances over my shoulder and sees Dad. She smiles crookedly and then looks back to me.

"What happened, Archie?"

"I think I can help there." Dad steps forward, but still leaves a wary space between him and Mum. "Shall we go and get a cup of tea?"

A hospital coffee shop wasn't quite what I had in mind when I fantasized about a family reunion. Dad goes to get the teas, while me and Mum go and perch on bar stools that overlook the hospital's gift shop.

"You OK, Mum?" The weight of the situation seems

to have pulled at her features, so that even her smile takes more effort than usual.

"Yeah. Better now. A cup of tea will sort me out." Her eyes flick to find Dad in the queue; they're full of wariness and old memories. "What happened, Archie?"

IM: *And now for a game of conversational Buckaroo...*

I know how much is at stake here, so I try and tread carefully, giving a sketchy account of the car-boot sale. My EM tries to cover any glaring omissions, but the Human Polygraph is having none of it.

"And what's the bit you're not telling me?"

IM: *D'oh!*

"Dad's moving to York next Friday."

"What?!" This isn't quite the reaction I'd been hoping for. In fantasyland, Mum would suddenly realize that she couldn't live without him, and Dad would probably look at her and resolve to win her back. Instead, the look Mum throws at the queue is the eyeball equivalent of a karate chop. As if directed by some mischievous god, Dad wanders cautiously over, carrying a tray and wearing an expression that wouldn't look out of place on a shop-window dummy.

"Tea?" He knows something's up, but seems to think that a cup of tea will somehow make everything all right.

310

"Thank you." Mum's reply is curt, reinforcing the invisible wall that has sprung up between them. "What's this about you moving to York?"

At this moment in time, I might as well not exist. Mum and Dad have locked eyes and the tension is practically visible.

"Ah…" Just the one syllable confirms everything.

"And when were you thinking of telling me? Haven't we been down this path before?"

"How long is it since we've spoken?" I can hear knives in Dad's voice.

"And whose fault is that?" Mum's got a spear in hers.

IM: *Pointless! This is pointless!*

My EM concurs by causing me to blow out a pointed sigh and apparently removing the muscles at the back of my neck, so that my head lolls back and I'm looking at the ceiling.

IM: *Which is a damn sight more interesting than listening to this.*

For once, my actions seem to have an effect. Dad looks at me, at Mum and then at his tea. Mum suddenly seems to find her cuppa endlessly fascinating.

Then there's some sort of sighing competition, while my parents gaze into the middle distance, searching for answers. Eventually, and as though someone has applied glue to his bar stool, Dad stands up.

"Let's leave it, shall we?" There's an air of resignation about him.

Mum wins the sighing competition with a monster exhalation, her eyes still fixed firmly on her tea.

"No," she says, as though she's trying to convince herself of something. "You're moving and we might not be able to do this again. Sit down. Let's try and work this out."

Dad sits down and there's another elephantine silence.

"Archie," Mum says, "do you want to go to the shop and get a magazine or something?"

IM: *Which loosely translates as "Get rid of the kid."*

"No. I think I ought to be here."

Dad flicks a glance at Mum. Mum flicks a nod at Dad. The fact that they're able to agree on something – no matter how small – seems to relax them a bit and they start to talk. Dad explains about his new job and how much better life'll be for everyone with the money he'll earn and how I can take the train to York and how he'll have to come down now and again anyway. An argument starts to build when they discuss who's going to see me when, and Mum suggests that Dad's going to need to be a "bit more reliable" and not cancel a weekend "at the first sign of a cold". This obviously gets under Dad's skin and he goes into some bristling rant about how "some of us have to work for a living", but Mum refuses to rise to the bait and changes tack.

"Archie? How do you feel about this?"

IM: *You've just been promoted to "grown-up". Don't blow it!*

I take a deep breath and for once in my life say exactly what I think. Not what I think people want to hear.

"OK," I breathe, taking the crown as Overall Sighing Champion. "What you both don't seem to get is how hard it is that you don't talk. And because of that, I don't talk to you about each other. I don't talk to you…" I lock eyes with Mum, "…about Dad and I don't talk to you…" Dad's turn, "…about Mum. So I talk to myself. Probably a lot more than you know. And that's when I get things wrong." Something akin to shame settles like a ceasefire between my parents. "In an ideal world, I'd like to see you both all the time. But I know that's not going to happen. So, if there's a way that I can call Dad…" I shoot another look at Mum "…without worrying that you're going to be upset, that'd be good. And if you can mention Mum…" Dad's not off the hook either, "…without it being such a big deal, that'd be good, too. You're both a part of my life, but it's like you're each trying to pretend that the other doesn't exist. And from where I'm standing, that's pretty lame."

IM: **Applause**

Mum and Dad look at each other, embarrassed, and then simultaneously start nodding to themselves, each lost in their own thoughts. I deflate a little and listen to my heart rate calming down.

"Truce?" Dad asks finally.

"I think so," Mum agrees with a tired smile.

"OK, then." The glue on Dad's seat has obviously evaporated. "I'll leave you to it. Archie, I'll give you a ring tomorrow and let's get together before Friday. Go out or something."

"'K."

"OK, then. Bye."

"We're going too. We'll walk out with you."

IM: *Steady on, Mum!*

The walk to the main doors is like wading through treacle, but they manage it with me walking between them. Eventually we make it out and, after some staccato goodbyes, my dad leaves and I head with Mum to the car. As I close the door, I switch my mobile on, just because I can.

Sarah's number is down as a missed call.

As the car starts up, a silence consumes us, but neither of us notice. Mum's eyes are staring at the road ahead, but her mind is somewhere else. Mine too; when can I call Sarah?

IM: *Best wait and see how Mum is before you*

do anything.

"Archie…" It's that tone that lets me know that this is something Mum has thought about for a while. "About Tony…"

"Yeah?"

"I know he can be a bit…"

"…of a Tosser?"

IM: *Sorry. Just came out.*

Mum squints through the windscreen, looking as though someone has just trodden on her toe, but she's trying not to show it.

"That wasn't quite what I was going to say," she says through pursed lips. "I was going to say that he can be a bit 'difficult'." She places enough emphasis on the last word to make it sound like a new one that I ought to absorb into my vocabulary. "But you've got to remember, Archie, that as much as you're learning about him and finding out what you do and don't like about him – he's finding out the same about you."

IM: *Incoming! New thought alert! Prepare to be boarded!*

"What? He doesn't like me?"

"No! That's not what I mean!" The gear change signals her frustration, while her gentle braking signals her cooling down. "Tony doesn't have any kids. He doesn't know about kids. And he's trying to learn."

"Well, I've never had a stepfather before." It's sulky and petulant, but Mum rides it out.

"But that's what I'm saying, Archie. I know this is hard for both of you – especially living together for the first time. But you haven't been the easiest of people recently, have you? And Tony's noticed; he's not stupid. He might be a tosser, but he's a tosser who cares about you and is trying hard to get to know you."

IM: *Your mum just said "Tosser"! Twice!*

"Yeah… OK. Sorry. I've been a bit stressed lately."

"I know that now. Why didn't you say anything before?"

IM: *It's a good question. Deserves a good answer.*

"Dunno."

IM: *Steeeee-rike!*

Mum communicates her dissatisfaction with another crunching gear change. I need to be honest.

"I didn't want you to be upset and I thought I could deal with it."

"Archie, I'm your mother…"

IM: *Well, that's cleared that up, then.*

"…and you should be able to talk to me about anything. That's what I'm here for. People need to talk; bottling things up only makes things worse. If you can't talk to me, talk to your friends or your dad."

"Or Tony…"

"I'm not expecting an overnight transformation, Archie, but yes, in time. Talk to people who care about you."

"OK. Sorry."

"And stop being sorry."

"OK. How are you doing, Mum?"

There's another silence while Mum considers my question.

"I'm OK," she says finally. "In a strange way, I think this has happened for the best. Obviously, I'm worried about Tony's health, but the doctors seem confident that if he stops smoking and eats better, he'll be all right."

"And at least you and Dad are talking again. What happened, Mum? Why did you stop speaking? What was it?"

Mum's answer is measured and considered, like she's trying to work through a tough Sudoku.

"If I answer you, Archie, you have to ask your father the same thing. I can only tell you what happened from my point of view and he can only tell you what happened from his. What you might get are two different stories, and you might hear us saying unpleasant things about each other. If you can handle that, then I'll tell you my side. But you'll have to ask your father as well – and then you'll have to form your own opinion."

IM: *Never a straight answer when you need one...*

"I'll get back to you on that."

Mum smiles.

"Good for you."

"Are you going to be OK?"

Mum's Agenda Detector fires up. She has an astonishing and often unnerving ability to tell when I'm trying to ask a question without actually asking it.

"You need to be somewhere?" There's a tinkle of mischief in her voice. I silently curse my transparency.

"Can you drop me in town?"

TWENTY-THREE

I could've asked Mum to drop me off at Sarah's, but part of me still wants to pretend that nobody knows what I'm up to; that my secret is still my secret. It also buys me a little time to think about what I'm going to say to her. With everything that's happened in the last few hours, thoughts are racing round my head like Superman on a sugar rush.

I pull out my mobile and before I lose my nerve, I take a deep breath and call Sarah back.

"Hello?"

"Sarah?"

"No, it's her mum. Who's that?"

Images of well-packed bras leap like mountain goats through my mind.

"Oh, hello. It's Archie. Sorry, I thought you were Sarah."

There's a faint giggle on the end of the phone and I realize I might just have inadvertently flattered Sarah's mum.

IM: *Store that one away for future reference.*

"Sorry, Archie, no. She's gone into town to meet a friend. Do you want to leave a message?"

I could ask her for Sarah's mobile number but, in my head, it feels as big a deal as asking for her daughter's hand in marriage. Bravely, I chicken out.

"Uh … no, thanks. I'll call later, if that's OK."

"OK. Bye." A dark part of me thinks I can hear a little disappointment in her voice. All I can think of is bras.

IM: *Sarah's in town!*

I could seek her out. Despite the best efforts of the gymnastic squad that have suddenly started performing in my stomach, I resolve to embrace the idea. I now have a Quest – something to focus on. I shall find Sarah. Where to start? All the files in my head concerning the daytime habits of the female of the species have yet to be written; what do girls do on a Saturday in town? Do they go shopping? What do they buy?

IM: *Bras.*

While the idea of scouring bra shops fills me with a frisson of anticipation, the idea that Sarah might be out shopping for the latest over-the-shoulder boulder holder doesn't quite ring true. I think she'd be somewhere more spiritual, somewhere more fulfilling, somewhere like…

IM: …*the Shop For Unrequited Love!*

It takes me seconds to race to the alley and just as I'm rounding the corner, the Gods of Fate smile upon me: Sarah comes out of the shop. Just as quickly, the Gods of Fate decide it's time to empty their bladders, which they do with formidable precision – right on my head.

Jason Humphries follows Sarah out of the faintly jangling door.

IM: *All communication frequencies are jammed! *Sound of static**

Jason Humphries follows Sarah out of the shop.

Jason Humphries follows Sarah.

Jason Humphries.

My EM has been entirely neutralized and I stand like a cardboard Dr Who standee at the top of the alley. Luckily, my IM goes into manual override and I manage to pull myself back round the corner.

IM: *Therehastobeanexplanationtherehastobeanexpl anationtherehastobeanexplanation!*

I risk another peek; Jason and Sarah are walking my way, but they seem too wrapped up in conversation to notice me. Jason's got a small paper bag that he puts in his pocket and Sarah is obviously trying to explain something to him; she's all animated hands and earnest expression. Despite his fading bruises, Jason looks like a freshly resurrected Frankenstein's monster. I briefly wonder whether Sarah's mum has rubbed arnica into his wounds as well and, once more, my mind is awash with bras.

I duck round the corner again and quickly find a shop window to appear absorbed in. Perfume has never been so interesting.

IM: *Come on, Sherlock – use the window!*

I catch the reflection of Sarah and Jason as they pass behind me, deep in conversation.

IM: *Which must be stretching Jason to the limit.*

They pass to my left and I risk another look: stopping under the clock tower, Jason jerks a thumb in the direction they've just walked. Some sort of goodbye is said and, although there are no kisses, there are plenty of smiles and Sarah says something meaningful before she continues on her journey. Jason starts to retrace his steps, so I return my attention to *Eau de Something Or Other*.

I'm giving so much consideration to the contents of the pink bottle in front of me that I fail to notice Jason until his meaty hand grabs me by the scruff of the neck. With as much effort as it would take me to pick up a kitten, he hoiks me round the corner and into the alley.

"Geek," he hisses, as he slams me against the wall. His forehead ripples and his blue eyes stand out against the bruises under them. "Thought I hadn't seen you?"

IM: *Our Father, who art in Heaven…*

The accumulated knowledge and experience of my Geek ancestors have programmed me for this moment; it kicks in without me even having to think about it: with lightning speed, I bravely shut my eyes and cower.

IM: *It's not going to be an open casket after this…*

Images of my parents weeping, Tony wailing and

Sarah gnashing her teeth over my battered body play on my inner cinema screen, as I wait in terror for the blows to land.

"Look at me when I'm talking to you!"

IM: *Anythinganythinganything!*

I peel my eyelids fearfully apart and gaze into the Face of Death. Which smells of cigarettes. Jason looks like he's wrestling with something – probably a thought. Even his little yellow teeth seem to be joining in, grinding together so hard that, by rights, there ought to be sparks.

"You're a very lucky boy," he growls, sounding like an evil Father Christmas. "Do you know why?"

In the absence of a functioning voice box, I shake my head as quickly as I can. My hands seem to be massaging his wrist, as though my gentle ministrations might cause *his* hand to let go of my throat.

"Because that girl likes you." I note he doesn't use her name, which suggests to my ever-active Paranoia Department that there is still some distance between him and Sarah. Hopefully not just emotional. There is also some subtext going on here: by telling me that I'm lucky because Sarah likes me, he's also telling me that he likes her too and, in order to maintain any relationship with her, he can't give me the usual thrashing that is second nature to him.

IM: *But I wouldn't start relaxing just yet… Not with his hand round your windpipe.*

"OK," I stutter in a voice that sounds as though I've been inhaling helium for the last four hours. "OK".

"But you tell your little mate that if he hasn't got rid of that shit on Facebook by tonight, then I'll be looking for him. You get me?"

Oh, yes, I get him. I get him quicker than a dose of the flu. I communicate my understanding with a series of animated nods and a couple of affirmative squeaks that are so high every dog for miles must be on its way. But Jason's not done yet; he leans in closer, just so that I don't forget every scar, every line and every rippling muscle in his bowel-loosening face.

"Lucky," he growls and throws me to the ground. "Get up. And piss off. Geek."

I have never obeyed anyone's commands with such enthusiasm. Slipping, skidding and scraping to my feet, I turn to face him and instead of responding with some killer line, I actually thank him. Then I piss off. At speed.

Before I go charging off to the Elven retreat that is number seventy-eight Davenport Road, there's something important I've got to do. Fuelled by the adrenalin boost bestowed upon me by the benevolent threats of Jason Humphries, I race round the corner, partly just glad to be alive and partly just in case he's had a change of his little black heart and is thundering after me.

IM: *No dust clouds on the horizon – but keep running*.

I tear into the Hovel, instantly soothed by the almost church-like atmosphere inside. My explosive arrival sends heads turning, as peace-seeking Geeks register what might be a threat on their detectors; even Big Marv half raises himself off his seat, before returning to the miniature he is painting behind the counter. As I expected, Matt, Ravi and Beggsy are here, looking through the blister packs, in search of new mountains to climb.

"Beggsy!" I pant a little too heavily into his ear.

"Dude? What's up?" There seems to be no hint of recrimination in his face, merely concern.

"Beggsy... Just seen Jason ... Humphries... He's seen ... Facebook... You better ... get rid of it ... or ... you're toast...!"

Beggsy responds in the classic Geek fashion: he turns white and looks around for help from nowhere in particular.

"By ... tonight..." I manage.

"Dude! Shit! I'm on it!" he squeals, sounding weirdly like Lisa Simpson, and without a goodbye to anyone, he rushes out of the Hovel to go home and save his skin.

I put my hands on my knees and pant at the floor.

"What are you doing here?" Matt's not quite so easily won over. "I thought you'd 'quit'."

IM: *One thing at a time.*

As my breathing slows down, I straighten up and, ignoring Matt, I turn to Ravi.

"Ravi, mate," I begin. Throwing in "mate" is a Geek method of showing that you are unarmed. Unless, of course, you're in an argument, when it hints at hostile intent. It's complicated. "I owe you an apology. I'm really sorry. I've just been going through a weird time and you caught me at a bad moment this morning. I'm really sorry."

The problem with Geeks is that they remember negatives. Over the course of a year, you could compliment a Geek a thousand times and insult him only once. On New Year's Eve, you could then ask him what he remembers about the past three hundred and sixty-five days and, as sure as Gandalf is a Servant of the Secret Fire, he'll only remember the insult. It's how we protect ourselves. Some might argue that this isn't a particularly life-affirming way to exist, but it's what we do.

"And that's what passes for an explanation these days, is it?" Ravi's obviously using telepathy to speak through Matt; they both look unconvinced.

IM: *Promote them to "grown-up"; see how that goes.*

"What're you guys doing now?"

"Standing here, talking to you," Matt deadpans.

"OK. Let's go and have a Coke or something."

"What do you mean?" An invitation to sit in a café might not sound out of the ordinary, but Geeks tend to avoid sitting in public places.

"Come on." I jerk my head left and head for the café across the road, without waiting for any argument.

By the time they arrive and stand conspicuously in front of the sandwiches, I've got a tray and three Cokes. I nod them to a table by the window and we all sit down, trying not to scrape our chairs.

Another of the problems of being a Geek is a bit of a paradox: Geeks are convinced that everyone's watching them and yet they only make themselves more noticeable by trying too hard to be invisible. While this hints at a huge sense of inferiority, it also points towards a massive, if fragile, ego. I'm dealing with two Ming vases here.

IM: *Time to start talking, Archie. With a capital "T".*

"OK, guys," I begin, "I owe you an explanation…"

"Yes. I think so." Matt's response fires me up to approach this as responsibly as I can. I start with Dad's revelation that he's leaving, then talk about seeing Sarah and Jason Humphries, then go on to the boot sale and Tony. It's not particularly chronological, but I spill it out as it seems most relevant.

"So why were you selling your stuff?" Ravi asks. "Are you still in the Game?"

IM: *Thought you were going to avoid that one, didn't you?*

It's true. I deliberately hadn't mentioned Sarah and my aura-reading and the IM and the PS – partly because I know how nuts it sounds outside of the protective enclosure of my head and partly because I don't want Sarah to cop the blame for me being a dunderhead.

"I think Archie's got more to worry about than the Game just now." I'm grateful for Matt's diversionary tactics. I can see in his eyes that he knows there's more to my story than I'm telling, but it doesn't need telling now.

"God ... yeah. Sorry, Archie..." Ravi stutters. "Hope everything's OK."

"Don't worry about it." I know why he asks; as much as he's trying to understand what's made me reject the Geek world, he's also trying to work out how it affects his life. "It'll be OK. And, yes, I'll be back in the Game. Gonna have to start all over again, though – sold all my paints and my figures."

"Why didn't you tell us all this before? We're supposed to be mates."

IM: *Lord Chief Justice Matt will require a good answer.*

Weirdly, I only know the answer as it comes out of

my mouth: "I guess because talking about it would make it seem more real. If I keep it in my head and no one else knows, then I can sort of pretend that it's not."

"Ah," Matt nods sagely. "Like an ostrich, you mean."

IM: *Touché!*

"Yeah," I grin ruefully. "Just like an ostrich. Sorry about that."

"Forget it. Welcome back. You Geek." The word has never sounded so good. "So, what're you up to now?"

IM: *Sarah!*

"Actually, I've got to get off and see someone before it gets too late. Can I ring you tonight?"

"Sure."

I leave Ravi and Matt to their Cokes. While the Fellowship might have temporarily disbanded, for me the Quest is still on.

Despite the ragged motions of my under-used and over-exercised legs, I am walking a fine line. I need to see Sarah and I'm hoping she's headed for home after her tête-à-tête with that knuckle-dragger. But what am I going to say to her?

IM: *Marry me?*

I'm in love. There's no getting away from it. She's the

Galadriel to my Frodo, Uhura to my Spock, Snow White to my seven dwarfs.

IM: *Happy, Dopey, Sleepy, Sneezy, Grumpy, Bashful and … Geeky?*

And there's the problem: I'm a Geek to my core. Like a stick of rock, I've got "Geek" printed all the way through me, probably in archaic runes. It's who I am and I can't get away from it. I've tried being something else and it just doesn't work.

IM: *Or did it…?*

Or did it? Maybe there's more to this psychic alignment stuff than I first thought. Maybe going through that has helped me create a bond with Sarah that I couldn't have done before. Maybe we are now psychically in tune with each other, to the point where I don't need to do my affirmations every morning. Maybe I've turned into a man, finally worthy of someone as beautiful as she is?

IM: *Still think a moustache would cap it off.*

Maybe I'm finally beyond the world of moustaches and bras. Perhaps this is True Love, the sort that transcends facial hair and undies. I don't think I'll ever look at a Next catalogue again. It all makes sense: it's not about my aura and my PS – they were just vehicles for me to finally, fully understand what it means to be In Love For The First Time.

Like that bit in *The Lord of the Rings* where Frodo uses the light given to him by the Queen of the Elves, I can feel this revelation taking hold and I know what I'm going to say to Sarah. It plays out in my head, underscored by a full orchestra.

I enter her room and, without saying a word, she perceives the difference in me immediately. Our eyes lock and everything else seems insignificant. She rises from her chair, dropping the picture she has just painted and walks towards me. We are both radiant with the spiritual light that shines from within us. As she crosses the room, she stumbles and trips, falling straight into my arms. I catch her and manage to scoop up the picture she has let fall. It's a fairy, but not one of the sultry nymphs that adorn her walls. It's me.

Music swells to a climactic crescendo.

I smile at her and then our lips lock in a final confirmation of our psychic unity.

IM: *These bloody jeans are too tight.*

Despite pausing to adjust my trouser furniture, I practically glide the rest of the way to Davenport Road, once again soaking up the mystical energies that seem to bleed out of every tree, every twitter of birdsong and the black and white cat that lounges in the late-afternoon sunshine outside number seventy-eight.

"Hello, Aslan." The name suddenly seems

331

appropriate and I give the cat a reassuring stroke. "You knew all along, didn't you?" Aslan offers his chin up for a scratch and purrs in agreement.

There's no sense of foreboding, this time – no sense that I'm unworthy of what is to come. The Quest is finally reaching its end; like Aragorn, I have shed my earthly garb and transformed from a humble Ranger to a King, who is finally deserving of his Queen.

IM: *Jason Humphries isn't going to like this.*

It doesn't matter who doesn't like it; Sarah and I will have each other: the psychic shield of our love will fend off all who seek to drive us apart. I open the gate and stride up the gravel path.

"Hello, Archie." Sarah's mum stands up from watering a rose bush, briefly affording me the opportunity of another view of her Misty Mountains. But I don't take it. I am above such things and wouldn't want to demean either her or myself with such thoughts.

"Hello, there. Is Sarah in?"

"Yes. She's upstairs. How's your eye?"

"Working perfectly, thanks," I smile, a picture of confidence and spiritual alignment. I even throw a wink in, just to show how healed I am.

IM: *We seem to be having a malfunction here, folks. Please be patient.*

"Go-od," she says, drawing the vowel sound out,

as though she's distracted by something. Perhaps she's already picked up on my transformation.

IM: *All systems appear to be offline. We will attempt to repair the fault as quickly as possible. Please be patient. And avoid operating heavy machinery. Or talking.*

"Can I...?" I jerk my thumb to the front door, which is slightly ajar.

"Yes, yes, of course. Go on up. I'll bring some drinks up in a minute."

"Thanks." With a final winning smile, I turn and walk into the house.

The smell of incense draws me like a charm up the stairs to Sarah's room. Her door's closed and I take a brief moment to run my fingers through my hair and take a final breath. I'm going to do it. I'm going to lean into the wind.

It's Now or Never.

TWENTY-FOUR

"Come in."

Sarah's room is just as I remember and the air is thick with patchouli. It's like a temple. Sarah is sitting on one of the cushions she has arranged on the floor, dressed in white jeans and a white T-shirt. She is Beauty itself.

"Oh, hi, Archie," she beams, closing the book she was reading. "Mum told me you'd called and I tried to call you back, but your phone was off. Couldn't stay away, huh?" She follows this question with a raise of one of her eyebrows and a laugh that makes my stomach want to melt.

"Something like that." I smile and sit down on the cushion opposite her.

IM: *Good answer. It playfully confirms her coy suggestion. All systems online. We are now cruising at a comfortable speed.*

"How's your eye?"

"Yeah, good. That arnica's pretty good, isn't it?"

IM: *Excellent work! By finishing your answer with a question, she'll be forced to elaborate and the dance can begin.*

"Yeah."

IM: *D'oh!*

The conversation threatens to die, but Sarah offers it mouth to mouth.

"How're you doing with the psychic stuff?"

IM: *Perfect! A foothold! Start climbing!*

However, I think I've just discovered I've got vertigo; my heart starts playing a drum roll and my palms start to sweat, causing me to rub them together like I'm trying to set them alight.

IM: *Slowly does it.*

"Yeah… I … uh… That's kind of what I wanted to talk to you about."

"OK." Another tinkle of laughter and another flip of my stomach.

"Yeah…"

IM: *Come on! Pull it together!*

"…Yeah. This psychic stuff. I have noticed a change."

Sarah nods; she's all anticipation and wide eyes, like a puppy that's just seen a bone for the first time. I think about what I want to say, but the reality is much more terrifying than the fantasy. Talking to my parents was easier than this, but it's time to take the plunge.

"Yeah. I feel that I'm making important connections with people close to me." The words are slow and clumsy, like they're the wrong shape for my mouth and I can't seem to get them out right.

"That's great, isn't it? That's just what you wanted?"

I have another go.

"Yeah. It's great. But I'm receiving connections too. From other people. People like me."

"Everyone is born with psychic abilities, but we forget how to use them. All you've got to do is take some time to concentrate on what you want out of life and those around you, and you'll be surprised how quickly things change. Suddenly, people become clearer to you."

IM: *This could be a hint.*

IM: *It might not be.*

IM: *But it might.*

Christ, this is difficult. But it's a way in. My EM opts for extra sweat and to remove all the blood from my face – probably to stop me blushing at any point. Unfortunately, I probably look like a sweaty bag of flour.

"That's what I mean. It's like I can *see* people better now. I can see what they are afraid of."

"Like what?"

"Like saying what they really mean." I try to give this statement some significance by leaning forward and staring into her eyes, but I'm quickly conscious that I might look like some sort of serial killer, so I pretend I've got something in my eye and rub at it with my finger. This isn't going quite like I'd planned.

336

"Most people never say what they really mean."

IM: *Could be a hint!*

IM: *But, then again...*

"I know! And I wish people would just be honest with me! I mean – if you had something to say to me..." Here my heart rate accelerates beyond the speed of sound. "...you'd be honest with me, wouldn't you?"

IM: *Good call! Ball in her court! A touch cowardly, perhaps – but there's nothing wrong with that.*

Sarah contemplates my question with all the grace of a swan. Her eyes search the ceiling, as though the answer will come to her from the ether, and I find myself entranced by the delicate curves of her neck. Not that she's like E.T. or anything. After a moment or two, her psychic antennae obviously tune in to the right frequency.

"If I thought you could handle it, yes. Yes, I would. If it was something serious."

IM: *GO! GO! GO!*

"And is it?"

"What?"

"Serious?"

"What?"

"What you want to tell me."

IM: *GENIUS!*

Sarah blinks at me. Like she doesn't know what I'm talking about.

IM: *But that won't wash with you – the Master Mind Reader!*

"I haven't got anything I want to tell you, Archie."

Now *I* start blinking. I think I'm sending out an SOS with my eyelids.

"Haven't you?" I don't mean to sound quite so shocked. But I think I do.

"No!" Sarah laughs and frowns at the same time. "Like what?"

"Like…"

"Li-ike…?" She repeats my words, coercing the thought out of my mouth. I decide to try another tack. I don't think she quite gets what I'm trying to say. Brutal truth should do it.

"Like I love you."

Ear-splitting silence.

"What?" Disbelieving laughter. "What?"

IM: *You, sir, are an arsehole.*

"I'm in love with you." I am fully aware that this is not going to have the result I thought it was going to, but for some reason, my mouth won't stop working. "I've fallen in love with you."

"Ar-*chie!*" Her eyes are wide with shock/horror/disgust – pick one. It doesn't matter now. I can feel the supporting structures in my head crack and splinter as she utters her next words: "But we're friends!"

Friends. There can be no more desolate a word. Friends means barriers. Friends means that your dreams will remain just that. Friends means that your hand will go for ever unheld, that your lips will for ever remain unkissed. Friends means that you should have known your place and stuck to it.

"But I thought…" I wish my mouth would shut up.

Sarah's face softens into a portrait of concern.

"Archie… I'm really sorry, but … I don't feel that way."

My EM responds with a series of silent nods. Sarah looks at me; she's so beautiful it hurts to look.

"Archie… When did this happen? How long have you…?" The question hangs like a highwayman. And now I'm expected to cut the corpse down and dissect it in front of her. The sad thing is that I'm prepared to do this, just in case pity will change her mind.

"When I saw you in the shop."

More disbelief.

"I'm so sorry…"

IM: *Scalpel*.

"No. It's fine."

IM: *First incision*.

"And then what?"

IM: *Bone saw*.

"I just thought… You liked the Game…" Brilliant stuff.

IM: *Rib dividers.*

"And then?"

IM: *Major organs intact.*

"After the fight… You invited me round here…"

IM: *Hang on…!*

"I thought I could help, Archie!"

IM: *This man's heart appears to have been ripped out!*

"But you kissed me!"

Sarah's voice softens even further.

"On the cheek, Archie! You were a friend. You were having a bad time."

I fall into a deep, still silence. There's nothing like watching your hopes swirl down the plughole and into the drain to take the fight out of you.

"Is it Jason?" It's a low card, but I play it anyway.

"What?"

"Jason. Are you in love with him?" I'm amazed at how childish I sound.

"Why would I be in love with him?"

IM: *Not an outright denial, eh?*

"I saw you in town together."

With this statement, I've given Sarah the entitlement to Righteous Indignation, which she takes with both of her beautiful, treacherous hands.

"You were spying on me?"

My silence is all the confirmation she needs.

IM: *Shit.*

"For your information, Archie, I was trying to make sure that he didn't try and beat the crap out of you! I met up with him and took him to Manisha to choose some incense for a reading! I'm going to read his aura!"

The supporting structures in my head finally give way with a resounding crash and I revert back to my hideous, Geeky self.

"He's only letting you read it because he wants to go out with you!"

"Isn't that what you did?"

"I've brought some biscuits as well!" Sarah's mum announces, pushing the door open with her backside and lowering the tray on to Sarah's dresser. I can't even be bothered to look down her front.

"Mu-um!"

"Sorry, love – have I interrupted something?"

I stand up, balancing on weak and wobbly legs.

"No, it's OK. I ought to get going." I manage a feeble sketch of a smile. "See you."

"See you, Archie." I can hear the "not in this lifetime" connotations attached to this statement.

"Thanks for the biscuits," I say stupidly to Sarah's mum, and leave.

IM: *Nice going, Romeo.*

TWENTY-FIVE

The flowery lanes of Lothlórien have morphed into the cracked, black paths of Mordor. When I first came to Sarah's house, my senses were heightened to the beauty and vitality of my surroundings. In that same, heady way, my senses are again working on overdrive, but now they only take in the morbid aspects of my environment: the crumbling brickwork, the screeching of kids who seem to be fighting rather than playing, and the fact that I nearly break my neck tripping over Aslan as he stretches and coils under my feet.

IM: *Dumb animal.*

How could I have got it so wrong? How? It all made perfect sense, it all seemed so right. I did everything; I even bought into all the psychic stuff – anything for Sarah to get to know me. And all she wanted was friendship. I just don't get it.

IM: *You do, though.*

I do. Of course I understand. I'm a Geek and she's gorgeous and it was never going to happen. I'm an idiot to ever think it was.

IM: *Come on, there's more to it that that.*

I avoid the thought, shoving my hands in my pockets

and ambling down the street, staring at my feet. Walking has never seemed so pointless. I don't know where I'm going and I don't really care. I feel like a waste of time.

IM: *But you know what went wrong, don't you.*

I do know and it only adds to the wretched feeling that makes my soul feel as heavy as lead. What was I thinking? I must've been mad to even think I had a chance.

IM: *You're going to have to stop kicking yourself eventually.*

Perhaps she *is* going to go out with Jason Humphries? He's got muscles, he's got that "screw you" attitude that I could never have and he's probably got some kernel of vulnerability that makes him ridiculously attractive to women – the rough diamond, the bruiser with potential.

IM: *Bullshit and you know it. He can throw his fists around, but he couldn't have a meaningful conversation if his life depended on it.*

Just to rub a little more salt into the wound, my mind spews up pictures of them laughing, kissing and holding hands. But the pictures I'm seeing are empty and without foundation; they're just a way for me to enjoy the exquisite torture of the moment and try to ignore the truth that's tapping gently at the back of my head. I know what went wrong and I know where the blame lies in this whole, sorry mess.

IM: *Time to look in the mirror, Archie.*

I put Sarah on a pedestal from the moment I met her. Talking to her made me feel good about myself and I tried to be something I wasn't, in the hope that she would like me. I am…

IM: *…a Tosser?*

Oh, God. I am. I'm a Tosser™. Even Tony's crimes pale into insignificance compared to mine. I am Lord of the Tossers.

IM: *There. Isn't that better?*

The admission of my Tosserism™ doesn't feel like an absolution, no. I suppose it rids me of any feeling that I've been somehow misused. But it doesn't do much for my opinion of myself. I've hurt someone. I stop for a while, wondering whether I should go back and apologize. But it's a mental mime; I know I'm not going to. She wouldn't be ready to hear it and I'm still too full of self-pity to make a decent job of it. I need to wait until I'm feeling a bit more adult about the whole thing.

IM: *Let's not wait THAT long…!*

No. Let's not. But let's at least wait until tomorrow. That's if she's still speaking to me. Which she has every right not to, I guess.

The horrible realization that I'm not quite the dashing Casanova that I wanted to be is draining. I suddenly feel very tired, but like I need to talk to someone.

I want to talk to Sarah.

IM: *Matt'll do.*

I call him on my mobile, and find the energy to do the old left-foot, right-foot thing, just as Matt's mum answers the phone.

"Hello?"

"Hi, is Matt there? It's Archie."

"Hello, Archie, love. How are you?"

IM: *Strap yourself in and I'll begin…*

Some mums have this crazy idea that it's them that you actually want to talk to. Matt's mum is a prime example of this phenomenon; give her just enough of an opening in conversation and she'll keep you on the line for ages. I opt to give her a gentle push in the right direction.

"Good, thanks. I told Matt I'd give him a call." This tactic hints at a prearranged conversation of Some Importance. As if I do have psychic abilities, she says she'll go and get him – but I know she'll give her son a gentle grilling later on to try and eke out anything that might be of interest. Matt'll put her off the scent with some story about homework or the Hovel and the last atom of dignity that I own will remain mine for a little longer.

"Archie."

"Matt. Hello, mate."

"Hey. How you doing?"

This is an interesting question. I'm doing fine. I've sort

of purged myself of any anger or bitterness; all that remains is a sense of my own stupidity and that's something we Geeks live with on a daily basis. On the face of it, I'm OK.

IM: *But it's what's going on underneath that he's asking about; he's your mate, remember. "How you doing" is a very probing question.*

"Well, I'm still single." It's a fairly fluffy answer, but I know Matt will pick up the nuances involved.

"Uh-oh."

IM: *Like a true friend!*

"Yeah. I've pretty much blown it with Sarah."

"What happened?"

"It's a long story…"

"Cool. I could do with a good laugh…" To anyone who doesn't know Matt, this could sound a little insensitive, but I know that he's letting me know that it's probably not as serious as I think it is and that he's happy to listen.

A thought hits me like Jason Humphries on steroids. *"Shit!"*

"What?"

"Oh my God! Oh. My. God. Oh my *God!*"

"What? What is it?"

"I winked at Sarah's mum!"

"What? You did *what?"*

"Oh my God! I did! I am such an idiot!"

I dissolve into laughter, made worse by Matt

demanding to know what the hell happened. By the time I've explained the scenario, Matt's cackling darkly down the phone. Between jokes, I manage to sketch an outline of what happened at Sarah's house, giving him enough background to join the dots himself.

"You idiot," Matt reprimands me in that way that only a friend can.

"I know."

"What're you going to do?"

"I don't know. Say sorry, I guess."

"Yeah. You probably should. Idiot."

Geeks have a strong sense of right and wrong; we seem to have an inbuilt fear of authority and a genuine desire to keep the wheels of the world turning as best they can. Which means that if you upset someone who doesn't deserve it, you apologize. Matt's moral fibre is strong enough to clear out a constipated giant. And, in a peculiar way, I know he shares my sense of shame. Because he'd have behaved the same way in my position.

"Archie?"

"Yeah?"

"You didn't really think you had psychic powers, did you?"

I have to think about this one. There's definitely something in what Sarah said: I do have connections with those around me, friends and family. And while it

347

might not be psychic, there's definitely more to it than just being around someone a lot.

"I don't know, mate."

"What am I thinking, then?" Quick as a flash, he's back taking the piss.

"Kirsty Ford, I reckon."

"Jesus! That's amazing!"

"Ha, ha. Hey – Matt?"

"What?"

"Do you ever talk to yourself?"

"All the time. Don't you?"

Mum's sitting at the kitchen table, looking very small and alone. I squeeze in on her chair and put my arm round her.

"OK?"

"Yes. I think so. I've checked in and he's doing fine."

"Cool."

We both go quiet, listening to the unfamiliar stillness in our new house. For me, it's like a symphony of peace: I can hear the faint tick of a clock and the distant whine of a lawnmower. For Mum, it's a gap, a space, a blank canvas that needs to be filled with the colourful cacophony of her boyfriend. I give her a squeeze, which seems to ignite her get-up-and-go.

"Tea?" She's at the kettle before I can even reply, so I just laugh in the affirmative.

"How'd it go?" she asks, rooting around for tea bags.

My EM instinctively responds with a general sweep of my body, looking for any signs that might give me away. With not a little effort, I decide to pull the power and instead allow my feelings to register in my posture. Which is a little stooped.

"You needn't worry about any grandchildren just yet. Put it that way."

At the mention of anything that might allude to the fact that her son has a functioning pair of gonads, Mum snaps to attention. I can almost see a Condom Parade playing through her head. I decide to put her out of her misery as quickly as possible.

"I mean we kind of broke up."

"But I didn't think you were going out with each other."

IM: *Doesn't miss a trick, that one.*

"We're not. We weren't. It's a bit … complicated."

"Oh." Even the sacred ritual of tea-making can't disguise her confusion. She takes a moment before asking me if I want to talk about it.

This is a tough one. After all the talk we've had about talking, I suppose I should try and tell her everything that's been going on. But I'm not ready to. Not yet. Not that Mum would judge me in any other way than a loving mother would; she'd probably find a million reasons to excuse my temporary insanity and probably pin the blame on Sarah somehow. But I know the truth and I need to live with it a bit.

"Not really. Do you mind?"

"Just as long as you're OK." She ruffles my hair, trying to displace her obvious disappointment. But I stick to my guns. It's the right thing to do.

"I'm cool."

IM: *Let's not go that far…*

"Oh!" Mum says, as though she's just realized where she is. "There's a film on tonight; one of those ones you like…"

"Oh, yeah?" I grin, knowing exactly what's coming. "What is it?"

Mum smiles back, knowing exactly what I'm thinking. "It's that one with the monkey in it. You know…"

"The one with the monkey in it?" Despite my fatigue and the feeling of having been a dunderhead that's hanging over me like a dunce-capped cloud, I can't help laughing.

"Yes! You know the one…!"

I do, but the potential for an impromptu game of charades is too much.

"No, I don't! Which one?"

More laughter.

"There's a monkey!"

"Tarzan?"

"No! A monkey and some aeroplanes!"

"*King Kong*?"

"*King Kong*! That's it!"

At this point, we're helpless with laughter. A monkey and some aeroplanes. Through my giggles, I realize that there's nothing I'd like to do more than to sit down with my mum, drink tea and watch a film about a monkey and some aeroplanes. Everything else seems like a long way off: visiting Dad in York, Tony coming home, starting up a new miniature collection and returning to my Geekhood.

And Sarah. While I may not have achieved the Geekhood Holy Grail of actually having a girlfriend, I have made First Contact; had a Close Encounter.

IM: *That's one small step for a Geek, one giant leap for Geek-kind!*

Maybe I need to learn a lesson from *King Kong*... Maybe, instead of trying to fit into her world and standing out like an oversized gorilla, maybe I need to draw her deeper into my world...

I need to think about this. Carefully.

IM: *It's all in the details.*

ACKNOWLEDGEMENTS

There have been a few books, films, TV shows and comics that have Changed My Life in some way. Of them all, here are the biggies:

BOOKS: *The Lord of the Rings*. The creation of a world in such depth rocked my eleven-year-old brain. It's also the only book that is guaranteed to make me cry.

FILMS: *Star Wars: A New Hope*. The sight of the Star Destroyer flying over my head in the opening shot was the beginning of a lifelong love affair.

COMICS: Marvel's *Spider-Man* gave me enough hope to try and find spiders in my garden that might bite me and give birth to a superhero from Devon.

THANK YOU

As I've discovered, there's a lot more to writing a book than writing a book. I'd like to offer my heartfelt thanks to Alex Garland for being kind enough to stop and chat, along with Jenny Savill at Andrew Nurnberg Associates and Jane Harris at Stripes Publishing, and their respective teams, for rolling the dice.